SHANGHAI PATROL

SHANGHAI PATROL

TOM WRIGHT

NAVIGATOR BOOKS

Published by Navigator Books
Ringwood, Hampshire

ISBN 0 902830 37 6

Typeset by Moorhouse Typesetters
Printed by The Cromwell Press, Melksham, Wiltshire

SHANGHAI PATROL

LOVE TO JACKIE FOR HER SUPPORT

Thanks to Philip and Richard

SYNOPSIS

SHANGHAI PATROL

Anna Pang, the beautiful intelligent daughter of the Pang family, ran the laundry at the British Consulate in Shanghai.

They had now to accommodate the washing from a naval patrol of a visiting warship billeted temporarily in an annexe in the Consulate grounds near to the laundry.

The young sailors were wartime only ratings, due for discharge from the Navy at the end of the war and their experiences were limited in coping with libertymen. The vast American 5th Fleet at anchor offshore and U.S. Army units ashore in the largest and toughest seaport in China, did not make the job easy.

When their ship sailed in an emergency and they were left stranded in Shanghai 1000 miles from the nearest naval base in Hong Kong.

Befriended by the Americans and pretty Chinese girls the story in the true traditions of sailors stories of returning home through the China seas and finding love, romance and a fight or two on the voyage home.

CHAPTER 1

The welcome sound of the ship's cable as it thundered down the hawse-pipe with the anchor, was heard all over the ship when the destroyer H.M.S. Battener anchored in the waters off Shanghai.

Three weeks ago they had been in England, with some men expecting to be demobbed at the end of the war, and now they were thousands of miles away from home surrounded by the large American 5th Fleet.

From the upper deck of the fo'c's'le you could see quite clearly the people in great numbers walking along the famous waterfront known as the Bund.

The landing steps on the waterfront attracted their own little crowd of sightseers, watching the passengers coming and going in boats of all shapes and sizes from sampans to large powerful launches from the warships anchored off shore.

On the destroyer's seamans mess-deck, there was more than the normal interest in the ship's orders being clipped to the notice board.

Wiggy Bennett, may have been the shortest seaman in the ship, but he was the first to reach and read aloud the good or bad news.

Shouting so that everyone could hear, he began "Leave to the Starboard Watch of hands, from 1800 to 2330 (6pm-11.30pm). Patrol will land at 1900. All ratings detailed for patrol duties are to report to the Coxswain's office immediately, Leading Seaman Wilson, Able-Seamen, Weller, Evans, Bennett, Edwards and two Misc."

Seeing his own name included on the patrol list, Wiggy turned a little pale and stopped reading. Moving away, he flopped down on a mess-stool next to Taffy Evans, muttering to himself, "I've got to go ashore and I've never done it before!"

Taffy, putting down his book, said cheerfully, "You couldn't have picked a better place, those little Chinese dolly birds won't half go for you!"

Wiggy, squaring his shoulders snapped back, "I'm talking about patrol duty, you bloody fool, what did you think I meant?"

Taffy replied, "Sorry, I thought you were talking about women."

Wiggy, still hoping to keep Taffy's attention said, "Doesn't it bother you that your name is down for patrol duty?"

Looking away from his book, Taffy answered, "Sonny, all I'm interested in at this moment is my book or a woman if I can afford it, with all these Americans ashore with their golden dollars."

Wiggy muttered, "Dirty Devil" and moved off to intercept Leading Seaman Wilson who was about to read the bulletin on the notice board. Knowing Wiggy, Wilson put his hand up to stop him talking, whilst he read the ship's orders.

Noting the P.T.O. on the list, Wilson quickly turned it over cursing as he read it.

"Bloody Hell, Petty Officer in charge of patrol, W. Willard, that's all I need to make my day!"

With a wave of his hand he signalled the patrol to follow him to the Coxswain's office.

The door was open as they gathered outside, the Coxswain, sitting at his desk gave a shifty look over his shoulder and then beckoned them to come closer.

"I shouldn't be telling you this, but you have been selected by me, for this special patrol duty to represent your ship and the Royal Navy to the Chinese and the American Navy, so don't let me hear any rumours about you lot talking Gun Boat diplomacy, or Anglo-Saxon bullying of the locals or you will all be in trouble! Are there any queries?"

Wiggy, quick to speak complained, "Why did you pick me, I'm about the last one for a patrol as an eight stone flyweight."

"Wiggy, my son, there are thousands of little women out there who think small is beautiful so think yourself lucky, my boy."

The Coxswain shouted cynically. "Dismiss and don't miss the boat!"

Wilson, arriving back on the mess-deck, told the men that his patrol was no different from patrols he had done before, but could be more interesting, he emphasised, "It might be much more fun than you think."

By the time it came to board the motor-boat, they were dressed in white suits, boots belts and gaiters carrying a small steaming bag of extra's and were in high spirits.

Bungy Edwards keen to be the first one to land leapt from the boat as soon as it touched the steps and called, "China, here I come!"

A harsh voice shouted from the top of the steps, "I'll give you China here I come, get up those bloody steps and make it snappy!"

Willie Willard, Petty Officer had landed from an earlier boat to arrange a lorry.

Willing child porters tried grabbing the bags in the hope of earning a dollar or two, while Willie urged them to go in the direction of the lorry.

Climbing aboard and hanging on for dear life, the lorry moved forward in a series of jolts and grinding gears to join the flow of traffic along the Bund.

It was not far to go but a very rough ride and the passengers cheered at the welcome sight of the Union Jack flying over the Consulate building.

Entering the gate, they were driven to an annexe away from the main building and partly shrouded by shrubs and hedges. The entrance to the annexe was some way from the main building and Willie directed them to carry their bags inside, whilst he made for the main building to inform Marcus Beatty, Comm'd Gunner, R.N. that the patrol had arrived and were settling down into their new quarters.

The patrol had been told nothing about being billeted ashore and the mess in which they were allotted came as a pleasant surprise with seven beds, clean sheets and lockers with a generous size table for meals and comfortable chairs.

Willie's room and office were through a door to the left with the bathroom and showers opposite, whilst the door to the right led to the kitchen and laundry.

The patrol members soon decided who they wanted to sleep next to and the disadvantages of a bed too near the kitchen. Taffie soon called, "What about a cup of tea, is there anyone in the kitchen?"

Wiggy remembering that Bungy was the first ashore, pointed to him and called, "Chinese Edwards was the first to land, send him!"

Bungy getting up smartly from his chair, flipped his face flannel over his forearm like a waiter, walked to the kitchen door, opened it slowly, looked inside and saw a Chinese cook.

"Hey, cook-boy, any chance of a cup of tea?"

The Cook reacted at once and picking up his chopper, began waving it wildly and speaking rapidly in Chinese as he walked towards Bungy who backing out of the kitchen quickly, closed the door. Looking white faced and quite shaken Bungy said, "I only asked him for a cup of tea and he came at me with a bloody chopper - the bastard!"

There was silence until the kitchen door flew open and Am Ling, the cook, stood in the doorway with a tray and seven cups of tea.

With a curt little bow, he addressed those in the room in pidgin English.

"Me not cook-boy, Me COOK!. Me not bastard, me have Chinese Papa and Mama."

With another curt little bow, he put the tea on the table, he left the room.

There was a hush in the mess, then they all began laughing after the shock of being confronted by Am Ling the cook. Taffy turned to Bungy saying, "Good job he wasn't a barber, he might have given you a Chinese haircut!"

Willy the P.O. entered from the other door without any warning and snapped out, "Get this place tidied up, I'm bringing the officer in shortly" and left by the front door.

Getting rid of the cups and saucers and tidying up did not take long. Wilson then allocated duties. Kemp the signalman as postman, Wiggy - Messman, Weller - Laundry, Taffy - Willie's office, Bungy - Food and Kitchen, Black - Hot water, Shower etc.

"Remember." said Wilson, "No women allowed in the quarters. If you fancied anything like that, keep it outside."

Wiggy stood up, being the youngest and cockiest, said with a certain amount of bravado, "About what you just said, where do we get our French letters now we have no Sick Bay like on board?"

Wilson, remembering what the Coxswain had said about little Chinese women waiting for Wiggy replied, "You had better talk to Petty Officer Willard about that."

There came a distinct knock on the door and they all stood up.

The peacetime navy was a bit dull to say the least, and Marcus the officer welcomed this chance for a bit of action ashore.

Willie arrived with a map of Shanghai and Marcus wasting no time showing them the limits of the municipal authority and the outline of China's largest seaport.

A lot of political activity was going on and local crime was increasing with the influx of refugees. The patrol tonight would operate within the area of the Bund and adjacent streets to direct ratings to the embarkation jetty. With all things going well they should be back in the quarters by midnight.

P.O. Willard would be in charge and in the morning they could lay in, but not too late.

Beckoning the Petty Officer to come with him, they left the patrol to have a meal, before going on duty. Bungy, keen to establish himself as the food member, rose to his feet and croaking in a dreadful imitation of Am Ling, said, "You likee fish and chips?," headed for the kitchen as he had done once before. When he reached for the door it flew open before he touched it and Am Ling handed him a pile of hot plates straight from the oven.

With burning fingers, Bungy just made the table as Am Ling in a great hurry laid finger bowls, cloths and chopsticks on the table.

Still hurrying Am Ling returned with a large dish of what appeared to be pancakes. Not thinking any more about Bungy's burning fingers, they all helped themselves, devouring the tasty cakes on the large dish until they were all gone.

Wilson, who was in the process of pulling a small fishhead from his mouth, coughed, picked up his cloth and cleared his mouth.

Wiping their fingers with the cloths they all blissfully waited for whatever was to come. Wilson hoped they did not ask for dried fish pancakes too often.

The next course was Chop Suey, although Bungy didn't recognise it. The pork pieces were succulent with a generous mixture of Chinese vegetables, ginger, bean sprouts, mushrooms, noodles, celery and black fungus with its tangy flavour. Only the bamboo shoots and wine were missing but not knowing, it made no difference as they stoked their mouths using chopsticks with a great deal of laughter.

Apples and tea finished the meal and they had all eaten too much, to feel like going on duty.

The call for the patrol to muster outside came soon enough and Willie could find little wrong with their smart appearance.

With Wilson in front, followed by two pairs, they marched through the Consul gates and soon were mingling with the crowds.

It became interesting, the way the dense crowd of people flowed towards them and passed them, without bumping and barging, it was a disciplined politeness, with no time for rudeness.

The first hour or so was an experience of meeting thousands of hurrying busy people. They could have been Chinese themselves for all the notice anyone took of them

Apart from a few American sailors making for the landing steps they saw no one who even looked like a member of their ship's company and wondered if anyone had bothered to come ashore.

At about 2300 (11pm) Wilson spotted someone a little under the weather, cap on the back of his head, wandering a bit aimlessly along the Bund.

Wilson and the libertyman recognised each other as they got closer and he was greeted by, "Hi-ya, Tug," (Wilson's nickname), "Had a smashing time, never known so many women smile at me and I'm half drunk."

Wilson spoke to him quietly, "Put your cap on straight Wallie, take your hands out of your pockets and see that light over there?" He pointed and turned Wallie by his shoulder in the right direction and shouted in his ear, "That is the landing jetty. If you hurry you will just catch the boat."

With a gentle push he started Wallie on his way and rejoined the patrol reporting to Willie, "That was Wally Barnes, he's had a few, but he's quite harmless and I've sent him on his way."

Willie snapped back, "I'm in charge of this patrol and I will decide who's drunk or not!"

Wilson did not like being corrected in front of juniors and replied firmly, "O.K., if that's the way you want it," and taking up his position at the head of patrol they began to march off once more.

Another sailor came into view rolling unsteadily and again Wilson recognised the rating. It was Paton a tough Scot who had met a merchant seaman from a ship discharging cargo from Bonnie Scotland. To commemorate such an occasion they needed a wee dram and Paton's fellow Scot knew just the bar to get it.

They drank too much and had been thrown out by a small waiter in a white coat who threatened them with the police.

Paton lost his mate and hated that little bloke in a white suit. He also had a headache.

Taffy had also seen the Scot and reporting it to Willie said bravely, "I think it's Paton, shall I talk to him?"

"Stay where you are" ordered Willie, "I'll speak to him, I think the man is drunk," then added, "You had better come as a witness."

Willie striding off on his own approached the tipsy Scot and ordered, "Come here that man and put your cap on straight."

This shortish figure in a white suit ordering Paton about was rather blurred and still resenting the bumptious little sod in white who had got him thrown out of the bar, Paton's temper snapped when this other man in white began shouting at him.

With a highland yell, fit enough for the Scottish Games, Paton seized the white figure by the crotch and neck and threw him into the Huangpu River.

The patrol rushed to rescue Willie who with the help of a nearby sampan rescued his cap, as he was brought to a jetty.

It took some time to get him back to the quarters and with a hot shower, a cup of hot tea, was little the worse for his experience.

It had however, dented his bossy ego and he did not sleep well that night.

Nothing was reported although Marcus Beatty the officer heard about the incident somehow.

The patrol, enjoying a lay in during the morning, did not stop Am Ling the cook. There was also plenty of activity going on in the laundry, where the girl had arrived early to begin her first day running the laundry.

Lee, the younger sister now fifteen years, had volunteered to light the fire under the large copper used to boil the clothes. It was not as easy to light and she was already in tears as she puffed at the stubborn paper and wood to get the fire going.

Lee's pretty face was already scarred with sooty marks, before she thought of Am Ling, the cook.

Lee had never spoken to him, having been warned by her mother that he was a wicked man, although her elder sister Anna, who knew him well, thought him ugly but kind. Terrified that her mother would not let her work in the laundry if she could not light the fire, Lee plucked up courage and knocked on the kitchen door.

Am Ling, hearing the knock, peered round to see the pretty smutty face of Lee peering round the door.

Grinning through his large teeth he welcomed Lee, "Good morning, I know what you want my pretty Lee, Anna told me you were lighting the fire."

Taking the end of his clean apron he gently brushed her smutty face to wipe the tears away and turning round, picked up a cup of fat and a hot poker he had already heated in the fire.

Looking round carefully, he entered the laundry. Telling Lee to stand back, he filled his mouth with fat and spat a stream into smouldering ashes and then inserted the hot poker.

There was an immediate burst of flame and reaching up he pulled a cord to open a vent in the chimney. The fire roared like a dragon and Lee kissed him on the cheek. It was a wonderful fire.

When the fire was burning safely, Am Ling looked at Lee, his ugly face smiling and happy, saying in a an earnest voice, "Do not say I, Am Ling, helped you with the fire, I will lose my job as Cook."

Picking up his cup and poker he happily left the laundry, as Lee washing her hands and face, saw Anna walk in, clapping her hands loudly at the sight of the roaring fire.

Working quickly together, they sorted the smalls, pillow cases and such, to go into the sink. Adding soap and soda to the water in the copper it now bubbled like a cauldron as they added the heavy linen and polled it with a dolly.

Stirring with a dolly was not easy work, but slender though Lee was, it seemed easy to this eager young girl. Later when the sheets had to be wrung, she threw them expertly over the hooks fitted overhead an twisted them almost dry.

Mother Pang arrived later in the morning and, not speaking, walked quickly round the laundry, her sharp eyes everywhere. All but satisfied, she commented when she stood by the door, "I smell pig! - what pig has been in my laundry?"

Ma Pang knew that Am Ling would be listening, and standing clear of the door as it opened, watched as Am Ling appeared with his chopper at the ready.

"Of course you smell pig, you old sow, you leave young girl to start work." Chuckling, he went back to the kitchen.

In case Am Ling came in again, Ma Pang ordered the girls to go to the linen room to collect ironing. Ma Pang was certain that Am Ling was a devil and able to spirit her daughters away if he got the chance. She had to be on her guard.

Someone seemed to be looking out of the window in the annexe as they passed, it could be the extra washing Mother had expected.

Ma and Pa Pang had managed the laundry and linen room at the consul for many years and were now getting old.

Their two daughters, Anna the eldest, 17 years, and Lee 15 years, mixed freely with the children of the staff and shared language classes in the classroom for their mutual benefit. Anna was the brightest of them all but Ma Pang thought that natural for she was quite tall for a Chinese girl. Ma Pang, more than anyone, realised the business potential of a bilingual daughter or two and retain the consul contract.

Ma Pang still held on to old beliefs, having seen young girls disappear after speaking to men in her own village. To her, there was a devil in all men. That was why she disliked the cook.

Ma Pang smiled when her two beautiful daughters entered the laundry and placed two bundles of ironing on the table for inspection. Ma Pang stroking the monogrammed pieces on the linen, smiled saying, "You have both done very well. Now I must show Lee around the wash-house so that she can begin tomorrow and light the fire under the copper."

Ma Pang slipping her hands up her sleeves, slowly began walking round, giving advice to Lee.

"Don't over fill the bucket, when topping up the copper, or you won't be able to lift it."

Moving on, she spoke of soda, soap, scrubbers. bowls and buckets, until she came to the two large linen bays.

Realising the girl was losing interest, Ma Pang asked, "What do you think those are for?" nodding towards the linen bins.

With a giggle, Lee replied, "For keeping little pigs," moving quickly out of mothers reach.

Turning to Anna, Ma Pang said, "We must now talk to sailorman about washing!" Ordering Lee to open the kitchen door, she held her wrinkled face high, tugged the hem of her tunic, put her hands up her sleeves and pattered into the kitchen. Not looking at the cook, but talking to him, she ordered, "Fetch me sailor-man, I talk laundry business. Now!"

Am Ling moved over to his spy hole in the wall behind the Yok and peeping into the mess he could see Wiggy dressed in shorts and naval singlet. Tapping lightly on the door, he entered and beckoning to Wiggy said quietly, "Big Washee woman from big house want to talk to sailor man. Now!"

Wiggy, glancing around and not seeing Sam Weller who dealt with the laundry, decided to deal with it himself. Stepping into the kitchen, Wiggy was surprised to be confronted not only with Ma Pang but also her two beautiful daughters.

Ma Pang, a little disgusted at the lustful stare from Wiggy, began a rapid dialogue in Chinese to her daughters about what she thought of this dirty little foreigner with the eyes of a rat who had the cheek to even look at her daughters. Reluctantly, she nudged her youngest daughter to try out her English on this odd creature. Happily, Lee began talking quickly but getting a little muddled said, "Me come room for bed-things to wash now take off clothes, come to bed now, Yes!"

Wiggy, hearing Lee's "come to bed", could only think of sex and nothing else. Confused, he replied, "You can't come to my bed in there," and shuffled back into the mess.

Almost everyone was present when Wiggy, boasting, shouted, "That young Chinese bird wants to take me to bed!"

Angry that his orders had been disobeyed, Wilson now towering over Wiggy said sternly, "What have you been up to now and what were you doing in the laundry?"

Wiggy, with a humble "I'm sorry."

Ordering Weller to get into the laundry and sort things out, Taffy and Bungy tagged along to see what all the fuss was about. Seeing Ma Pang and the two girls in a line as they entered the kitchen, the trio formed up in a row to bow.

Ma Pang acknowledged their presence with a brief bow, to which the sailors politely responded in Ma Pang's eyes like nodding donkeys.

Turning to Anna, Ma nodded her approval for her to talk to the sailors. Choosing Sam, by far the most handsome with black curly hair and smooth skin, it was apparent that he was very taken with her, for he had looked at her since he had walked through the door.

Anna liked the attention and with a smile she handed him a price list scrolled in Chinese just to see his reaction.

With a look of disbelief he smiled and shrugged his shoulders, pleading with his eyes for guidance.

Anna watched his face light up, when she spoke to him in English saying, "Those prices are for American dollars and Yuan, do you have dollars?"

Sam shook his head and said with a smile, "We have Hong Kong dollars, which are much better!"

Ma Pang nodded approval and Anna asked, "How many Hong Kong dollars to American dollar?"

Sam thinking quickly because he did not know, smiled hopefully and said, "Thirteen Hong Kong dollars equal one pound British."

Again Anna consulted Ma Pang and back came another question, "How many sailors are you?"

Sam brilliantly put up eight fingers.

With a smile, Anna proposed twenty Hong Kong dollars for one week all in. This was ridiculously cheap by Hong Kong standards and Sam wanting so much to impress this beautiful girl Anna, said, "Make it forty dollars in advance in case we sail."

Taffy and Bungy nodded their approval and leaving Sam to work out the details they returned to the mess.

Sam standing still as Ma Pang and Lee left the kitchen, Anna raised her hand for the price list. Sam instead took hold of her fingers and pressed them against his warm lips.

Neither spoke, but the look in their eyes told each other something.

Grabbing his towel as soon as he reached the mess, Sam hurried to the shower, whilst the water was still available. The shower room being almost as warm as the kitchen he opened the window.

Entering the laundry Anna felt radiantly happy. It seemed to begin when she had felt the touch of Sam's warm lips on her fingers. Anna had never been kissed by any man. So to be kissed by this smiling curly headed sailor had sent romantic tremors of delight to her mind and sparked a desire to kiss Sam on the lips if she got the chance.

Knowing Ma Pang's keen eye was watching her closely, Anna picked up a basket of washing for the clothes line, grabbed a bag of ties and calling, "I'll be back in a minute," she disappeared out of the back door and round the corner towards the drying area.

With her mind on Sam she almost bumped into an open window jutting out over the path. Normally these windows were always closed and without thinking she leaned in and un-hooked the stay, glancing inside.

Mesmerised by the sight of a naked body lightly tanned with a white bottom, she was transfixed as the sinewy muscles, glistening under the shower, rippled under the skin.

In a panic she slammed the window and fled back down the path and round the corner. Leaning against the wall and puffing a little, Anna could not make her mind up, whether to face Ma Pang or return to the drying area. Deciding on the latter she retraced her steps back to the drying area.

Sam who having quickly dressed had come outside.

Looking at each other and smiling they both reached for the bag of ties and their fingers touched. His thoughts were, "Oh what a beautiful face", whilst Anna thinking, "Oh what a beautiful body."

Anna, knowing that Ma Pang would soon be out if she took too long, they began hanging the clothes. With the empty basket and surrounded by washing she kissed Sam for helping and it lingered on her lips as she fled back to the laundry.

Looking at Anna, Ma Pang queried, "Where have you been girl, day dreaming in the garden?"

Anna bowed and joined Lee at the sink.

After the previous night's patrol, lying in bed was like being on leave. Am Ling had not been too noisy, and his early morning cup of tea was most welcome. Am Ling's breakfast was not too bad, with slices of fresh boiled bacon, mushroom, fried cucumber, with his hard chunky rolls and butter. Seeing Bungy bashing his roll on the table to penetrate the crust, mad Am Ling lost face and he grudgingly threw half a dozen knives on the table for the heathen sailors to use.

With Wilson's rule, no shop to be spoken at the meal table, no comments were passed about Willie's involuntary swim in the harbour.

They all enjoyed a pleasant idle day, most of them sleeping in the afternoon. No one seemed interested in walking round the shops, but idled their time away as though another patrol that night was not going to happen.

After supper Willie's voice soon reminded them it was time for them to commence duty.

Wilson asked Willie for a change of route to add a little interest. Willie spoilt it by saying, "March in the street and avoid the shit!"

They covered the Bund and waterfront once that night and Wilson seeking a change turned into a narrow side street although the lighting was poor.

The houses were shrouded in shadows with glimmers of light through cracked shutters or dim lights behind drawn curtains giving a sensation of being watched. Wilson suddenly raised his hand to stop when he heard someone calling in a weak voice, "Help Buddy - help me."

Undoing the metal whistle draped round his neck and slipping it over his wrist, Wilson approached a darkened doorway making a couple of practice swings with the chain and whistle. He then saw a moaning naked body slumped in the darkened doorway.

A short peep on the whistle brought the patrol at the double. Wilson, helped by Taffy gently raised the bloodstained body, laying him prone on the pavement. Using his cap Taffy placed it as a pillow under the victim's head who was bleeding freely from a head wound.

Sam and Bungy began removing their jumpers and stripping off vests and singlets to make rough bandages for the man had been cut and stabbed.

A boy age about eleven years appeared out of the shadows and thrust a crumpled sheet and bottle of water into Bungy's hand and then ran away. Wilson ordered Bungy to remove his underpants to cover the man's penis.

Bungy always willing, did as he was told. Suddenly the street was illuminated from two large bedroom windows being opened by half-naked and topless girls giggling and laughing at some sort of orgy going on below. Bungy caught in the lights with his pants down but never at a loss in a crisis waved something at them with a good old English sign with two fingers and pulled up his trousers.

Turning round now decently dressed Bungy helped Taffy and Wilson to get the man to bend his knees and slip on the underpants. Cleaning and bathing the stab wounds in the back, they used the rest of the sheet as a toga.

Slowly they lifted the naked sailor and carried him back to the jetty. He was an American sailor foolish enough to pick up a street prostitute.

With a hug for Wilson and a handshake, he was then handed over to a ship's medic amongst the libertymen returning to their ship.

The patrol, looking as though they been in a battle with blood on their clothing, were well looked after by Am Ling who still awake, made them tea and taking their dirty clothing, placed it in soak in the sink of the laundry.

Last night's patrol had been a messy affair and Kemp the postman, having had an early breakfast, was on his way to the ship for some fresh clothing which he could pick up with the mail.

Marcus congratulated Willie and the patrol, then wrote a full report which might be useful if the American Military Police were to ask questions.

Marcus the Gunner showed his appreciation of their efforts by granting two days unofficial leave, with the proviso that they would turn out in an emergency. He also permitted the wearing of non-uniform shirts off duty provided they were not too conspicuous.

A general rush to go shopping began and the mess was soon empty except for Sam who had things to do in the laundry.

Now the mess was clear, Sam moving quickly, stripped the beds and gathered the dirty washing. With his arms full, he walked through the kitchen and into the laundry.

This really did please Ma Pang as the girls moved to take the washing. Anna touching Sam's hand as she took some of the washing wanted so much to kiss him. Sam seeing Anna thought she looked gorgeous and whispering together Sam asked, "When will you be hanging clothes?"

Seeing Ma Pang was watching them, Anna turned to Sam with a very business-like tone and said, "Thank you Sam the laundryman, it should be ready and dry by 3pm. Here is the list," handing him a note. Sam with a bow to Ma Pang, then left the laundry. In the mess, Sam read the note quickly.

"We bring in the clothes at 2.20, Anna."

Remembering Anna had said 3 o'clock, Sam had to make sure. Returning to the kitchen, he asked Am Ling, "Are there any spare sheets?"

Am Ling with a crooked wink went to the laundry door and shouted, "Anna, sailorman Sam want clean sheets."

Anna appeared at the door handed him the sheets saying, "Remember 2.20."

With a kiss on his cheek and a pile of clean sheets from Anna, he breezed into the mess as happy as a Chinese cracker. Wasting no time he began making up the beds as though it was an Admiral's inspection day.

All the pillows were smooth, the sheets turned over an equal amount on all the beds, and the blanket tucked in and squared at the corners like wrapped biscuits.

Am Ling was well ahead with the lunch and it would not be long before the shoppers returned to make a mess of the place.

When they did turn up you would have thought they were on the front at Blackpool for all had replaced their naval singlets with gaudy Chinese Summer shirts, with Wiggy wearing a Chinese Coolie hat that made him look like a walking coloured mushroom. Wilson bought a Zeis Ikon camera for fifty Hong Kong dollars. Bungy a beautiful bone mah-jong set for about the same and a lacquer tea set for Mum. Wiggy had something wrapped up and was reluctant to say what. Eventually, they got it out of him.

Undoing his parcel, Wiggy produced an exotic pair of white silk pyjamas emblazoned with red dragons on the front and the back.

Slipping them on over his trousers he posed for Wilson in the sunshine wearing his coolie hat and pyjamas.

The lunch of Chinese eggs boiled in tea and salad was all right after the initial shock of seeing the funny colour of the eggs for the first time.

The shoppers, keen to visit a bazaar they had found, were soon off to the town again as soon as lunch was over. Wilson had noticed the tidiness of the beds with their clean linen.

Sam, watching the clock, was anxious for them to go for the time of his date with Anna was getting closer and closer. With a sign of relief, Sam watched them pass through the consul gates. With ten minutes to spare, Sam washed and did his hair and was delighted to see from the shower room the lines of beautiful washing blowing gently in the breeze were dry.

Admiring the girls hard work, he could only think of Anna as she appeared with an empty basket from round the corner. Dropping the basket, she ran to Sam as though they had been parted for years saying, "Oh Sam, I could only peck your cheek!" Reaching for his hand, she briefly held it to her face. Then, back to business, Anna said with a straight face, "I must now get the washing in on my own, Lee is required at the big house."

Working together, they quickly cleared the lines. Sam carrying the basket, followed Anna down the path to the laundry, throwing the washing on to the pile already in the clean bin.

Anna, looking nervously at the windows, took Sam's hand and led him behind the partition of the linen bins.

Here, out of sight of passers-by, Anna snuggled up to Sam and raised her soft lips to be kissed, whilst Sam with his hands on her slim waist, slowly drew her curvaceous body to him. Slowly, holding the kiss, they lowered themselves on to the sun-warmed washing in the bin.

Snuggling down, they kissed and fondled, his hand passing over her small well formed breast and resting there. Softly they whispered to each other of their growing love, enjoying the intimate closeness of their bodies.

The click of the latch on the outside door made them freeze for a second, before burying into the washing, scarcely daring to breathe.

Again the click of the latch and a door closing was heard. Leaving quietly by separate doors, not knowing who the intruder could have been.

CHAPTER 2

Major Joe O'Brien, veteran of many campaigns during the war, was enjoying his present appointment, his wife being a Chinese American, had family links here in Shanghai.

He was interested in a report brought to his notice by Sergeant Borkowski with his morning mail who commented, "It's blue Major" meaning the U.S. Navy.

The Sergeant, smiling all over his rugged face said, "They even got the Admiral to sign it."

Reading the report, Joe came to a tasty bit and said to the Sergeant, "Listen to this Admiral's comment," "....and my men pursuing recreational pursuits are in constant danger from local thugs who the Military Police are supposed to etc. etc."

"I'd like to see a bit of brass around the town watching these recreational pursuits! - My Butt - These fish-heads have three things in mind as soon as they step ashore, Females, Fighting and Frothy beer. God! We picked up three in the meat wagon last night and that guy was very lucky being seen by the Royal Navy, he too could have been in the meat wagon!"

Sergeant Borkowski coughed to catch the Major's attention and reported, "I have made an appointment for you to see the Officer of the British patrol today at 10.30. He requested to meet you by phone this morning. The way he spoke, it was like a guy reporting for duty."

"Paying his respects, or something."

"Shall I tell the corporal to get out your suit with medals?"

The Major nodded, saying "Borrow a decent chair, that thing you clean your boots on is crap."

The corporal's private Chinese ornate throne was brought in and dusted. The Major met Marcus outside and after shaking hands invited Marcus into his office. Marcus removing his cap, was amused to see the ornate chair.

The Major wasting no time sat at his desk, and with a wave of his hand, indicated to Marcus that he should sit there on the throne. Taking it all in his stride as though he was used to such treatment, Marcus sat down with his briefcase beside him, and crossed his legs.

Joe did not want the conversation to drift away from Navy matters too much, and began to talk of the activities of gunboats of the American Navy like the S.S. Patan sunk by the Chinese before the war and the Amethyst, a British ship that ran the gauntlet of steaming down the Yangtse whilst being shot at from both sides of the river.

Holding up the Admiral's letter and saying, "Nowadays, we have to worry about sailors being stabbed as well as drunk these days."

Now the subject had been raised, the Major asked "Can you tell me exactly what happened last night?"

Marcus, who had been expecting this matter to be raised, gave a full account and also the observations of the patrol. The building from which the sailor had been dumped was a brothel from whose windows the whores had been jeering and laughing. This was music to Joe's ears, last night's incident had been one of a series of such attacks on sailors in that particular district. The Major, not one for cutting corners, came straight to the point.

"Can you cooperate and show us this brothel and we'll close the joint down."

Marcus, not wanting to commit the patrol at this stage or appear to be chickening out, agreed, saying quite casually, "Of course, our men are unarmed, but we have whistles."

Both the Major and the Sergeant burst out laughing and, the Sergeant saying, "Whistles, Sir - in Shanghai!"

At that point, Marcus leaned over and recovered his briefcase standing by the chair. He took out and placed a parcel on the desk.

"Accept this, Sir, with the compliments of the Royal Navy," then added, "Of course, we will cooperate."

The parcel helped to break up the conversation, for Marcus did not in fact have a free hand, in what he could and could not do.

The Major, not knowing what to expect, accepted the parcel graciously and encouraged by Marcus unwrapped the box.

He first of all withdrew a brass and enamelled ship's crest mounted on a plinth. Placing it in a prominent position, he said to his Sergeant, "Now isn't that something Borkowski!"

Returning to the parcel and undoing the wrapping he was confronted with a large bottle of genuine Scotch Whisky. Placing it firmly on the desk, he extended his hand, saying, "Uh?"

Marcus said, "Marcus." Giving his name once again.

"Thanks again. Now let us celebrate something Marcus!"

Borkowski needed no orders and quickly returned with three glasses and an ice box on a tray. Looking at the Major for a signal, the Major nodded and Borkowski began to pour generously. Handing round the tray adding the ice as required, they all raised their glasses to the toast by the Major.

"America and the King's Royal Navy."

There was a reverent silence as the high gravity strength of the whisky tantalised their palates.

Mellowed by the warmth created by the drink, the Major said, "Do you usually do this sort of thing in the Royal Navy?"

"Oh yes" said Marcus, "we have been doing it for centuries, offering the natives gifts for young maidens as we jumped from our long boats."

Marcus then added, "In China, it is an old saying, 'obligate your brother first' and we in the Navy just follow the local customs."

Reverting to duty, the Major enquired, "What are you using for patrol transport, after all, you cannot row round Shanghai."

Marcus blandly replied, "We have no transport."

Both of the Americans laughed out loud, Borkowski saying in disbelief, "You're using your feet!"

The Major and Sergeant Borkowski turning away from Marcus, went into a private huddle. Borkowski poured another round of drinks and the Major, raising his glass, proposed a toast.

"To Marcus's jeep, God help those who ride in her."

Marcus was a bit overcome, they were giving him a jeep.

"Thank you. Does it come with a Chinese driver?"

Borkowski and the Major looked at each other and smiled. Borkowski, asking to be excused, then asked Marcus the name of his Petty Officer and noting it down, left the office.

Hearing that his car was outside, Marcus and the Major shook hands, Joe saying cheerfully, "See you at nine tonight!"

Stepping into the car, Marcus was driven away.

It was about midday when he phoned P.O. Willard and cancelled leave that evening and asked him to display a notice in the mess than an early supper would be served at 1800.

Willie entered the mess for a second time to pin a notice on the temporary notice board. All leave cancelled. Patrol to muster at 2100. Thinking to himself, "Just wait and see their faces."

The patrol members were in high spirits about the shops in Shanghai when they returned, until they saw the notice on the board. Some thought they had been recalled to the ship to be replaced or that the ship itself was leaving.

Am Ling improved their spirits with a splendid lunch of Chinese Rolls, luscious vegetables and rice.

Making themselves comfortable after a heavy lunch, most of them fell asleep in chairs, but Taffy liked his bed and got in between the clean sheets. Willie the Petty Officer didn't relax so easily and feeling warm and uncomfortable, headed for the showers with a towel round his waist. Adjusting it and getting the full benefit of the pressure, he soaped and splashed to his heart's content.

A loud banging on the outside door woke everyone with a start. Bungy, being the nearest went to open the door, but it opened suddenly and a six-foot plus G.I. said, "Where's Mr Willud, buddy. I'm in a hurry!"

Bungy, not really awake, pointed to the door leading to Willie's room and the showers. Marching in and through the door, the G.I. brushed the shower curtain to one side and smacking the only bare backside in front of him, said, "Hey buddy - you, Willum, I've got it outside and I've got to present it to you in person man, here grab that," handing Willie his towel and taking his elbow the G.I. led him outside.

Standing outside was a brand new jeep, marked Royal Navy with a white ensign on the bonnet. Holding up Willie's towel with one hand while he signed the requisition form, he dropped it as his buddy, waiting in another jeep, impatiently honked for him to get aboard. Holding the keys and papers in one hand and his towel in the other, Willie headed back to his room to get dressed. In no time at all the whole patrol were outside admiring a U.S. jeep in navy colours.

Willie appeared now in shirt and trousers and ordered, "Get your hands off that. It's mine."

Walking round the jeep, he felt quite proud of himself, until someone shouted, "Who is going to drive it?"

Marcus now appeared in the driveway and patting the jeep on the bonnet, said to Willie, "Give me the keys."

Climbing into the jeep, Marcus invited Petty Officer Willard to join him and together they drove round the consul grounds.

The left-hand drive proved a little odd to Marcus at first, but he soon got used to it and they arrived back with the jeep still in one piece.

Before getting out, Marcus asked Willie, "Have you anyone in mind yet to drive the jeep?"

Willie replied quickly, "Leave that to me, Sir. I've made a few contacts!"

Not wanting to embarrass Willie by asking who these contacts were, Marcus instead instructed Willie that he needed Leading Seaman Wilson and the four seamen for a patrol that evening, whilst Petty Officer Willard, could use Kemp and Black for jetty duty.

Checking the fuel gauge, he handed the jeep keys to Willie, saying, "I'll see you at 9pm (2100) with a driver."

Was it wise, he thought, as he walked away, to leave the question of a driver to Willie.

Willie, on leaving the jeep, was followed into the mess by an interested patrol. Without knocking, Willie entered the kitchen and immediately the shouting began, with Willie retreating from an excited Am Ling waving his meat chopper, jabbering in Chinese.

Sam Weller, about the only one who could get Am Ling to calm down, walked between him and Willie and said to Willie, "Would you like me to talk to him about the driver, Petty Officer?"

Willie, blustering said, "All I asked him was did he know a driver," and he began clucking like a bloody hen and waving his chopper.

Then, nodding to Sam, he said: "OK, be careful - he's a nutter!"

Sam, entering the kitchen, moved two stools together and inviting Am Ling to sit next to him, he mimed a driver, then taking him through the laundry showed him the jeep in the driveway.

Now Am Ling understood everything, and with his best English, said, "Chung Ling, all Ling, drive jip jip, sleep jip jip, clean jip, no pay pay."

Sam and Am Ling went back to the kitchen and Sam conveyed to Am Ling to bring Chung Ling here, and said "Now!"

Removing his apron and cap, Am Ling mounted his bicycle and sped off towards the big house.

Willie, still sitting in the mess, listened to what Sam had to say, but disagreed that if the driver was any good, he had to be paid. Marcus would decide that and anything else, about the jeep. Dealing with Am Ling had been enough for Willie. Going outside, Willie ordered Wilson, Edwards, Evans, Bennett and Weller into the jeep to satisfy himself that the seating was ample. He also checked a generous first aid and tools.

Just as they were about to dismount, Am Ling appeared with another Chinaman, looking very much like Am Ling who said, "Chung drive jip."

The Chinaman's eyes shining at the sight of the gleaming jeep, seated himself behind the wheel. Willie, seating himself in the passenger seat on the right, turned to Wilson, saying, "I'll just give him a short driving test to see how he manages the traffic."

With a slap on the back he ordered the driver to start. The engine fired first time and with a thump, the clutch was engaged. Then with a jerk and a roar of the exhaust, they changed to second, followed by a blast from the horn as they shot through the gates and into the traffic.

Willie in the passenger seat gripped the safety bar, and the sailors, almost unseated, clung on for dear life.

Honking his way forward with a curse or two at the policeman on traffic duty, he sometimes leaned out and pushed the odd pedestrian for being too close to the jeep. To Chung, all rickshaws seemed to be fair game.

In the seven minutes that Willie was aboard the jeep for the so-called test, they had covered almost a circuit of Shanghai.

One upended rickshaw man stood cursing at the consul gates. Willie needed no assistance to get out of the jeep and simply fell out into the driveway, while Chung helping him to his feet said cheerfully, "You like Shanghai. Good?"

Wilson, Bennett, Evans and Weller tumbled out like wounded men, rubbing arms and legs and Wiggy, who had sat on his cap and crushed it flat, and still in a kneeling position in the jeep, cursing, "I'll murder that yellow bastard, if I can get my hands on him."

Willie's troubles were not yet over and recovering a little, he asked Am Ling to ask Chung for his driving license.

A dirty folded piece of paper covered in Chinese characters and stamps meant nothing, but, if Willie was asked, he could at least say that he had seen some documentary proof, hoping that Marcus would accept his word and choice of a driver.

Willie retired to his room to eat his evening meal and reflect over his own decision to choose and examine Chung for the post of driver. The license Chung had produced was a folded piece of paper with stampings and Chinese characters, which could easily have been for a driving offence.

Hoping that Marcus as an officer would not probe too deeply into Chung's background and that all went well tonight, Willie was secretly pleased not to be going with the patrol this evening.

Promptly at 2045 the patrol mustered. From Marcus came the question, "What about your driver. Is he satisfactory?"

"Well Sir, I have been driven round the town by him and he didn't kill anyone!"

Amused Marcus turning to the patrol, he ordered L/Seaman Wilson, Weller, Edward and Evans into the jeep, leaving Willard with the other for embarkation duty on the jetty.

Expecting to be back by midnight and hearing the sound of the jeep's horn at the gate, he ordered Chung to drive off.

Chung took off much too fast and had to brake hard which didn't please Marcus at all.

Seizing Chung by the scruff of the neck, he shook him like a rag doll, saying, "You stupid fool."

Chung hung his head in shame and with a further signal to drive on, drew up behind the Major's jeep, and they were on their way.

Now indicating a right turn, they followed the Major, leaving the rest to go straight ahead.

Again the Major's jeep indicated a turn and entered a side courtyard of a private entrance to a smart restaurant, with a flower covered trellis.

The Major and his American-Chinese driver Benjamin stepped from the jeep and waving to Marcus to follow, entered the private door to the restaurant.

The Major's driver Benjamin ordering Chung to move over to the passenger seat, drove away to meet Sergeant Borkowski and his men, who were having a little entertainment of their own elsewhere.

A beautiful Chinese woman, taking the Major's cap and hanging it up on a hat stand, turned to greet Joe saying: "Joe darling, I am pleased you could come home tonight."

Placing her slim, elegant fingers against his cheeks, she drew his face to hers to softly kiss his ready lips. Much to Marcus' surprise, another girl entered with an older Chinese gentleman, saying, "You must be Marcus?"

Hearing his name spoken, Marcus turned to face another Chinese girl equally beautiful to the first, though rather taller, holding the arm of an older Chinese gentleman, who bowed as Marcus looked at him.

"Meet my Papa", said the girl, giving Marcus an appreciative look. With a simple bow the older said, "Welcome to my home Marcus, meet my daughter Lita, Una's sister."

He turned to greet his wife, descending the stairs.

Lita, taking Marcus's cap and fingering the golden cap badge before handing it up, confided, "Joe told us all about you and your present of a ship's crest - he's been showing it to everyone."

Smiling, Marcus attracted to the exciting presence of this beautiful girl answered, "We in the British Navy have been doing it for hundreds of years, bribing fathers, to give up their lovely daughters."

Together they laughed and she replied, "I'd better not tell Papa that or he'll be exchanging me for one, too!"

"Come on, we'll join the others."

They moved to enter the restaurant. Seated at a half circular table with the parents in the middle looking out on the octagonal centre floor, she placed her hand on Marcus' thigh as though they had known each other for a long time and commented, "Joe cannot handle chopsticks, so we have provided knives and forks this evening if you want them."

Marcus was pleased to be able to say, "No, I have been using Chopsticks at the Consul, after all, it is an art, and I like to be able to join in and do as the Chinese do."

Without thinking, he placed his hand on hers resting on his thigh, while Lita continuing to chatter happily about America, spoke with great affection of where she had been at college in Seattle.

The waiter hovered, then the meal was served quickly to meet Joe's wishes. Each couple were too wrapped up in themselves in the intimate atmosphere of the restaurant to begin a general conversation and ate the meal in silence.

Lita being such an uncomplicated beauty, brought out the best in Marcus and he already felt that his love for the Royal Navy was under attack each time he looked into her beautiful face and her eyes welcomed him.

Still holding hands and touching each other's thighs, their intense attraction for each other grew.

Marcus was one of those remarkable young Canadians who had joined the R.N. to fight for King and Country. When he would return was uncertain for he loved being a naval officer.

When Joe stood up, Una pleaded with Joe to come home soon. Lita hoping Marcus would do so too,

Joe always put duty first and with a kiss to each of the women, followed by a kiss from Lita to Marcus, they boarded the waiting jeeps.

The time was 2320 when the first pair of jeeps eased their way silently into the shadows, adjacent to the brothel. The following jeeps dispersed a short distance on the other side. Marcus' men were to remain in the jeep until Wilson, who was the decoy, had entered the building. Marcus and the Major were already in position against the wall by the brothel door. Wilson took his part seriously and broke into a nautical version of "Nelly Dean!" before knocking loudly on the brothel door.

Getting no reply, he banged a great deal louder, an old painted face appeared in the sliding panel in the door. It flew open then snapped shut. Wilson was about to knock again, when the door opened wider to let him in. Barely inside he was roughly pushed from the back and flattened against the wall as Joe's military police rushed in.

These were followed by more soldiers passing through and Wilson worried about the unconscious woman who let him in. He took a chance, picked her up and finding a door unlocked, carried her inside and laid her on the floor clear of the door.

Using a cushion as a pillow he raised the woman's head and gently placed it on the cushion. A dim light suddenly came on and in the half darkness, Wilson could make out a number of half-naked or topless girls appearing from behind draped mosquito netting curtains and coming towards him.

Silently whispering and giggling, they gathered around him, not taking the slightest interest in the unconscious woman.

Slowly, although not pushing him, he found himself eased on to the bed with no resistance on his part to lash out and free himself.

Soft lips touched his cheeks, his hands were held by smaller hands firmly against soft firm breasts and soft tongues penetrated his mouth. All his efforts to raise himself from the bed were wasted having no leverage from the bed against the clinging fingers of his tormentors.

He could feel himself being slowly unbuttoned, exposed and then fondled in an exciting way until a light came on, and a man's voice said harshly, "Let go of that," and fondling ceased.

The whack of a stick on a female bottom and a scream, broke the silence.

Marcus ordered Wilson to get dressed as the girls retreated to their beds, covering their faces with the flimsy sheets.

Wilson's embarrassment was compounded by his feeble explanations of the charging soldiers and an unconscious woman and gang rape by a bevy of Chinese beauties just didn't add up.

Locking the room with the girls inside, Wilson returned to the patrol now standing in the hall, eagerly awaiting orders from Marcus on what to do when the action began.

Although they were on a serious investigation, Marcus could not help having a little chuckle to himself about Wilson getting himself captured by females, as he climbed the stairs to rejoin the Major on the first floor.

Knocking quietly and entering the bedroom on the first floor, Marcus was surprised to see the Major sitting down, obviously thinking. He didn't have to wait long, before the Major stated, "I think we've drawn a ghost, Marcus - the place is empty, apart from the girls."

Benjamin, the Major's driver and never very far from the Major's side in Shanghai, called, "Sir, I'm sure those reports we had were first class and the gang is here somewhere!"

Suddenly Marcus swore, "Bloody priest holes - they were at it long before we were, no wonder we have been puzzled by those double doors."

Pulling up a chair next to the Major and speaking in a soft voice, he began, "In England, there have been secret stairs and priest holes for centuries. It is a hidden space with a secret opening where the families can hide a priest or dodgy relative who cannot pay the rent. The Chinese are past masters with their carvings. In a ship we have double bottoms and watertight compartments, where you could hide the crown jewels if you wanted to, let us look at those double doors."

Together they quietly closed the bedroom doors then opened them. Everything seemed normal. Marcus then closed the door and the quiet click of a lock engaging could be heard.

Another feature was noticeable on closer examination, the carving on the door and wall matched and keyed together. Open or closed the wall looked solid, but was actually half a door wide. Getting Benjamin to examine the wall behind the door, he lit a cigarette and easing away a piece of the beading around the panel, he directed the smoke from his mouth towards the crack. It was sucked up as with a chimney.

Dispatching Borkowski and another soldier to carry out tests on the space behind each bedroom door directly above, they all thought that Benjamin's idea of a mock Chinese fire, to smoke out anyone hiding in a priest hole or hideaway, would be most effective.

It was the same in each room with double doors Borkowski reported.

The Major's plan was simple, but effective, based on Benjamin's idea, who was already in the kitchen collecting items he would need.

A Yok, dirty cooking oil, a taper, old rags. A couple of fire extinguishers from the jeep would also be needed and smoke masks from sheets, to avoid too much discomfort for those who would be close to the stinking fire to be created.

Taking up agreed positions around the panelled wall behind the opened half-door, the beading was eased away to increase the flow of air through the cracks. At a signal from the Major, guns were drawn and pads for the face held ready. Benjamin lit a concoction of dirty oil, smelly rags and something he would not name held in the yok. Placing it close to the panel, he lit it with a lighted taper. With a 'whoosh' of burning oil, it settled down to a smoking, stinking putrid black smoke which could be seen being sucked into the cracks like smoke in a fireplace. Giving the job of keeping the smoke going to another soldier, Benjamin began shouting, in Chinese, "Fire! Fire!" throughout the house, whilst downstairs the sailors unlocked the room with the girls inside who welcomed them until the sailors began shouting and slapping their bare bottoms with their caps, and drove them screaming up the stairs.

The acrid smell of burning was now strong and the repeated shouts by Benjamin of, "Fire!" added to the fear and hysterical screams made by the girls as they rushed up the stairs.

In the swirling stinking smoke in the bedrooms, things began to happen fast and a panel in the wall shot up and an evil looking dagger appeared grasped in someone's hand.

Borkowski reacted instantly with a savage kick that must have broken the wrist, he then seized the forearm and dragged the screaming man into the bedroom to be silenced by the soldiers. Borkowski instinctively drew his gun when a gun appeared and twisted to fire into the bedroom. Before the hand could be withdrawn, Borkowski had fired two rounds smashing the hand and wrist. Again seizing the bleeding stump above the shattered wrist, he dragged the demented gunman into the bedroom.

Removing the smouldering yok and oil by throwing it into the backyard, Benjamin was able to coax a sobbing girl from behind the panel. It was a distressing sight as she wiped her bloodstained hands down her flimsy nightdress and wept.

Wrapping her in a sheet, the girl curled up on a bed still sobbing.

Bringing the first aid box into service, the medic soldier did what he could for the wounded men.

Upstairs, the soldiers had the same success, capturing four of the gang with one soldier receiving a bullet in the leg. He took the wound as a bonus being on active service, for it meant he would be on his way home. The sound of a Police siren was the signal for Sam to leave.

They were all soon in the jeep with Chung driving from the area like a getaway car.

All of them agreed that the girls were too young and pretty to be hurt and Wilson knew it was an experience he would not forget.

There was little activity in the mess this morning and the only noise was the occasional clatter from the kitchen, as Am Ling preparing breakfast, moved around the kitchen.

Being busy, he did not notice Ma Pang slithering in her tiny shoes and raising the yok hiding hole to peep into the mess, where the sailors were still sleeping. Allowing the yok to swing back into place, she began muttering, "Lazy foreign devils, laying in their beds like pigs, while we wait for the washing."

Am Ling, hearing this and incensed that she had the arrogance to use his peephole without his permission, shouted angrily, "Get away from my peep hole, you dirty old woman, looking at sailors dickies. They all work late last night - now lie in bed."

Am Ling opening the laundry door, pointed to the uniform in soak in the sink with other pieces of clothing and again shouted: "Now get out your scrubber, you old crow, and get on with that lot. Let the pretty girls collect the laundry!"

It was Ma Pang's turn to be angry, "Don't you speak of my daughters through your evil mouth, you dirty ugly peasant or I will put some taste into your lousy soup with a bar of soap!"

Picking up his meat chopper and waving it wildly, he ranted, "Go Go GO before I pigtail you."

Ma Pang sniffed and pattered into the laundry. No-one could sleep once Am Ling was aroused and having already prepared the breakfast, and still shaking with temper, he seized the piglet he was preparing for lunch in his shaking hand and raised his meat chopper.

Wiggy at this moment entered the kitchen to ask for a cup of tea. Seeing the angry face of Am Ling, the raised chopper and shaking piglet, he turned away shouting as he entered the mess, "He's killing a little pig out there, the rotten sod!"

Taffy, always ready with a gibe, called, "Are you sure it was a pig? These Chinese eat funny things!"

Am Ling appearing at the mess door, held up the bloodied carcass of the piglet and shaking it at Taffy replied, "Chinese not eat funny things - Chinese eat pig!"

With a final wave of the carcass, he returned to the kitchen.

Not losing face to Ma Pang or people like Taffy, Am Ling began serving the breakfast of egg and bacon, tomatoes and fried courgettes on plates and laying them out on the table with bread rolls, left it to get cold. If they couldn't use the chopsticks he threw on the table, it was just too bad. Wilson now sitting at the table, ordered Taffy to get up. He didn't like Taffy's attitude to the cook, who after all had been most helpful last night when they returned after midnight.

An apology to Am Ling would put things right. Taffy grudgingly agreed.

Wilson's troubles were not yet over, for his order that meal times were not for talking about what they got up to the night before.

Wiggy had more than a chip on his shoulder and the cold breakfast had not helped. He stood up at the table and looking like a man prepared to walk the plank for his principles looking at Wilson, he complained. "I heard what you lot got up to last night, whilst I was on duty on the jetty - don't give me any more of that no sex at the table, when you lot have been having a good time chasing Chinese dolly birds up the stairs and having a bit. It was bad enough having to stand on the jetty listening to the Americans going on about the women they had been with."

He then pointed at Wilson saying, "You're worse than my Mother about sex and she's a Presbyterian!"

Picking up his cap, he swaggered from the mess.

Wilson, having let Wiggy get it off his chest, said nothing and got on with his breakfast. The silence that followed emphasised Wilson's intention to keep the meal table a sex-free zone.

The laundry was the next subject that Wilson wanted to bring up for some of the uniform whites had got pretty grubby last night.

Sam was more than pleased to talk about the laundry and it was unfortunate that Taffy also had ideas on this service and was quick to point out, that if it came to fixing prices, he would have something to say.

Breakfast over, they all disappeared, leaving Wiggy brooding at the table with the subject of the laundry unsolved.

Am Ling looking through his peephole and seeing the table clear except for Wiggy, decided to clear the table and pass on the laundry message for a meeting at 9am this morning, that he had received from Ma Pang.

Entering the mess, Am Ling asked, "You see, Sam the laundryman?"

Wiggy shrugged his shoulders and got up, to join the others then said, "All right, I'll come," and followed Am Ling into the kitchen. Expecting to see Ma Pang and possibly the girls, Wiggy was disappointed and seeing Am Ling pick up his meat chopper, decided to get Sam after all.

Sam, followed by Taffy, Bungy and Wiggy all trooped into the kitchen as Ma Pang entered with the girls for the 9am meeting.

Ma Pang moving forward slowly, a girl on either side, stopped a clear distance from the sailors and with a slight nod of the head acknowledged the presence of the sailors, who she thought nodded back like donkeys.

The girls, looking down, also bowed, keeping their faces lowered. They were both extremely beautiful and Ma Pang, not liking the lecherous look of one of them commenced a tirade of Chinese abuse at the man, before nudging Anna to speak.

Anna raised her head and first looking at Sam, then Taffy, Bungy and Wiggy, wondered if they came any smaller, as each one was shorter than the one next to him and Anna was taller than Wiggy.

Looking back at Sam, Anna smiled a little, saying, "Ma Pang, the linen lady for the big house has agreed to permit Lee and I, to do your washing."

Taffy unable to resist talking to this English speaking beauty, piped up crudely, "You can do my washing anytime, darling."

Anna replied quickly, "Can you pay American rates in U.S. Dollars?"

Taffy was flummoxed having to think in dollars and Sam, quick to exploit Taffy's hesitation, replied at once: "We can pay in Hong Kong Dollars which are just as good."

Anna, thinking what a soft voice compared to Taffy and turning to Ma Pang for approval and to Sam with a gentle smile, she asked, "How many Hong Kong Dollars for one American Dollar?"

Needing time to think, Sam replied, "There are thirteen Hong Kong Dollars to a British Pound, but we can pay fifty Hong Kong for us all for one week."

Anna smiled this time, saying, "Sam, when can we have the washing soon perhaps."

Ma Pang ordered her daughter Lee to speak.

Lee, excitedly said, "Me come bed now, take off clothes, no extra dollars."

With a look at the rest of them, Sam quietly said, "Get out." As Wiggy was about to comment.

Lingering behind the others, Sam, now quite close to Anna said, "It is better I bring the laundry to you, it is safer that way." For a brief moment, they touched each other's hand.

As Sam entered the mess, Wiggy, talking to Bungy, was turning the young girl Lee's words into a personal invitation for him to go to bed with the youngster. Sam, stripping Wiggy's bed and grabbing any clothes of his that he thought could be washed, said to the astonished Wiggy, "This is what she meant, you dirty little sod." And disappeared through the kitchen door on his way to the laundry.

Ma Pang, so pleased to see the first bundle of washing arrive from the mess, began sorting it. Taking a chance with Ma Pang in the laundry, Sam whispered to Anna, "Can I speak to you, please?"

Without replying, Anna touched the string bag and shook a piece of clothing. Understanding, Sam bowed to Ma Pang and the girls and left the laundry.

Kemp, the signalman, caused a stir after returning from the ship with extra clothing for the patrol and mail, saying that he had heard a rumour. Communicators were usually the first to know and it was confirmed very soon afterwards, when the Gunner Marcus appeared and announced the ship had sailed and there would be no libertymen tonight and no need for a patrol. They could please themselves and take the leave that was cancelled last night.

Willie of course quickly began issuing orders when the news reached him, even though the ship may only be gone for an hour or two. Anyone going into the town were advised to go in pairs and put their names in the leave book now in the Petty Officer's room.

The ship's departure was taken very calmly by everyone who was already talking of walking round the city and seeking bargains in the shops.

Sam, not wanting to go, was quite happy to arrange the washing, hoping to meet the charming Anna. Willie was glad to get rid of them for an hour or two and it did not take them long to get ready, sign the leave book and be on their way into town.

Sam, equally keen, grabbed sheets, pillow cases and anything washable and marched calmly into the laundry. Anna seeing Sam enter, went to give him a hand, but Ma Pang waved her aside. Lee now joined her mother, sorting the washing, It took all Ma Pang's time to control her enthusiastic daughter Lee, who was keen to fill the copper and begin her first wash.

Unseen, Anna and Sam slipped out through the rear door into the grounds. Taking his hand, she led him around the corner and across the path to a small enclosed garden with a wooden seat and sitting by side, they naturally sat close together. Not really knowing how to begin, Sam, who was completely fascinated by the aura of her lovely face, just sat there taking in her lovely eyes, soft lips and perfect complexion. Sam almost in a dream that he was here with the most beautiful girl he had ever seen. Anna, in these few brief moments had become something very special to him, and leaning a little towards her, she turned quite instinctively to kiss him softly on the lips. Sam never wanted to forget that kiss and raising her hand to his lips, said, "Anna, I have something important to say, I think I am falling in love with you."

She nodded her head not quite understanding what Sam really meant, although the light in his eyes told her a great deal more.

Taking hold of her hand he told her, "Our ship has sailed and we may be here a little longer."

Anna's eyes said she liked the idea, but she said nothing and offered her lips to be kissed again.

Suddenly she said, "Sam you are sweet like honey, I must leave you." And she kissed him again and hurried back to the laundry.

Sam in a dream made his way back to the mess. Throwing himself on to his bed he thought, "God, she is really beautiful."

Suddenly, Sam was brought back to earth, as Petty Officer Willard walked in and shouted, "What the hell is going on here, get off your fat backside and get this damned mess cleared up. If it's not tidy in half an hour, there will be no leave for you, my lad."

Working as rapidly as he could, Sam made up the beds, folded towels and generally tidied up, before Willie once again passed through to see if his orders had been obeyed.

Satisfied, he still extracted a price, saying, "Weller, could you arrange for one of the girls to iron my shirts?"

"Of course, Petty Officer. Can I take them now?"

Willie, returning to his room, produced three shirts for Sam to get ironed. Wasting no time, Sam again passed through the kitchen into the laundry. Seeing Sam, Anna quickly moved to take the shirts and moving away from Ma and Lee, she raised her beautiful eyes and said in a soft voice, "Oh, Sam, Sam, I think I'm loving you all the time, can you come back after we have finished?"

Sam nodded and smiled. Anna, glancing round to see if anyone was looking, planted a kiss on his cheek and moved off.

Giving Ma Pang a brief bow, he quickly left the laundry.

Amongst a dozen or so letters that had been collected by Kemp before the ship had sailed, was a letter for Sam from a friend.

Taking a chair outside, he sat in the sun, reading his mail until the shoppers returned for lunch.

A happy lot they were too. Everyone had bought something and Wilson, who had bought a Zeiss Ikon camera for five Hong Kong Dollars, couldn't resist using it when he saw Sam posed on a chair, sitting in the sun. Wiggy had a coolie hat that covered him like an umbrella. Black and Bungy had picked up a mahjong set for twenty Hong Kong Dollars.

A further shopping spree was planned for this afternoon to buy shirts in a bazaar, that sold everything from carpets to clogs. Looking at the mahjong set, Wiggy commented, "All we need now is some opium and we have our own sin bin!"

It was a warm sunny day and with the windows open, it became an open-air restaurant when Am Ling brought in plates of mottled Chinese eggs boiled in tea, salad and rice. Getting used to Am Ling's cooking, they found that the taste of the eggs wasn't bad at all.

Bungy reading his Mum's letter, for she thought the food in the ship was not very nourishing, told him to ask the cook for a good bread pudding.

Before the shoppers once again left for the shops, Sam asked Bungy to get him two white short-sleeved shirts.

Whilst Am Ling cleared the table, Sam sat outside in the sun and watched his messmates disappear through the gates into the crowds.

A little later, Am Ling called Sam from the mess to tell him that Ma Pang had now left the laundry. Still a little apprehensive, Sam asked, "Does Ma Pang come back?"

"No" said Am Ling "the old crow go home."

With a token piece of washing, Sam confidently entered the laundry. Peering round, then crossing the floor to where Anna stood, he was about to put his arms around her, when she pointed down to the floor. Kneeling down beside her taking something from a shelf, was Lee, her younger sister. Anna, looking at Sam with a sparkle in her eye, said: "Someone here wants to meet you," and touching Lee on the shoulder, the girl stood up, wiped her hand and with dancing eyes, held out her fingers to be kissed.

CHAPTER 3

Sam, not seduced by this youthful coquette, obliged and said, "You have been talking to your sister."

"Yes" said Lee and looking at Anna, giggled and said, "Can I feel you hair?"

Bending his head, the two girls ran their fingers through his curly black head of hair.

It's soft springy texture seemed to please them both and with a final giggle, Lee picked up a bundle of linen and giving a knowing smile, left them to go home.

Taking Sam by the hand, Anna led him behind the framework of the sorting bins and out of sight of the windows, looking into each other's eyes, they kissed passionately, he sensing and feeling the touch of her firm breasts and softly curving body and hips, whilst Anna, feeling the sinewy strength of his shoulders, fantasised about the beautiful body of Sam she was now holding.

Together their faces turned and looked at the sun warmed pile of sheets and slowly sank together intimately kissing her gently and fondling her beautifully formed young breast.

The metallic click of the door latch, chillingly froze them together for a moment. Burying deeper, they lay perfectly still. Slowly, the footsteps approached then stopped and began to recede. With a click once again, the door closed.

Clinging together, they remained amongst the sheets for a minute or two.

Slowly they got up, smiling and relieved then laughed when Sam said: "We should have locked the door. Never mind, we'll remember it next time, Anna darling."

Anna smiling a little said, "That was the tenderest moment I have ever felt." It left her with a desire and a longing for Sam she had never had for any man before.

With a farewell kiss, they each left by different doors.

From then on a routine of mock patrols were arranged by Marcus as a training programme and included the use of the jeep.

Weller and Taffy were keen to become drivers. Marcus had already obtained a permit via the Consul to drive providing they always took Chung, in case of any incident, where his language might be useful.

Marcus could not get Lita out of his mind and was glad, when a telephone call from the Major gave him an invitation.

"I've been meaning to phone you Marcus, but I've been busy and Una and Lita have been giving me hell for not inviting you over. Can you make this evening? - You can, that's great. Don't worry about a driver. Lita wants to use her own car. See you at 7pm. A jacket will do. OK Buddy. Be seeing you." With that he rang off.

Marcus could have brought down the house, if he could sing, the way he felt. The Navy held the promise that he would one day meet the King and Queen, but that was fading fast now he had met Lita.

What am I going to wear, passed through his mind, feeling like a poor relative. After all, he had only expected to be ashore for a short spell. I wonder if Chung could help.

Chung could more than help, for after his disastrous beginning, Marcus had become appreciative of Chung's efforts to please.

Within a few minutes of Chung reporting to his room and a quick trip to a tailor, Marcus was back in his room, admiring the excellent fit of a smart cream linen suit and silk shirt.

Even the footwear of light brown leather had a touch of class and all for less than one hundred Hong Kong dollars.

Telling Willard he was dining with the Major, he hoped the patrol would have a pleasant evening.

Lita arrived a little early, but Marcus was already outside the gates waiting, Smiling in an ancient Chevrolet, she could have been in America the way she looked.

Marcus, sitting in the passenger seat, was too far away from her to steal a kiss, although they touched hands before she let out the clutch and heaved the steering wheel to join the procession of traffic flowing along the Nanking road.

Lita did not appear to notice the dozens of cyclists alongside, within inches of the car, as she slowly increased speed. In the midst of all these vehicles and people, she calmly began a conversation, "Have you been waiting long, Marcus?"

"Yes, from the moment I first saw you" he replied.

Turning round to look at him, they both smiled and she spoke again.

"Like your suit, makes you look very young."

Smiling at the compliment he returned it in good measure by saying, "You're the prettiest driver I've ever been in a car with."

Lita, just missing a rickshaw, laughed, saying, "Have there been many?"

Marcus, feeling the conversation was going in the wrong direction, asked, "Will the Major, I mean Joe, be there this evening?"

"Sure, he will, it takes a lot to part him and Una."

They were soon easing their way into the rear of Jung's restaurant. As soon as they stopped, she ran round the car and threw her arms about his neck, "I've waited for this" and clutching his arm, she said, "Oh Marcus, I wish you could stay with us a little longer."

Marcus said, "I was going to tell you inside Lita, but I cannot keep it to myself any longer. The ship has sailed and I cannot say when she will be back. So I'm here for a few more days at least."

Looking into his eyes, she whispered, "Kiss me," clinging to him still as Joe opened the door.

"Hello Marcus, glad you could come," said Joe, shaking his hand warmly. Una also came forward and taking his hand Una led Marcus away before Lita took possession and planted a kiss on his cheek.

"That's for helping Joe, although Joe has never really told me what happened that night you went out together - he has been so quiet!"

Lita joined them, saying to Una jokingly, "Hands off my man!" cuddling into Marcus's arm.

Una smiled at them both, saying, "I never hear any gossip, like we had in the States."

Leaving them together, Una joined Joe at the bar. Lita began walking towards the stairs that led to the bedrooms, saying as she walked, "I'm just going upstairs to change into something comfortable" then added: "You can come up if you want to. I shall only be a minute or two."

Marcus, looked round at the others. Lita laughed, saying: "Don't worry about those two. I'm a big girl now."

Taking his hand, they walked up the stairs together. Her room was a delightful mixture of East and West, with an exotic oriental carpet with a floral motif, copied and matched by the inlaid flowers carved into the white wardrobe furniture and doors. The modern mirrored dressing table contrasted with the ornate Chinese bed. There was a feeling of harmony in the room, with motif matching curtains.

Sitting at her dressing table, Marcus tried not to look at her as he moved around the room. For a brief moment or two she was topless and he just happened to look. Lita, asking him to zip the side of a low-cut Chinese style dress, then teased Marcus, saying, "That wasn't too bad, was it? You cannot say now, you have never been in lady's bedroom."

Marcus, with Lita on his arm, walked slowly down the stairs and into the bar. They were a handsome pair and radiated happiness.

Whilst Una wanted her sister to confide in her all those tasty titbits of gossip about the new man in the family.

Joe was a pleasant host and most interested in how Marcus came to be in the Royal Navy. Marcus' mother being Welsh, which accounted for his dark hair, had married a Canadian soldier, who took his bride away from the hills of Wales, to the mountains of British Columbia, where his father worked as a forester. Marcus's impulse to join up had come from his mother's love for Wales.

Marcus and many like him from Canada and America, wanted to defend the old country. Looking at the two beautiful women, Joe and Marcus now had a lot in common.

Ma and Pa Jung now joined them for drinks and accepted a glass of Chinese wine and their delight at meeting Marcus again with Lita was a joy.

Again, he welcomed Marcus to his home. This time however, Pa Jung raised his glass to Marcus, saying, "May all your children be beautiful."

Marcus, thinking quickly, replied, "And may all your grandchildren be wise."

They all liked that reply. Ma Jung, taking hold of Marcus' arm, nodded to her husband as Marcus led her into the restaurant, waiting for her to be seated. Lita grabbed the tail of his jacket and pulled him towards the seat he had last night. No sooner was he seated, than she stroked his muscular thigh, saying, "I hope mother does not steal you from me, she has been a great charmer with the men in the past!"

"I'm sure you'll follow in your mother's footsteps - you've already charmed me. You're too beautiful for words!"

Placing his hand on her thigh, he softly traced a heart.

These were difficult days in Shanghai but it did not seem to be changing the standards of the Jung's restaurant. This evening a small dance band played softly and later there would be dancing.

The Chinese meal and chopsticks had been expected by Marcus and very much to Lita's surprise, he handled them with great skill, having used nothing else since he arrived and dined Chinese fashion at the Consul where it was encouraged. The food favoured Joe and Marcus with familiar names they could recognise, although Joe had no problems with menus.

Vegetable soup, Chinese chicken and shrimps, sauces and varied rices. The Chinese wine served in different colours added to the reflecting colours on the table from the dimmed restaurant lights shining from above.

It had everything that made the evening a real party, for everyone loved someone.

From the days of the hornpipe, sailors usually danced well and Marcus moving gracefully with Lita looked as though they had always been partners just dancing dreamily in each other's arms.

Ma and Pa Jung got their pleasure watching the happiness of their daughters, as they danced. The head waiter approached bowed to Ma Jung and then whispered in her husband's ear.

With a nod of his head to Joe as he danced past, Joe and Una left the floor and walked through the private door to answer the house phone.

It was Borkowski reporting that there had been some trouble with sailors smashing a jeweller's workshop window.

No-one entered the premises and nothing was stolen, but the owner who is French wants to arrest the whole fleet.

Leave it until the morning was Joe's answer, he knew just the guy to deal with a Frenchman and rang off, with a chuckle.

When they got back to the table, Joe put it to Marcus, "Do you speak French, being a Canadian?"

Not knowing what Joe was on about, Marcus replied, "Yes, enough to get by on."

Joe, smiling and taking Lita's hand for the next dance said, "I was hoping you would say that!"

The interruption had reminded them all of the time and the Manager came over to report to Mr Jung before he retired to private quarters.

After a nightcap, Una and Joe retired and Marcus and Lita, alone at last, sank onto the comfortable empty settee.

Lita was a seductive creature and was already telling Marcus to show how much she cared. The graceful way she curled her arms around him to help him remove his jacket. The unbuttoning of his shirt to cool him and removing his shoes from his dancing feet slowly fired his desire to feel her soft lips kissing and the sensation of her smooth skin beneath his fingers.

Her fingers beneath his shirt passed over the hair and nipples on his lightly tanned chest. Their kissing became more passionate and only the closing of a door and the dimming of some lights checked Marcus from stripping away the flimsy veils of modesty that hid the beautiful body and breasts of this lush Chinese beauty.

Whispering softly, Lita crooned, "Let's go to bed." Clinging to each other, they turned out the lights and climbed the stairs. The subdued lighting in the bedroom greeted them silently, as they began to undress.

Experimenting a little, then laughing and loving they occupied the Chinese bed in painful pleasure, relief and ecstasy as their bodies met in love for the first time.

Those who love. They lay in bed like lovers in the morning, not wanting to let go, until a rustling on the bed caused their sleepy eyes to rise above the soft silk sheets where lay an enormous bouquet of flowers.

"It's our wedding day." Said Lita, handing him a flower.

The rest of the Chung family were already seated and having breakfast when Lita carrying her flowers appeared at the head of the staircase waiting for Marcus to show. Lita looked radiant and taking Marcus's arm when he appeared, made a handsome pair as they came down the stairs and took their places in the dining room.

Marcus kept stroking his unshaven chin, but no one took much notice of him apart from a smile. Joe was the first to speak and addressing Marcus he asked, "Marcus, are you doing anything special today?"

Before he could answer, Lita, putting her arm on Marcus protectively replied, "Yes, he is, we're going out to lunch and seeing the sights of Shanghai!"

Joe calmly sipped his tea, then said sweetly, "OK honey, I just wondered if he could talk to a Frenchman for me," Joe went on, "it will only take a minute or two this morning, if you can spare him Lita, it is not really duty!"

Knowing Joe's devotion to duty, Lita asked, "Are you sure, Joe?" looking at Una, who nodded reassuringly.

Having reclaimed her man, Lita turned to Marcus saying, "Promise?"

With a kiss on the tip of her nose Marcus promised and finishing his breakfast he joined Joe outside where Chung was waiting with the jeep. Waving as they moved off he called "One o'clock, darling, OK?"

Dropping Marcus off at the Consul after giving him the details of the incident involving the Frenchman. Marcus agreed to see Pierre as soon as he was in uniform and once dressed asked for volunteers. Everyone that was there volunteered, Wilson, Bungy, Wiggy and even Sam.

Bundling them into the jeep they were soon on their way to the jewellers clinging on for dear life as Chung weaved his way in the traffic. During the day it was best not to speak to Chung as he moved around Shanghai. It was better to concentrate on hanging on, as some of the patrol found out.

Giving the address of the jeweller's workshop, Chung had no difficulty in finding it.

It was a double fronted premises with black painted windows, one of which had been demolished and roughly covered with boards and nailed canvas. Ordering the patrol to dismount, they waited until Wilson, standing outside the outer door of a central porchway with no bell or knocker, thumped on the door.

A small woman opened the door and seeing Marcus in his uniform, invited him into the lobby. Automatically the patrol squeezed in as well although the woman was holding her hand up for them to stay. Unlocking the inner door she called out, "Pierre!"

A thin, angular man with thick lens glasses appeared and peering at Marcus he addressed him in English. "You're not Americans, you are Angleterre" and threw his arms around Marcus, kissed him heartily on both cheeks, saying, "Come in, Englishman, I am Pierre, again you come to help me!"

Pierre then giving a lengthy account of being released by the British from a P.O.W. camp in Hong Kong.

Entering the lobby with the patrol trailing behind, Pierre entered what appeared to be a workshop which dumbfounded Marcus for it was full of naked girls sitting around an enormous oval table covered with a black cloth, stringing together pearls of all sizes from numerous oyster shell dishes around the table. Marcus remembering the men behind him and getting Wilson to try and close the door, he had to help Wilson himself as the patrol, pressing forward to get a better view were all thoroughly enjoying the show. The Frenchman just took no notice until a girl in the confusion, with a flick of her thumb, shot a pearl into her mouth.

The old minder an aged woman as wrinkled as a prune spat out her name and together they left the room. From some other distant room came the sound of muffled screaming which went on for some time. The older woman returned but not the girl. Wilson, in the room with Marcus and the girls were a little disturbed by the screams. But Pierre shrugging his shoulders commented, "Examinations are part of the job and these girls know all the tricks and it's a deadly business between them and the minder. Each loses face if they are caught or not caught, depending on whose side you are on."

Wilson doubting his ears, "Where can they hide them without clothes on?"

Pierre said, "Come with me," tapping the minder on the shoulder as we left the room. Entering a smaller room a gorgeous woman in a kimono sat using an eye glass inspecting individual pearls.

With a brief word in French from Pierre, she seated herself at a small table and scattered a few pearls on the cloth. Removing her kimono, her figure was fuller than the girls in the other room and very attractive with it.

Each time Wilson or Marcus looked at her, she looked them straight in the eye and smiled confidently with a blink of her long eyelashes. Occasionally she passed her hand across the table or stroked her hair and admired her nails all very feminine and yet, before their eyes the pearls disappeared.

Pierre kissed the woman as she replaced her kimono saying, "Meet, Madam Yvonne, my wife."

With that they withdrew to the workroom.

Pierre, seeing Marcus and Wilson were still mystified, explained that every crevice in the ear, mouth, nose and hair were used, including most favoured of all, the flick into the mouth and the swallow. Fascinated by the experience and particularly Pierre's wife, Wilson kept it from the others for he doubted if anyone would ever believe him.

Pierre never expected any help from the U.S. Navy and had already taken steps to have it repaired.

CHAPTER 4

Chatting to Marcus and Wilson they promised together they would join Pierre and his wife for a meal, he wanted to repay at least a few Englishmen for helping to free him from the P.O.W. Camp.

The novelty of watching the girls at work in the nude soon wore off when they were completely ignored by the girls.

Promising Pierre they would dine with him, as they parted, Pierre handed to Marcus a small parcel heavily wrapped, before kissing him once again on both cheeks.

Phoning Joe to report the outcome, he refused to meet Joe for a drink. But changing quickly into his new suit and shirt and patting the parcel in his pocket, he returned to the waiting jeep, Chung already knowing the destination.

Chung did try hard to make the jeep look very smart. He had refused a wage and even took umbrage when Marcus suggested he should pay for the polish that Chung was constantly using.

Chung, on his way to the restaurant with Marcus to meet Lita, handed Marcus an envelope written in Chinese at the same time, shrugged his shoulders and grinned.

With his thoughts on Lita, he stuffed the envelope into his pocket to read later.

Lita looked beautiful as she came through the archway of the private entrance to meet him. Taking his hand and gently pulling him into the hall, she couldn't wait for him to kiss her, as she threw her arms around his neck saying, "Marcus," kissing him as though they had not seen each other for months.

Marcus, hungry for the feel of her in his arms reacted passionately too. Without a further thought for lunch, they ran up the stairs, into the bedroom and standing in front of the mirror on the dressing table, they undressed each other.

Next, in the shower, they played like children showering and spongy soaping each other, until she tormenting him soon had him deliriously hard happy against her.

Suddenly, he lifted her and carried the soft, beautiful body towards the bed.

Calling excitedly, Lita said, "No, No - not the bed - the carpet!" as she swept her dripping hair from her face and wrestled his willing body to the floor and gently straddled him.

They were very late for lunch and did not mind a small table in the corner for they liked to sit side by side and touch thighs.

After the meal, like lovers, they touched each other's fingers which reminded Marcus of Pierre's present. Taking it from his pocket he laid it on the dining table and said casually, "Open it darling, it may be something nice, for you."

Curious and with a twinkle in her eye, she removed the plain brown paper that covered a plain brown cardboard box.

Opening it, she gasped as she lifted out a perfect double-stringed necklace of pearls, draping them over her slender fingers.

Marcus was more astonished than Lita and preened himself a little as he watched her unclip them and drape them round her slender neck.

Reflecting in the lightness of her complexion, they looked warm and glowing.

With a longing kiss, she thanked him, sitting there holding his hand and fingering the pearls, she sighed for life was so good with Marcus.

Feeling something else in his pocket, he withdrew the note that Chung had given him on the way to meet Lita.

Flipping it onto the table, he commented, "Read this for me dear. It's probably a love letter from Ma Pang in the laundry."

Looking at the seal, Lita frowned and half-turning away, opened it carefully.

Reading it quickly, she replaced it in the envelope and stood up grasping for Marcus's hand.

In a quiet voice, she asked, "Darling, let's get out of here."

Taking his hand, they left by the door leading to the private rooms.

Sitting together on the settee, she cuddled into him like a child. Not wanting to intrude on her thoughts Marcus remained quiet.

After a while, Lita rose and walked to her father's desk, placing the note inside.

Returning to Marcus, she cuddled and said quietly, "It was not for us, dear but for my father I am a little worried that's all."

Joining her parents who were now enjoying tea together in the dining room, Lita mentioned the letter quietly to her father. With Marcus and Lita for company Mrs Jung excused her husband and bowing he collected the letter and retired to the prayer room.

He was still there when Joe arrived with two of his officers for a drink or two.

Delighted to see Marcus again, he asked him and Lita to join him. Lita, preferring not to drink, stayed with her mother for company.

It was a casual meeting of, "Hey buddy," as one of them fingered Marcus's suit, saying, "Is that Saville Row?"

Marcus answered in good Canadian, "No Buddy, pure Chinese for one hundred bucks, plus the shoes in Shanghai."

The second officer was curious how a British naval officer came to be out and about in civilian clothes in Shanghai of all places.

He may have had ambitions to be in the FBI and thought of Marcus as MI5, but when Marcus told him a story of disappearing pearls performed by a naked woman, he did not believe it and was only interested in Marcus' tailor.

They both had to return to duty very soon and Marcus little knew that they were to meet again very soon. Now both Una and Lita had joined their mother. Joe called Marcus to the end of the bar and asked, "What is this letter you have delivered to Pa Jung?"

As the letter was written in Chinese, Marcus explained that all he knew was that his driver was handed the note for delivery through Marcus to one of the family.

Without waiting for Mr Jung to leave the prayer room, Joe left Marcus and lightly tapped the door of the prayer room.

Mr Jung opened the door and waved Joe inside with a polite bow.

"I've been expecting you to knock," began Mr Jung as he offered a space on a wooden stool for them to sit close to each other.

"I've opened the letter, for I thought with that seal on the outside, it was important."

Lifting the letter from the shrine, he handed it to Joe and it read, "You have trespassed on the ground of the house of Kia for which we demand payment of two million Yuan. A warning as a punishment will follow soon."

There was no signature, but the stamp of the KIA tong.

Joe, having read it, turned to Mr Jung now at the shrine and queried, "What do they mean by a warning as a punishment?"

Mr Jung, now facing Joe, looked very solemn and came forward and put his arm round Joe, for they were close friends.

"My son, this is the worst part, for the ransom is only money. These criminals are cruel people, it could be an ear or hand of a loved one, we must be on our guard, it could be something worse."

"God" said Joe, "To think this could happen to us! Who are these people?"

Mr Jung said, "We have a number of criminals, Tongs, growing up in the spreading slums which are difficult for the police to contain. Thousands of migrants are coming to Shanghai, which makes rich pickings for the criminals. Opium, other drugs, prostitution, extortion, in a city of millions, the crime gangs are already out of control."

Joe, comforting the old man, took him back to join the women, whist he and Marcus went into a huddle. Dinner was announced and they all moved to their usual table in the restaurant. Knowing Marcus would be here overnight, they arranged to talk with Mr Jung about the threat later after dinner in the prayer room.

After the meal, Joe opened the talk by asking Mr Jung: "What about calling in the police. I'm on very good terms with the chief and he will have some idea who these people are."

Mr Jung shook his head saying, "It is not as easy as that, Joe. I have customers from some of the Tongs, who dine here at my expense, but if I were to ask anyone for help including the police, they would find a way of closing me down and turning this restaurant into a casino."

Mr Jung continued, "There are some things I can do, but first I must pray, for my family are in danger."

Joe and Marcus, leaving Mr Jung to his prayers, continued talk in a corner of the bar. Joe told Marcus the full contents of the threatening letter and apart from being very alert in the house, any investigation they did, had to be kept in the family for spies were everywhere and not knowing who to trust.

Joe included his staff and Marcus' men as part of the force for the protection of the family.

The Jung family, spent the rest of the evening together and apart from the appearance of one or two beefy newcomers amongst the restaurant staff and houseboys, everything went on as normal.

Marcus left promptly after breakfast, after Joe had given his blessing for Marcus to do anything he thought might help to safeguard the women.

Lita was very understanding for the whole family now knew that something very serious had come about since the delivery of the letter.

Joe could not go along with all that Mr Jung had said, although he was very fond of him.

Joe commanded a lot of respect from the Chinese Chief of Police, as did Joe's Chinese/American driver Benjamin who helped with the more difficult parts of their usually argumentative Chinese conversations.

As police go in China, the Chief was rather less corrupt than the rest, although American cigarettes 'Camel' were his weakness.

He welcomed Joe that morning, by offering him an empty cigarette case.

Joe replied, by placing a packet of two hundred 'Camel' cigarettes on the desk and came straight to the point in Chinese, and demanded, "I want a list of all the Tongs in Shanghai now!"

Joe's voice was quite aggressive,

The chief looking at the cigarettes, shouted back, "That is very dangerous for me, I could get my throat cut." drawing his fingers across his throat.

The chief then leaned over, looked around the office, where everyone seemed to be busy, and held up five fingers quickly, to which Joe nodded, then added two more.

Beckoning to Benjamin to put two more cartons, making it seven hundred, brought a smile like a squeezed lemon to the Chief's face, as Joe stopped him from sweeping them into his open desk drawer.

Half shouting, Joe bawled out, "I want my list now!" Still, with his hand over the cigarettes.

Turning round and opening a filing cabinet, the chief flipped through the files and finally handed a printed list to Benjamin to look through.

With a nod from Ben, the Chief pushed the cigarettes into an empty drawer.

In return for the cigarettes the Chief complimented Joe on his improving ability to speak Chinese well. Saluting, Joe took his leave.

Joe's wife Una had always been the gardening enthusiast of the family. With her coolie suit and a head band over her pretty face, she could have encouraged anyone to take up the art of trimming garden flowers.

Una's pruning was done with the help of an old gardener, who enjoyed the company of his employer's daughter, who ordered rice cakes and tea to be sent to his little shed whenever she was working in the garden.

Wearing no rings and dressed in a coolie two piece with gardening gloves, she could have passed as his daughter, but for her ravishing looks.

They had been working steadily for an hour or more when the wheel barrow now full, was wheeled round the hedge by the old man to empty on the hidden compost heap.

Una, with another armful of cuttings became concerned when the old man did not return straight away. Deciding to look for him she carried her bundle of cuttings behind the hedge to find him.

Before she could cry out at the sight of a crumpled figure half hidden by the pile of compost, she was seized, gagged and dragged painfully through a hole in the outer hedge, before being bundled roughly into the boot of a waiting car and driven away.

It was an hour later, when Lita, calling her in, for their usual cup of tea together, walked into the garden to find her sister Una.

The sight of the crumpled gardener, his upturned barrow and Una's broken sun glasses nearby sent her rushing into the house, calling for her father.

At the first cry, the two guards responded quickly, but only found the moaning elderly gardener, still half conscious.

Una had been kidnapped and taken as a hostage.

Lita was already on the phone to Joe and then phoned Marcus. Sitting in the hall, Lita was joined by her parents, anxiously waiting for Joe to arrive.

They did not have long to wait as Joe driven by Benjamin, arrived within a few minutes.

Comforting the two distraught parents, he was glad to see Marcus arrive and take a tearful Lita into his arms.

Pa Jung, still not wanting to call the police, begged Marcus to stay with the women, while he and Joe searched the grounds and garden. In the meantime, the two guards had revived the gardener, but he could remember nothing, except a heavy blow from behind before he passed out.

Ma Jung was now quite ill, and helped by Marcus, Lita took her to bed and gave her a mild sedative. Marcus, leaving the two women together, joined Joe and Mr Jung in searching the grounds. Marcus was quite astonished to find Joe and Mr Jung at the extreme end of the garden, looking at the masts and funnels of the not-too distant ships and junks berthed in the Huangpu River.

Marcus, having now driven to the restaurant a few times, had never been aware of the bend in the river as it flowed towards the Bund and on to the open waters of the estuary.

Marcus's thinking now turned to the river, where on the waterfronts in China were berthed the boats and junks of smugglers and raiders amongst the ordinary junk dwellers.

Speaking aloud, Marcus said, "If I had a boat, I wouldn't mind looking around that lot. You never know, I might find something."

Joe answered straight away, "We've a couple of sampans in the river further down and Benjamin looks after the engines. If you want to do some snooping, go by all means, but take Benjamin with you, he knows the engine well and you will need to change your clothes - you can't be too conspicuous down on the waterfront."

Joe putting his arm around Marcus said warmly, "I appreciate what you're doing Marcus and I believe you when you say, you think better on the water than you do on land, but for all our sakes, be careful, they'll slit your throat like gutting a fish, if they think you're on their patch."

Together they walked back to the house and Joe began to turn out a cupboard in the garage to find an old overall for Marcus to wear.

Wearing an old trilby, that looked as though it had been chewed by a mad dog, Marcus didn't look himself at all after an early supper and a change into his rather grubby overall.

The trilby, with a dirty face, finished his disguise for the trip up river.

Benjamin, with a can of petrol and a coolie hat, looked the part, for he was Chinese.

The sampan was bigger than Marcus thought, as he lashed on the steering oar to the hole pin on the sampan's gunwale.

Benjamin had no trouble with the engine, although Marcus worked up a sweat with the starting rope. It was not like punting on the Thames and it would have unnerved someone less experienced than Marcus, to drive a Sampan around this part of the river in the dark in the evening. Benjamin had thought of everything, A bright light marked U.S. Army property, shone brightly on the top of the canopy.

With just enough revs on the engine to give steerage way and a gentle movement on the oar, they slowly joined the up river traffic, staying close to the shoreline boats.

Some junks had cars on the jetty, but Marcus, not knowing what sort of car was used in the kidnapping, really did not know what to look for.

Most of the boats and junks all looked very similar and Marcus began to lose heart when there was a cackling laugh, as some ignorant crew man knowing the sampan was passing by, threw a bucket full of stinking slops all over the engine and it cut out dead.

Clinging on to the junk astern, they grappled their way against the running flow of the river, until Benjamin, by some miracle, found a junk ring bolt and passed a rope through, to give a head rope for the sampan to ride too.

Clinging on to the rope while Benjamin got rid of the filth all over the engine, Marcus stared at the stern of the junk ahead, cursing, as sailors can, at the stinking bastard who had landed them in it.

Faintly in the glow of the lights on the jetty, he could make out a name that had been roughly painted over. It read Kia Kia.

Marcus smelling a little himself, thought, "I won't forget that in a hurry!"

It was now quite dark and if they had not had the lamp they could easily have passed the berthing post to which the sampan was now secured. Marcus, rather disappointed with his evening's effort, went straight upstairs for a very long shower.

Lita, knowing he was also upset and that the evening's work had not gone well, did not offer to scrub his back.

Later, Marcus after his shower, joined Joe for a late night snack and a drink, Joe took the threatening letter from his pocket and reread it.

Marcus, seeing the letter for the first time since he had handed it to Lita, naturally wanted to look at it out of curiosity and held out his hand to Joe. The lettering and writing, although strange to Marcus, had an aggressive style and stroke, but what made Marcus sit up, was the wax seal on the outside of the envelope. Without saying anything to Joe or Lita in case he was wrong, he went to Mr Jung's desk and helped himself to a piece of paper and a fountain pen.

Carefully lifting the filling lever on the pen, he squirted a little ink on to his finger and wetted the seal on the envelope.

Carefully pressing the seal on to the paper, the word 'Kia' showed up well on the paper.

"That's it." Said Marcus firmly, holding up the paper for them both to see.

"Joe, get Benjamin to confirm it, it's the boat that covered us in s....!"

He just caught himself in time, as he looked at Lita's startled face.

Joe, getting up quickly, phoned the kitchen where Benjamin spent his spare time. In no time at all, he joined them and confirmed that the Kia Kia was the junk that swamped the sampan.

He too could read the painted-over name of 'Kia Kia'.

It was exactly the same form of writing as the pressing on the piece of paper. Not wasting any time, Joe got on to the Chief of Police and told him what they had discovered.

The Chief, keen to catch anyone of the tongs, immediately put the junk, cars and crew under surveillance.

The Chief also accepted that Joe himself and his special squad would also be in the area, for after all, it was his wife that had been abducted.

Marcus had already alerted his patrol that they may be needed at any time and were to act on any orders received from the Major until he could get in touch with them himself. Reports came back to the Chief of Police that there was still some activity on the junk Kia Kia, although it was quite late.

Kia Kia was without doubt, a fighting junk, with concealed exhausts to her two diesels. Night guards could be seen on deck and all her ropes and hawsers were clear running, to enable her to slip and get under way quickly.

Decisions were quickly made when Borkowski and two officers from Joe's other units arrived. Marcus would disable the Kia Kia or stop her sailing.

Knowing Marcus would probably need a boat, Joe had already arranged for one to be on standby, in addition to the two sampans available. The snatch squad, once they had a description of the victim and the possible hiding place, were already primed and an order to go would activate them immediately.

The soldiers, all of whom had seen active service, would flush out any resistance, with the armed Chinese police in support.

Berthed alongside the Kia Kia was an accommodation junk. It was used to house the women. Two gangboards ran between the junks and two more from the inner junk to the jetty.

Both the Kia Kia and her companion were unlit, but for the glimmer of the weak shore lights on the jetty.

A lorry dispatched by Borkowski with useful gear for use in the boat, was already on its way.

As more information was fed to Joe, it was assumed that Una was imprisoned on the accommodation ship. The sentries were to be taken out by silent methods.

Knowing pirates and raiders used heavy machine guns, an all out assault would begin as women and children were clear of the accommodation junk.

It was accepted that the Navy would have immobilised the Kia Kia.

Marcus's men had been supplied with military camouflage gear, which was far too big for Bungy and Wiggy. Half the legs in each case had to be hacked off and when standing, each looked no bigger than a camouflaged dwarf alongside the Americans.

With everything that Marcus had asked for, they were well equipped to stop the Kia Kia. The signal to commence was a flare, fired from down river by Kemp who was used to firing signals.

Black the stoker drove the sampan to a position where it would be seen by all those taking part when it was fired at 3.30pm.

Marcus, using the jeep and lorry, had been able to get the gear to the jetty, where the sampans were kept, with a berth for the motorboat, when it arrived.

Petty Officer Willard had chosen Wilson and Weller for the diving, as both were strong swimmers. They would man the second sampan, to which they transferred all the ropes, wire and shackles and prepared for the job of stopping the Kia Kia. A half dozen large potatoes seemed an odd piece of equipment, but ideal for bunging up a boat's exhausts.

With everything set but for the motorboat that was due any minute, Willie ordered them to check their seaman's knives, a vital tool for any diver.

Am Ling was the alarm clock and at 0200, he was creating enough noise in the kitchen to arouse all Shanghai. The strong tea he brewed and plates of hard biscuits that he made himself, left them feeling as though they had eaten a full meal.

To see the patrol in combat suits supplied by Sergeant Borkowski brought the first smile, as Wiggy stood on the mess-table to have half the legs cut off the bottom for him to be able to walk. With blackened faces they all looked the part of soldiers going into action.

Operating from Joe the Major's berth for the sampans and motorboat, near to the restaurant, Marcus was pleased to see an American soldier with a boat mechanic badge, ready and waiting by the motorboat. He was young, black and cheerful and was pleased to be going along.

"Call me Benny," was how he introduced himself.

Not knowing who Marcus was, he enquired, "You the boss?" Putting his arm round Marcus' shoulder and making him bend over the stern. Benny pointed down to where the exhaust came out of the boat, saying, "I've fitted her with a snuffer. OK." Then turning round he pressed the starter and a muffled throb of a powerful engine added to the night sounds of the estuary.

Marcus had no doubts that the wire girdle they had made last night would work, having seen it stop many boats. This one was made for the job provided it could be fitted quickly and silently.

Raising his arm and down again, Marcus dispatched the first sampan with the start flares, followed shortly afterwards by the second sampan with Taffy and Weller tending the girdle, strapped under the sampan with wire jackstays and sliding shackles attached and a signal rope from the sampan to the divers Weller and Wilson, who would be diving helped by nose clips only. They approached the Kia Kia by warping from boat to boat and slid under the poop quite unnoticed.

Wilson did the first dive and attached the safety and signal lines to the port propeller shaft quite easily.

Before Marcus dived, Wilson told him that the brackets holding the shafts were well out from the junk's side and Marcus could attach the first of the jackstays to the starboard shaft.

They dived and broke water together breathing deeply, but with a thumbs up sign that all had gone well.

Wasting no time, the stops and lashings around the girdle were undone and now hanging down, slung from the sliding shackles on the jackstays, were eased away as Marcus and Wilson, guided by the jackstay under water going to each propeller.

Surfacing for more air, they again dived and hooked the girdle of wire first through the frame then over the propeller.

After two or three more dives, they completed attaching the well oiled shackles around the wires. Throwing all ropes still attached to the sampan overboard, they allowed the sampan to slowly drift away from the stern of the Kia Kia, to meet up with the motor boat further down stream.

The only attachment now to the Kia Kia from the power boat was a single length of stainless steel wire being paid out from the sampan as they drifted astern was passed into the motorboat. All eyes were now on the Kia Kia. There were five minutes before the raid commenced.

Everyone in the motor boat was screwing up their eyes at the watches to check the time and on the dot, the flare soared high in the sky some distance down river and the raid had begun.

There were two guards on watch on the accommodation junk, both smoking and talking close to the forward boarding plank. Patiently, the snatch group waited within yards of the boarding plank. The guards then parted, one appearing to go aboard the Kia Kia and the other into the fo'c's'le of the accommodation junk. Within seconds, the first wave was up the plank and out of sight aboard the accommodation junk.

Only the glow of a distant night light on the jetty gave any light and the darkness on deck of the junk made movement difficult with the amount of gear and ropes cluttering the deck.

It was better to lie in wait and let the enemy come towards them.

Having seen the guard enter the fo'c's'le of the accommodation junk by the low midship bulkhead door, they waited one on each side for him to appear. They did not have long to wait and as his lowered head appeared, the dull thud of a cosh before they grabbed his falling body, made little or no noise. Even the splash of the lowered body into the water was lost in the throb of a slow-moving boat going down river.

Moving motor-boat on its way downstream.

Splashes occur at night, but the second guard on Kia Kia was curious at what his fellow guard was up to.

The gangboard rested on the junk's side amidships between the two junks and as the guard stepped down on to the deck, two dark figures rose from the shadows and again came a dull thud.

Catching the body before it hit the deck, they relieved the body of its gun and lowered it over the side.

The blink of a soft torch light brought Joe, Borkowski and Benjamin aboard, followed by Orlando and Lewis in charge of the boarding party for the Kia Kia.

The Chief of Police had insisted on being part of the boarding party, although Joe, the Major, had tried hard to persuade the Chief not to take part for his men were poorly armed, but Joe shut up when the Chief had threatened to go it alone, after all, Shanghai was his city.

Joe realised that a combination of policemen and American regular soldiers was a bad thing and the rescue of Una was all he wished to achieve.

A strategic withdrawal, the order of the operation, once Una was safely ashore and all units understood this.

It was a lucky night for the Major, for the soldiers who had disposed of the guards had also entered the confined space of the junk's fo'c's'le. A sleeping guard gave a throaty gasp as a strong hand seized his throat and a hard fist chopped down on his neck, as he slumped unconscious onto the deck.

Withdrawing a wooden staple from the hasp on the compartment door, the soldier felt around amongst a heap of dirty sails in the dark, until he touched a body and then held one of the bound legs of Una.

Running his hands up her body, he sat her upright and whispered, "It's me, Joe's man."

Untying her hands and feet, he took her hand and led her to Joe standing on deck. Not waiting, Joe led her silently and quickly off the junk to a waiting car and making her comfortable, ordered the driver to take them home.

In Joe's arms, Una shed a gentle tear, saying, "I knew you would come" and kissed him passionately.

Leaving Una in the caring hands of her mother and sister, Joe returned to deal with the Chief of Police.

With Benjamin, his Chinese American driver, he reported to the Chief that Una was safe. The Chief of Police gave a couple of hoarse chuckles and laughing at Joe, he said, "I put you under arrest, if your men don't leave junk, NOW!"

Benjamin then repeated the order in English adding, "Major he means what he said. It is his party and you are not going to get the credit, get off the ship at once!" pointing to about fifty armed policemen and another fifty sitting in buses on the jetty.

To capture or kill a Tong gang was a feather in his cap he was not going to give away to Joe or he would lose face!

Via a sampan, Joe got a message to Marcus to abort the operation, let go everything and get out of range.

Joe's officers and Borkowski had already got the order and just managed to clear the junks as the Chinese police charged aboard and began shooting at anything that moved.

Joe quietly wiping his brow said to Borkowski, "Thank God, we missed that lot." As a fusillade of rifle fire broke out with bullets flying everywhere.

All Joe's men and Marcus too, withdrew and left the Chinese police to it.

The restaurant was an ideal place to celebrate and it became more of a party when Marcus and his boat crews appeared. Not that they had achieved very much, but all the same, they were given a rousing cheer by the soldiers who must have found their appearance rather amusing, being led into the restaurant by Wiggy in the oversize jacket of his combat gear with half the trouser legs cut off.

Somebody called out, "Whose piccaninny is this?"

Marcus was quite proud of his men, who had shaped up very well in unusual circumstances. Joe was introduced to each member of the patrol and commended each one personally and shook hands.

Looking up at the tall figure of Joe, the American Major, when he was introduced, Wiggy said, "Sir, does a commendation mean I'll get a medal?"

Joe, quite amused by Wiggy's comment, answered, "You might well do that my son, if you stay here in Shanghai long enough."

Lita and Una, who had been circulating around the men, came over to join Marcus to meet his patrol members.

They were both a great attraction, Lita, with her direct manner and speaking in English, soon had them all falling in love with her.

Sam was able to talk to Lita alone as the buffet was served. He spoke of his girl friend Anna, who worked in the Consul laundry. Not aware of Lita's relationship with Marcus, he added, "Please don't tell our officer Marcus, we are not supposed to consort with any of the consul staff!" With a smile and a promise Lita nodded with understanding.

The soldiers were very interested in the patrol and keen to give them a good time in Shanghai. The drive back to the quarters was strangely quiet and what they all did first of all, was to head for the showers. It was better to see each other faces that smiled occasionally.

Am Ling as usual appeared from the kitchen and was soon walking into the mess with the proverbial pot of tea.

Wilson and Weller took the longest to shower after diving in the not too clean waters of the Huangpu River.

Wilson had some exotic aftershave he had received for his birthday last year and never used. Sharing it with Weller after they had showered they were greeted with some very odd remarks as they entered the mess together.

Am Ling pinched his nose and joined in the joking, laughing loudly at what he thought was a funny smell.

Sam Weller failed to see the joke for he had a good reason for wanting to smell fresh and clean. He had already gathered all the washing and once he knew that the girls had arrived in the laundry he would have something interesting to talk about, the restaurant. It would be a splendid place for him to take Anna one evening if he could get out of uniform. Clothes were so cheap and they made a suit in a day or less if you were in a hurry. He really fancied himself in a summer suit. It looked so cool.

Sam's demob was due anytime now and he had played with the idea of looking at the opportunities that were available in Hong Kong, if the Navy would permit his demob in Hong Kong especially if he were married.

Marcus had seemed friendly with the girl Lita at the restaurant last night.

Breakfast the morning after the raid on the Kia Kia was the headlines in the Shanghai Times, a commendable comment or two about the Chief of Police who had captured a few of the kidnappers.

Having no real authority to get his men involved in a shooting situation, Marcus was pleased the Americans were also excluded.

Apparently, according to Joe, all hell broke loose shortly after they withdrew. The Chinese police after much shouting, had lost patience and stormed the Kia Kia.

Everyone was firing at somebody in the dark and they reduced their own police by a dozen men before they even entered the fo'c's'le deck. Another problem was the door to the poop in the after part of the junk was armoured plate and the siege was still going on as dawn broke.

The outcome would have a bloody ending but when the police broke into the after poop there were but two or three dead or wounded prisoners. The rest had floated away down the river through escape hatches to the sea.

None of the patrol had fired a shot in anger and it was a topic that soon lost its popularity.

Willie Willard entered the mess as they were getting up from the table. Everyone stopped what they were doing and looked silently at Willie, waiting for him to give an order. Instead he took them all by surprise and with a smile, held up a knife saying, "Anyone lost one of these?"

It was a service knife and part of one's kit and after a pause while they looked, Sam held up his hand and said, "It is mine."

"That's the good part," said Willie, putting the knife back into his own pocket.

"Yours is down on the junk that we tied alongside last night and you have to pick it up from there, if you want to claim it."

Willie went on, "Naturally you will have to reward whoever found it if you don't want to spend the next ten years rotting in a Chinese dungeon having left it at the scene of the crime!"

To Sam it seemed a long way to go, the way he was feeling and he said wearily, "How the hell am I going to get down there, it's a hell of a walk." Really thinking more about meeting Anna.

Willie felt in a good mood and agreed, "If the jeep is available and Wilson willing, I'll let you go with him to collect it, but take some money and don't be too long."

With that Willie left the mess.

Willie had obviously phoned Marcus, for the jeep with Chung driving was very soon outside ready to go.

Putting on plain shirts and without headgear, they looked unofficial, apart from being British. Chung, familiar with where they were last night, stopped within walking distance of where the junk was tied up and indicated he would wait here in case a police cordon was operating in the area of the Kia Kia. The police were there.

By asking if they could step aboard the next inshore junk from the Kia Kia, with much pointing and nodding they were directed how to get to the outside junk to which they had laid alongside last night.

Indicating that they wanted to come aboard, a brown muscular Chinese and obviously his wife and four young children, came to the gangboard to welcome them aboard.

A couple of younger men appeared from the fo'c's'le and stood just watching the strangers led by the children come aboard and entered the poop, a living and sleeping area.

It was spotless inside. Neat bunk beds, a table and chairs and a small joss-house built into the junk's shipside, next to the gallery.

They all sat at the table, with the children climbing on their laps as though they were family.

It was an occasion for them and very soon, a pot of tea was brought in by a wrinkled lady from the kitchen. It was Grandma from a boat downstream. The tea cups were exquisite and politely nodding, Wilson and Weller waited for their host to offer his cup for them to drink. It was a quiet and friendly little tea party.

As soon as the tea was over the elderly lady cleared the tea cups from the table and gathering all the children but the eldest, ushered them outside to play on the midship deck.

The boy began speaking to Wilson and Weller in a mixture of Chinese and English, at the same time showing Sam's knife first to Wilson then Sam, who patting his chest, indicated it was his and named himself.

"Me Sam," he said.

The boy burst out into peals of laughter as though Sam had cracked a joke.

Everyone joined in, including Wilson. Sam finished up laughing himself, although exactly what they were laughing about he couldn't tell.

Holding out his hand to the boy for the knife the boy grinned back, but kept the knife in his pocket.

Suddenly two dice danced across the smooth surface of the wooden table. Sam, to show willing, scooped up the dice and shook them, but did not throw.

The boy then placed the knife on the table and held up three fingers. Sam shook his head from side to side, refusing the challenge and placed ten Hong Kong dollars on the table.

The boy shook his head this time and removed the knife. The old lady had now returned and with the other children, gathered round to watch the betting. Sam placed another ten Hong Kong dollars on the table and the boy half drew the knife from his pocket, but let it go back.

Sam suddenly realised he was betting against his own knife and could still lose it, if it came to a toss of the dice. Having got the dice that belonged to the boy, he placed them into his pocket. Looking at Wilson, Sam said, "What in the hell do I do now?"

Wilson looked at the father who with Wilson both shrugged their shoulders as though it was nothing to do with them, rose from the stool and together walked out on to the upper deck to look at the Kia Kia, where all was quiet once again.

Leaning over the side, they forgot all about Sam, it was such a nice day.

To throw dice for his knife had Sam a little puzzled, for he did not have all that much money to throw about. The old lady smiled at Sam and he raised his stake by another five Hong Kong dollars.

The boy again shook his head and slowly all Sam's loose change was extracted from him.

Sam needed that knife it was part of his kit, Sam didn't fancy doing it, but he took the dice from his pocket and placed them on the table.

The boy did the same with the knife and the atmosphere became as intense as any gambling joint in Shanghai.

Wilson and the boy's father entered quietly and watched the two faces of the gamblers. The boy's Chinese face was quite inscrutable to Sam as his face was to the boy.

Holding up three fingers, Sam nodded, as the boy reluctantly, took the dice and threw three and four, a total of seven. Sam threw a miserable pair of twos. The boy, still straight faced, threw a challenging two fours. Eight would take some beating.

It did. Sam could only make a four and a two. The boy leapt to his feet laughing and shouting. Ignoring the money, he slapped the knife on the table in front of Sam and still laughing, he ran out and began to play with the other children. The gamble meant more as a game to the child than the money.

The older lady accepted the money and indicated by producing a tin of sweets how she would spend it.

As men of the sea in a simple way, the father invited Sam to call again for tea and warmly shaking hands with everyone including the children, Sam and Wilson returned to the jeep with waves from all the family.

Wilson and Weller made up a cock and bull story about being dragged into a game of gambling for their lives amongst a gang of cut-throat Chinese pirates. Sam even pulled out his pockets to prove it, not that anyone fell for that. Sam felt quite attached to his knife now and promised to repay the visit with some toys in exchange for a game.

When Sam entered the laundry with a bundle of washing, the smiles he received from Ma Pang and the girls were so gratifying, his absence could have been weeks instead of two days.

Anna with sparkling eyes, looked into his face and feeling for his fingers as she moved to take the washing, a thrill trembled through her for she so loved this gentle man.

Sam anxious to get on well with Ma Pang for Anna's sake, had suggested to Lee that if Ma Pang wanted to wash the combat overall tunics, they would be paid for in American Dollars.

This work could be done at Ma Pang's convenience. Ma Pang beamed at Sam like a young girl when she heard this and amended her opinion that all sailors were foreign pigs. Anna's basket was already filled with washing for the clothes line and Anna with a nod to Sam, picked up the basket and left by the back door.

Sam, with a quick wave to Ma Pang and Lee, disappeared through the kitchen and mess, heading for the shower room and the drying area. Quickly hanging up the washing together, they surrounded themselves with the larger pieces to be hung up which covered the windows.

Looking at each they both appreciated how much they loved each other and their kissing was out of this world for them both.

The sheer happiness of their physical presence so close to each other aroused in them both a sensuous desire so needed it brought a gentle flush to the delicate features of Anna.

Reluctantly, they drew apart, as thoughts of the laundry and Ma Pang came crowding in. Love is such a private feeling. Even the laundry bin was more private than out here in the laundry area.

Sensibly they agreed to talk, for being caught making love would be the ruin of Anna.

They agreed to meet and talk about the future, for Sam had so much to tell her that could affect their future lives together.

Later in the afternoon, they were once again together, after Am Ling had given him the nod that Ma Pang and Lee had left for home.

Having gathered the clothes fresh and warm from the sun, they together folded the washing and filled the basket.

There was no reason why they should not have a kiss before they began sorting, in preparation for the ironing tomorrow, but it was so tempting not to draw apart.

Sam and Anna, as agreed, sat at the table holding hands, while he quietly spoke of his thoughts about leaving the Navy in Hong Kong, as he was certain his demob and release from the forces was imminent.

Would Anna be prepared to join him there and possibly get married?

They could teach other languages, for Anna was as intelligent as she was beautiful.

Hong Kong would be a new world for them both. Sam was sure that Marcus his officer who had an interest in a Chinese girl like himself would be helpful.

With no family ties in England, having lost both parents in the war, a new life with Anna in Hong Kong was romantic and exciting.

Sam was certain they could make a wonderful life together, if they were not foolish. Anna thought something would turn up to give them a little privacy and more time together.

CHAPTER 5

Anna did not want to have a baby without a husband. Her mother would lose face and consequently her post as the linen lady at the big house, where she had worked for so many years. Anna was a Christian at heart and had been taken to the English church with the Consul children, to sing songs at Christmas. She had liked it very much, perhaps Sam would take her one day for he wore a cross around his neck which had belonged to his mother. What a wonderful thing to be married in a church.

Her only doubt was whether she was too old to be baptised like a baby. Unfortunately the children she played with had returned to England, so she could not ask them.

After the wash that day, Ma Pang said before she left the laundry, "I am taking Lee with me, make sure the door is locked before you leave."

This was a change by Ma Pang who never in the past had let the girls walk home alone.

Sam was pleased when Anna told him, for he also felt he was trusted.

Sam told Anna about the family on the junk he had met and his gambling with the boy for his knife. Anna was delighted with the story and said, "If you would like to meet them again, I would love to come with you. I've never been on a junk!"

There came a knock on the door from the kitchen and after a discreet pause, Am Ling poked his head round the door and asked, "Would you like a cup of tea?"

Anna and Sam, who were sitting quite primly at the table, accepted with enthusiasm. After all, Am Ling was a friend whom they both trusted

"Why don't you join us," called Anna in Chinese, before Am Ling closed the door.

Smiling, Am Ling reappeared with a tray and three cups and saucers. This was an honour indeed. So too were the plates of soft pastries and slices of fresh lemon. Anna, speaking and smiling at Am Ling, invited him to sit next to Sam and facing her across the table.

In front of Am Ling, she reached forward and took Sam's hand and began speaking to Am Ling in a very confiding manner in Chinese. Sam was quite happy to sit and enjoy the pleasant tones of Anna's voice, as she expressed with stylish movements of her long fingers. Sam was now someone special and had to be guarded not only from Ma Pang, but also from the wagging tongues of the sailors, who would think evil of her for loving a sailor.

Am Ling drank his tea and waited patiently for them to empty their cups. Collecting the crockery neatly on the tray, he stood up and with a bow that would have pleased a mandarin, he picked up the tray and left the laundry. Am Ling was in fact a little overwhelmed by the trust these two young people placed in a simple cook like himself and felt quite honoured, almost paternal at the great age of forty years.

Sam, having said goodbye to Anna in the laundry, entered the kitchen and waved to Am Ling as he passed through. Am Ling with a solemn face, gave Sam a deep respectful bow.

Marcus in the quiet of his private room at the Consul, reflected on their present situation in Shanghai. The uncertainty of when the ship would return was a worry and he could see no easy answer to his own problems.

Lita was always on his mind. He was in love and for once the Navy was taking second place in his thinking, for a change.

He had put his men at risk and should now try and redress the balance. After all, they had proved their mettle in the affair of the Kia Kia. Accepting the situation in a very disciplined way. The fact that none of them had been shot at was pure chance. Having acted as the officer of the court, to escort the accused at a court martial, the experience had lived in his mind how he would face up to the severity and discipline of a court martial if he had lost one of his men in such a clandestine raid as that on the Kia Kia.

His loyalty was to the men he commanded and he must treat them more humanely in the future, after all for all he knew they were now civilians!

A few concessions would make amends, like wearing civilian clothes for they only had a limited amount of uniform to wear. They could come and go as they pleased but still subject to naval discipline should ever any occasion arrive that they had to deal with any trouble.

Another important factor was their 'Hostility Only' status which made them more free as individuals and any further offers to take part in Joe's little escapades in the near future, would be purely voluntary or in defence of the Consulate.

Marcus decided to phone the quarters and picking the telephone up, he called Willie Willard, the Petty Officer, to say he would visit the men in the mess in half an hour.

Looking in the mirror, he smiled to himself, saying, "Wear a human face if you can and get out of uniform." He did just that.

The mess looked neat and tidy and the men now that they knew Marcus better were much more relaxed. Without a cap, Marcus looked much younger and joining them at the table, he joined in a general mess conversation about where the ship was, the Kia Kia and also an invitation from Borkowski to join a party to celebrate rescuing Una.

She was a great favourite with Joe's men, many of them had known her in America, when Joe's unit was in the States.

Una had worked for the Red Cross and visited many of Joe's men who were hospitalised. Una was in fact a little welfare society on her own.

Lita was more involved with looking after Ma and Pa and attending to business matters.

If Una was to attend the party by Borkowski, it was certain that Lita would be invited too. Marcus would have to think about that, for if he was expected to attend, he could hardly keep it a secret that he was very very friendly with Lita. Also he didn't want to spoil their fun.

Lita would no doubt know what form these parties took. Personally Marcus rather like the idea, for it would help him form a closer bond with his men as if they were shipwrecked, all hands together.

Wiggy had yet to experience that all the girls in China thought that small was beautiful. Wiggy being the smallest, had visions of playing Romeo to every girl he saw and asked Wilson who had accepted the invitation on behalf of them all, "Will there be any girls?"

Wilson could but assume there would be and replied, "Can you imagine any party being given by the Americans without girls - I can't!"

Marcus added, "It will be civilians for us all, I hope."

Wilson replied, "Half and half, some of Joe's men are on call."

Taffy rather tactlessly said to Sam in front of Marcus, "You're pretty friendly with Ma Pang and the girls in the laundry, why don't you ask her if we can take the girls out to a dance?"

Supporting Taffy, Wiggy added, "Yeh, we can look after them, can't we?" giving a wink to Taffy.

Sam, looking at Marcus before he replied, said calmly, "They are not those sort of girls. In any case, they are members of the Consul staff."

Hoping to get a favourable answer, Taffy spoke directly to Marcus as the Officer, "Sir, I reckon Wiggy and I..." but he got no further as Marcus cutting him short snapped, "Evans, you're a married man and should know better!"

He then reminded them, "If any of you got one of those girls into trouble, it would not be me that you would answer to, but the Head boy of the Consul! I should not like to find you, Evans like our American friend the other night, with a Chinese hair cut!"

Wiggy, a little nervous and not his cocky self, then asked, "Sir, what's a Chinese haircut?"

"Um, nothing much really," replied Marcus, "They just grab you by your pigtail, lift you off your feet and slash off your hair, if they like you - if they don't, they take off your head with it!"

Changing the conversation, Marcus invited them all if they had any personal problems, he was always available to talk things over in the privacy of his room in the Consul.

A new atmosphere had been created in the mess by the informal visit and it was as if they had left their uniforms behind somewhere and were individuals once more.

At lunch, there was not a piece of uniform in sight. The brightly coloured shirts added an air of casual informality, with more conversation going on about leaving the Navy and how they were to spend this evening free from any restriction. They all needed an extra shirt or two and for some reason, trousers became a must. The flap on a sailor's uniform trousers was a damned nuisance anyway, if you wanted to go anywhere in a hurry. They all fancied the slimmer trousers worn by the Consul staff, even the turn-ups were not bad.

Wiggy and Bungy, the two youngest, were already plotting together to find a dance hall. Taffy, now taking Black the stoker under his wing, just fancied a night on the town with a drink or two, whilst Wilson and Weller were all ready to go shopping when lunch had been served.

Kemp the signalman, usually spent some time with Willie, but most of the time, he just disappeared in the big house. There were rumours he had been seen with the telephonist in the Consul, but as no one had ever seen the telephonist, it remained a rumour.

Marcus, seated in the dining room at the Consul, having lunch with one of the staff was called to the phone by Lita, saying that they had received a call from Pierre who had booked a table for the evening and heard by chance that Joe and Marcus were friends and would they care to join them, Lita then teased him saying, "You wouldn't refuse to stay here for the night, would you Marcus? I had to say, yes this morning, because I couldn't get you on the phone - they also mentioned something about you providing the transport so would you give them a ring and I will see you this evening at eight darling." Lita then rang off.

Marcus had Pierre's telephone number and as soon as lunch was over, he gave Pierre a ring. Pierre's wife answered in a soft sexy voice, which altered slightly when she heard the name Marcus. Pierre greeted Marcus like a long lost brother and did not give Marcus a chance to speak or refuse the invitation.

Pierre had no transport and distrusted taxis, being in the jewellery business. If Marcus could pick them up, Pierre would be obliged. With that he rang off.

Marcus was half inclined to ring and explain his transport was a jeep. It was smart and clean with blue seat covers that Chung had fitted and it would have to do.

Chung enjoyed the trips to the restaurant. They treated him well while he waited and he enjoyed the food, the kitchen staff and their comments on his new driver's cap on which was embroidered Royal Navy in Chinese with a large anchor. Chung dined well at no expense. Marcus was a good boss with a pretty Chinese girl.

Chung also had his own way of following Marcus's orders, Anna in the laundry read them for him and Chung now felt very important indeed.

Wilson and Sam Weller enjoyed their shopping spree and Sam felt sure he would create a good impression on Anna when he met her later.

New shoes, neat trousers with a light yellow shirt and black tie. Sam and Wilson had each had their hair trimmed, which was a great improvement to the uneven ends of a short back and sides.

Wilson too had gone the whole hog and bought the same coloured shirt and white trousers and shoes with a white tie. They just did not look like sailors anymore and that's the way they wanted it.

Willie, the Petty Officer entered the mess and asked Wilson in a friendly manner, "You doing anything tonight?"

"No," was the reply.

"Good" said Willie. "I have a little job for you."

That evening, everyone was surprised to see Wilson in uniform. All he would say was that he was required for duty and left it at that. Wilson seemed quite happy about it and couldn't have arranged a better evening for himself if he had tried, but the rest of it he kept to himself.

Chung in his clean white shirt and smart chauffeur's cap, opened the door for him to enter the jeep. Wilson, smiling, nodded for him to drive off.

Wilson already had his instructions and was looking forward to the evening in anticipation of seeing Pierre's voluptuous wife and escorting her and her husband to dinner at Jung's restaurant.

At seven pm dead on time, Chung glided to a stop outside the jeweller's shop. Coming out of the shadow of the porch, Pierre's wife climbed nimbly into the back of the jeep helped by Wilson's arm and then pulled him into the back with her.

Pierre seating himself next to the driver, turned round and graciously thanked Wilson for being so brave to escort them to the restaurant.

Pierre then began instructing Chung in Chinese how to get there, while his wife sparkling like a duchess and quite glamorous, snuggled up to Wilson, saying in halting English, "You look so young tonight."

Wilson overcome by the scent and voluptuous closeness of the breasts of this glamorous female broke out into a sweat as her fingers began to gently massage the inside of his leg.

Wilson looked at the driving mirror and could not see if Chung was watching or not and to be on the safe side, he took her hand and whispered in her ear, "Yvonne you're gorgeous, but let us keep it until later."

She settled for his hand on her thigh. Helping her from the jeep when they arrived Yvonne seemed quite petite, but for her beautiful breasts as she turned to thank him.

Chung parked at the private entrance but had left very little room in the driveway for Wilson to hand Pierre's lady down from the jeep without stepping into a flower bed. Not to be deterred from being a little gallant, he slipped his arm behind her knees and the other around her waist and lifted her gently towards him, then allowing her feet to touch the ground. They were so close and looking down at her bare breasts, made him naturally draw her towards him and instinctively she kissed him.

Pierre having got out first, was already at the door, giving his lady the opportunity to invite Wilson indoors for a drink after the dinner. Not really knowing what he was letting himself in for Wilson willingly agreed.

Yvonne appeared from the rear of the jeep as the light from the opening door beamed across the driveway. Pierre's lady would have graced any stage as she stood there extending her hand to Marcus, who had opened the door.

It was hard to believe that this gorgeous creature was the same woman who had sat naked in front of them, calmly making pearls disappear before his eyes for his education.

Marcus excusing himself after introducing Pierre and his lady to Lita, spoke briefly to Wilson, asking him if he minded escorting Pierre home later, he Marcus, had made other arrangements.

Wilson thought, "I am in luck tonight." As Marcus made his way back into the house.

What a feast Wilson and Chung had that evening dining in the kitchen. The Chinese wine was mellow and potent. Unable to talk to Chung, but enjoying his company, Wilson could not help thinking about the rest of the evening to come.

Marcus had been more than surprised to see Pierre's lady and thought what a beautiful picture these elegant women made collectively.

Ma Jung had also dressed for the occasion and her dress, traditional Chinese looked quite exquisite. Pierre nominated to sit between Mr Jung and Una, who sat with Joe, whilst Yvonne his lady chose to sit between Mrs Jung and Lita and Marcus.

To be with Lita was all Marcus needed to be happy. At first he did not place his hand on Lita's thigh, him being next to Pierre's lady. Lita was having none of that for she loved the feel of his strong sexy fingers lingering there.

Pierre's lady did notice this familiar gesture, but thought nothing of it, having the need herself for the touch of a young lover.

Pierre had been a wonderful husband although his internment in the P.O.W camp in Hong Kong had rendered him impotent. Pierre suggested she should take a lover, for she wanted a child by someone tall like her husband.

The young handsome sailor, Wilson, was her age give or take a year or two and Pierre himself had noticed the light in Wilson's eyes in the workshop, when he had admired her naked body.

Perhaps tonight, Wilson would find her desirable and for her part, she was already in love enough with the young sailor to have his child. A child sometimes brings lovers together. Pierre wanted to watch when it happened, in order to feel part of it. Both she and Pierre thought nothing of that and their rooms were located to enable Pierre to feel part of the creation, if it were to happen.

It was a delicious meal and perfect company. Such a happy mixture of East and West.

Like all good things, the meal had to come to an end and the contrasts between them all was sufficient to provide everyone with a high degree of pleasurable entertainment and form new friendships.

Marcus was a little taken aback by Pierre's lady's comments on the charms of their escort, Wilson. Marcus liked him too and wondered what he would do, for he was due to leave the Navy.

Marcus stroked down his own dark wiry hair, although he needed no further encouragement from Lita for within a few minutes of Pierre and madam leaving, Lita was leading him by the hand up to their bedroom.

Pierre and his lady had just left with Wilson their escort and Chung needing no directions from Pierre quickly arrived at the jeweller's home, which they entered from the building next door which had the appearance of being separate from the jewellers.

The buzz of an electric motor revealed a hidden sliding metal door into a carpeted foyer.

The door closed silently behind them. Pierre, turning to Wilson, kissed him on both cheeks saying, "Welcome to our humble home. A glass of wine before we change."

Pierre's lady had already entered the bedroom area and returned in a revealing dressing gown. Accepting a glass of wine from Pierre, she patted the settee by her side and adjusted the cushion for Wilson to join her.

They all drank to each other and Yvonne placing her glass on an occasional table, turned to Wilson, giving him a perfect exposure of her breasts.

His glass shook a little in his hand and he quickly placed it on the table.

Pierre's lady Yvonne smiled and said, "What is your name?"

Wilson hesitated, then replied, "It is Edward, but everybody calls me Teddy."

Pouting her lips, she breathed out, "Oh - I love Teddy" and leaned over him, scented, sexy and very desirable saying softly as though confiding a secret, "Teddy darling, I am still a virgin. Can you do something about it." Looking him seriously in the eyes.

Teddy had slept with a woman or two in failed romances but never with a virgin.

Picking up his drink, he downed it quickly and stood up. Pierre's lady looked quite unhappy as she stood up and drew him into her arms, thinking she had played her part wrong.

Looking round to see if Pierre was in sight, Teddy took her into his arms and kissed her passionately, then whispered, "I can, if you really want me."

Her eyes were sparkling with the thought of a young lover.

Teddy said, "I've thought of nothing else but your beautiful face and body since the demonstration - I can't get you out of my mind."

Yvonne was equally forthright, "Pierre wants me to take a lover and you are the man I have been waiting for. Pierre understands why he has been impotent since being a prisoner of war in Hong Kong. He wants a child to love and so do I."

Holding her with great gentleness, Teddy Wilson whispered, "I'd love it too, if you were the mother!"

They then kissed passionately and Teddy feeling a little warm asked, "Can I have a shower?"

She laughed happily as Pierre entered the room, saying "I love your laughter, Yvonne," cuddling her fondly like a father.

Showing Teddy the shower, she began to help him undress, for with Pierre it was necessary, but with Teddy it became much more fun.

With Teddy naked, they looked at each other with pleasure on their faces until she reached in and turned the shower lever on at the same time calling, "I'll play with my teddy bear later." As Yvonne left for the bedroom.

After the shower, Teddy towelled and she brought him a dressing gown of white silk.

Teddy felt refreshed after his shower and was soon aroused as Yvonne popped into see how he was getting on and rub his back down as an excuse to touch his healthy young body in the right places.

Later, together in their dressing gowns, they sipped a nightcap of a good French brandy. Two adjacent bedrooms each had an ornate

Chinese double bed and before retiring Pierre, recharging his glass and returning to his armchair, addressed them both, saying, "Isn't it time you young lovers went to bed I want to enjoy my brandy for a little longer."

Yvonne rose and as she leaned over to kiss Pierre goodnight, he gently fondled her beautiful breasts.

Taking Teddy's hand, Yvonne led him eagerly into the bedroom, lighting a joss-stick and standing at a small shrine for a moment or two before turning to find Teddy already lying naked under the silk sheets, his silhouette showing prominently in the dimmed bedroom lighting.

Lifting the top sheet, she slid between the sheets until her breasts caressed his downy chest and their lips touched in a first passionate kiss. With cries of pain and joy she surrendered to the pleasure of creation as the exquisite sensation of mounting satisfaction they created burst within her to leave them briefly in a heaven, clinging to the creation of love that had passed between them.

A soft voice from the darkness speaking in French was heard by the lovers, saying, "Elle - est - beau. Elle - est - beau."

The door then quietly closed. Again they made love, before going to sleep.

When Teddy woke up, he was alone, but for a beautiful bunch of flowers at the foot of the bed. It was long time since he had been able to smell the sweet fragrance of freshly cut flowers and reaching down, he picked up the blooms and was smelling them, when Yvonne's maid arrived with a tray of tea and biscuits. Removing one cup and a biscuit and singing cheerfully to herself, she disappeared into the next bedroom, where Pierre greeted her with affectionate kisses and together they laughed happily, as his wife spoke in an excited voice of the pleasures of her successful love making with Teddy during the night and the ecstasy she felt that it was going to be fruitful.

Pierre too, without a trace of jealousy, sounded happy and excited.

Teddy, still naked, got out of the bed to place the flowers on the table, when in walked Pierre with his lady.

Pierre smiled and with his arms outstretched embraced Teddy warmly smiled and kissing his passionately on both cheeks. Looking down, he turned and smiled at his lady, muttering, "Le faire Part." before returning to his bedroom.

Teddy could not stop himself laughing when Yvonne and he jumped back on to the bed, forgot the tea and began feeling each others bodies all over again.

It was not long after that, when the telephone rang in Pierre's bedroom. Marcus saying that he would pick up L.Seaman Wilson on his way back to the Consul. Chung having left him there last night had to tell Marcus in any case.

Wilson had quite enjoyed reverting to his own name for a few hours and intended to use it a lot more for she wanted him to be with her every night.

Pierre's lady was adorable, even though she was Pierre's wife. Wilson was quite content with his status as a lover.

Pierre and his lady continued to call Wilson by the name Teddy even when Marcus stopped to pick him up. Pierre and his lady both kissed Teddy (Wilson) goodbye affectionately before he boarded the jeep and with a wave from Marcus they were on their way back to the quarters.

Marcus, with a friendly smile said, "So you stayed last night - were they nervous on the way home?"

Wilson, from the back of the jeep and smiling to himself replied, "Oh yes, that's why I went in with them to see that everything was all right. Pierre's such a generous man, he'd give you anything - even his brandy!"

"Why do they call you Teddy?"

"My grandfather was fond of Edward VII and I am named Teddy after him. I couldn't use my naval nickname Tug, could I?"

Marcus agreed with that saying, "No, I don't suppose you could. It might mean something dirty in French," said Marcus with a chuckle, knowing the meaning of the word in that language.

Getting held up a little in the traffic, Wilson took the opportunity to raise the question of his demob and the others by saying, "Excuse me, Sir, off the record, can you find out for me if I can be demobbed in Hong Kong. After all, I'm technically a civilian now the war is over."

Marcus not knowing the answer, was stumped for a minute. They'd begun to move again and needing time to think about this, he asked, "Are the others worried about their demob numbers and groups being announced?"

Wilson thought before he answered saying, "Yes, I think so, but it's quite a treat to be ashore in Shanghai, it's the first and last holiday I'll ever have." Thinking of last night.

Having had a French breakfast of coffee and croissants before he said goodbye to Yvonne, Wilson was not hungry, although they all seemed to be eating a late breakfast when he arrived. Wilson quickly changed out of uniform into a shirt and went in to report to Willie that he was back.

The patrol were all itching to know what he had been up to, for he was smiling and seemed very pleased with himself. That was unusual for a start, for few people left Willie's office as cheerful as that, after being called out on night duty. To avoid a cross examination, he sat down at the mess-table and immediately got all their attention.

With a serious face, he began by saying, "I've been discussing the matter of our demob coming back with Marcus in the jeep and he is going to look into it for us. By the time we get back to U.K. it could take weeks, even months. I have no intention of joining a dole queue with a few medals in my pocket."

Bouncing it back, Wiggy enquired, "What are you going to do?"

"That is my business Wiggy, but I used to work for a newspaper and I'll consider that first." replied Wilson.

Back came Wiggy again, "You're a bit old for a newspaper boy."

Not expecting anything better from Wiggy, Wilson ignored him and asked them all to think about it and put it down on paper, for he was going to see Marcus officially or the Consul to discuss their future. After all as civilians it was the Consul's job to look after British nationals and in their situation they would soon be penniless, unless the Consul was prepared to pay them.

After all, in this situation and having tasted the sweet things of life in their few days ashore in Shanghai, Wilson and the others all felt they deserved something more.

As far as Wilson's future stood, if his relationship with Pierre and Yvonne prospered, he was quite happy at the moment in Shanghai, although Hong Kong would be better if Pierre and Yvonne were to be there.

Without the routine of preparing for a patrol each evening and the greater freedom of wearing non-uniform clothing, the patrol tended to split up into pairs.

Wilson and Weller unknown to each other, had begun a love affair with a Chinese girl and both were single without any strong family ties at home, had half-committed themselves to a life in Hong Kong if they could only get there.

Bungy Edwards and Wiggy Bennett were younger, but still due for demob and shared some commons interests in proving that Chinese girls were no different and therefore wiser than other men for their time on the China station.

Together they agreed to do what had been recommended by a soldier at the party after the raid.

There was a dance hall known as the Texas Dance Hall used mainly by the American 5th Fleet. You would be welcome if you went in uniform.

The entrance was free, but you bought books of tickets if a girl caught your eye and she just walked over, handed you a ticket and the next dance was yours and anything else if you could afford to pay for with the tickets.

Mind you, this advice was given by a soldier and could be dodgy, but everyone agreed when seeing them dressed in their expertly laundered sailors suits, British sailors always look smart, even if a little short as in Wiggy's case.

As the coxswain had said to Wiggy before he left the ship, "small is beautiful" to the Chinese.

Wiggy, with an extra squirt of hair cream on his hair, was ready to dance the night away.

It was about 2000 (8pm) when they left the quarters and recognising the rickshaw runner who hung around at the gates, Wiggy hailed him and they were soon on their way.

The entrance to the dance hall was impressive, with a carpeted foyer like a cinema, with large double doors leading to a further carpeted area with doors at the end, to enter the dance hall. Wiggy, paying off the rickshaw, entered the foyer as though he owned the place and had every right to be there. He was only small, but being dressed differently from the U.S. sailors they were intruders on the U.S patch as they milled around looking aggressive to find a table.

Dancing was in progress and spying an empty table, Bungy and Wiggy sat down quickly and waited for some service as they watched the dancing. Off the floor, standing in groups, were a number of girls, holding books of small tickets, which they kept flicking like a pack of cards as they scanned the customers not dancing.

Wiggy, wasting no time, asked Bungy for twenty Hong Kong dollars for tickets and telling Bungy to mind the table, skirted round the dancers until approached by a group of girls halfway round the floor wanting to sell him tickets.

One who spoke better English than the others who claimed the name of Rosie, looked up to Wiggy with a twinkle in her eye caught his eye, but appeared a little disappointed when he flashed his Hong Kong dollars.

She paused, before grabbing everything in his hand, twenty dollars, and handed him a book of tickets. At that moment the music stopped and the floor cleared.

With his usual bravado Wiggy took her arm and marched her across the empty floor directly to their table.

Seating herself and smiling, she said, "You Hong Kong sailor, come dance."

Her size made her an ideal partner for Wiggy who danced a lot with his equally small sister.

It was a quickstep and suited them fine jazzing it up between the larger U.S. sailors whom in the main had two left feet and towered over the girls.

Some dancers deliberately tried to push Wiggy out of the way, but light of foot he danced his way out of trouble. Envious and angry eyes looked at pretty Rosie and Wiggy as they returned to the table, although Bungy and Wiggy happy and enjoying themselves Wiggy and partner were oblivious of the resentment they were creating.

Joe's men had been on duty and spotted Wiggy and Bungy entering the Texas ballroom and knew they were in some danger poaching on American girls, however innocent they may be.

A phone call to Borkowski, quickly contacted Marcus who was in uniform at the time. Putting on his gaiters and taking his sword stick, he called the patrol and was on his way.

Pepe, Bungy's girl was persistent about ordering drinks holding out her hand for more money each time they had a dance. It didn't please Bungy's palate sipping an insipid wine with a drop of fizzy locally made lemonade and dipping into pocket he said to Wiggy. "Your girl is pestering all the time for drinks. Ask her to stick to dancing, I'm not a bloody Yank!"

Wiggy answered, "Why don't you tell her to Pepe off, you have hardly had a dance and it cost you thirty dollars buying stupid drinks!"

Sensing Bungy's feelings, Pepe grabbed his arm saying, "We dance, yes."

They began dancing. Wriggling into Bungy in tune with the music, he found it quite pleasant even if the tempo was Chinese. He managed to get her to say Bungy without tittering and make her understand he was English, not American.

Pepe snuggled up to Bungy and smiled a lot and speaking very softly, but loud enough to be heard over the music, she conspired and indicated cleverly with her fingers, that they should go to bed for twenty dollars.

All Bungy ever had was Phyllis against the coal shed and that wasn't much fun with the rain dripping down his collar.

"OK" he said, "but let us dance a bit more, I can get a girl anytime" and danced her quickly round the floor.

Pepe was not bad for a Chinese, but lacked a western sense of rhythm. Wiggy's dancing had been too energetic for Rosie and she was glad to get back to the table for a sip of her Texas Special of coloured water and a teaspoonful of Chinese wine.

Sitting next to Wiggy, she gave him a ravishing smile when Pepe was not looking and with a flick of her eyes, implied she would like to dance. Together they rose and the music being slower, Rosie was able to snuggle into Wiggy in much the same way as Pepe had done, saying, "You sleep with me?"

Wiggy was rather flattered that both girls wanted to go to bed with him and he continued to dance with Rosie.

This pleasant partnership was not to last, for already they were getting dirty looks from the table next door, where a bunch of half drunk Yanks not able to dance, began sniggering at Wiggy's fancy footwork.

The arrival of Wiggy and Bungy in the hall had caused a lot of comment in the first place, for the Texas Dance Hall was their joint, although owned and run by Chinese.

Oblivious of the impending threat, Wiggy and Bungy continued to dance, monopolising the girls who now found the Englishmen quite fun and very romantic.

There was an even chance that they would continue to need their services when the dancing was over.

In the meantime, Joe's patrol kept the dance hall under surveillance, because it was from this joint a lot of trouble began.

A routine report-in stated that foreign sailors had been seen entering the dance hall. Joe's intimate knowledge of the British patrol rang a bell and he automatically rang Marcus to pass on the information.

Marcus, in uniform, having just returned from a staff birthday party at the Consul, refused Joe's offer of help and phoned Willie Willard to get two patrolmen into uniforms, the jeep driver and be ready to leave now.

Weller and Wilson were nowhere in sight, leaving only the stoker Black and Kemp the signalman available. Black, a cheerful but dumpy lad, had to be half dressed by Willie, to make him look smart. Kemp on the other hand was neat and slightly built. Neither were actually patrol material and Willie, a bit of a Martinet, marched them up and down outside for two or three minutes in the hope of giving them an air of authority.

Willie at least looked smart and ushering his novice patrolmen into the jeep, he clambered into the rear also. Marcus sitting quietly in the front seat, ordered Chung to drive off. Marcus was somewhat surprised to be met by Sergeant Borkowski, who was surprised to see Marcus with just his walking stick.

Marcus and Willie had a quick word and Borkowski outlined the best way to extract the two British sailors from the stormy sea of resentment gathering from all sides in the dance hall, as they chatted up the two girls regarded by half of the American 5th Fleet as their property.

Marcus' orders were short and sweet. He and Willie would march across to Wiggy and Bungy after they had been sighted. If they did not stand up at the sight of Marcus, they would be ordered to do so. Kemp and Black would make quite sure they were handed their caps and made to put them on. They would hold one arm at the elbow of each man and march them out of the hall, through the door by which they had entered. Once in the jeep, they were to be driven straight back to the quarters.

This understood, they formed up behind Marcus and Willie and at the order quick march from Willie, they entered the foyer and marched through the door into the dance floor.

When the music stopped, Willie shouted, "Rise, you're under arrest, on caps" louder still shouted, "Quick March."

Willie leading stepped on to the dance floor like a cabaret turn and thinking he was on a parade ground and not a dance floor called out, "Left, right, left, right," as they marched across the floor to the door.

CHAPTER 6

The real show began when they entered the foyer and were confronted by a gang of half-drunk sailors led by a hulking great brute of a man intent on smashing someone.

Marcus, confronted by the mob, ordered the patrol to halt. Taking two paces forward, he shouted, "Gangway," at the same time, clicking the handle of his stick with his free hand.

The brute of a leader took half a fighting step forward like a fighter, but got no further, as Marcus, coolly drawing the sword from the stick, flicked it neatly down the man's cheek and the blood spurted like red wine down the leering face. Clutching his face and washing it in his own blood, he reeled back and the mob parted.

Wiping his blade on a clean handkerchief, Marcus gave the order, "Quick March."

Bundling the two dancing sailors into the jeep and climbing aboard, the jeep quickly roared off back to the headquarters.

A call to Joe as soon as he returned was treated confidentially and stabbings take place every day in this sinful city.

You couldn't really blame Wiggy and Bungy for being romantic and apart from a good telling off by Marcus, they were grateful to have been rescued. They still had plenty to talk about when breakfast was over and Bungy won the day, having been propositioned twice.

Wilson and Weller were getting better acquainted by the hour, now that demob had become the leading topic. Sam Weller being rather a loner and with different duties on board ship from Wilson, this was the first time they had ever confided intimately to each other.

Sam needed to confide in someone, although Wilson was Sam's superior, he told Wilson of his friendship with Anna. He didn't hesitate to say he was in love with her. Wilson seemed to understand straight away, instead of saying, "You shouldn't do that" he congratulated Sam, saying he also had someone in mind, but he didn't say who she could be. Wilson and Sam talked for sometime about leaving the Navy and both had considered Hong Kong, having found girl friends and with no one to return home for, at least in the near future.

Pierre seemed to have achieved a great deal in the time he had been free and not a P.O.W. Pierre was not in good health and might welcome Teddy (Wilson) as an assistant.

Wilson's ideas of the future were in advertising, although he and Sam joked about starting a paper round.

Pierre being a businessman would certainly be able to give them good advice and their plans to demob in Hong Kong were not as wild as first appeared. Sam still twenty, had a sound education and a good manner. He was gifted with common sense and in his talks with Wilson, he showed an aptitude for thinking up some sensible ideas. With Anna, who had good business sense, he was sure his future was with her.

Shanghai with an unknown future and a prize to be gained in the struggle between the Communists and Chang Ki Shek which was getting ever closer, British Hong Kong would be safer for Anna. Each had gained something from their conversation and with a promise by Teddy Wilson to introduce Anna to Yvonne soon and arrange an evening out together, they walked outside with arms round each other more like old friends.

Once outside their conversation changed and the junk where Sam had left his knife came up.

Sam rather liked the family, particularly the children. He said to Wilson, "I would love them to meet Anna."

He then spoke about Anna knowing nothing other than her life in the Consul laundry. She had thought a trip to see a junk and go on board would be a holiday for her. Together they agreed that they would have to do something about that.

Marcus, sitting in his room at the Consul, had spent some time writing up the log he was keeping on the daily activities of his patrol. So far he had managed to give a reasonable account of a routine nature without a mention of daily prayers.

This was one thing his own Commanding Officer in the ship was rather strict about and he must get hold of a prayer book and get something on record.

Marcus didn't know of anyone in the patrol burdened by religious zeal, but a single question to any of the patrol would give the lie, that Church Parade was the last thing he should have forgotten for the sake of his men.

Today being Friday, gave him a couple of days to prepare a short service for Sunday. With a congregation of eight, he hoped they were all Church of England. If he had to excuse half of them by saying fall out R.C's, it wouldn't be much of a service with a congregation of four.

The subject of church had never arisen in the Consul or at meals in the staff dining room. He could of course just have a parade and a prayer. Strangely enough, the men were quite content doing their own thing and one had even suggested that he, Marcus, should get out a bit and stop worrying about them, saying, "We are civilians!" Writing to finish the day's entries, he added, "Morale was high, with a high standard of good behaviour and discipline being maintained."

Talking to Wilson, Sam's future seemed more important and instead of just waiting for his demob to be received, he resolved to spend some time in looking for possible jobs here in Shanghai and Hong Kong, although the latter was a few hundred miles away to the South.

Am Ling seeing Sam at the door, beckoned him in and with a friendly grin, offered Sam a cup of tea. Sam declined saying, "Have we time for a little talk?"

Am Ling was more than willing and offering his seat to Sam, drew up a stool and facing Sam, his expression was solemn.

Sam struggling a bit with a mixture of syllables, he thought he had learnt he tried to convey, "I am leaving the ship, could I, work in China?"

Sam had to go over this repeatedly before Am Ling really understood.

Am Ling's first advice was to speak to big boss in big house.

"You speak Chinese - then job easy, here in Consul."

"Much paper, you not proud, why not speak to head boy." demonstrating humility and respect by making a slow respectful bow, he made Sam stand and copy him.

Am Ling was not the best of tutors, but he insisted that Sam should continue to do it several times, correcting the feet, knees, hands and fingers.

This ritual was being watched by Anna from the kitchen door. She had just opened it to give a message to Am Ling, to pass to Sam. The lesson ended when Anna said, "Ma Pang wants to see you, Sam."

Taking his hand she led him into the laundry. Entering the laundry holding Anna's hand, produced no objection from Ma Pang which Sam had expected. Instead, she indicated to them to stand before her, like a bride and groom.

Looking into Sam's eyes, she studied him for a while, then in slow but better English than he had heard her speak before, she said,

"You marry my daughter Anna in one month. How much? - I want thousands H.K. dollars."

This knocked the wind out of Sam in one sentence and he didn't know what to say. Struck dumb, he just stood there whilst he gathered his wits.

Looking at Anna, her eyes sparkling with good humour she said, "What have you been saying to my mother - have you made an offer for me?"

Finding his tongue, he turned to Anna saying anxiously, "What am I supposed to do?"

"Double it and ask her if we can go out together from tonight."

Sam's mind worked quickly and a thousand dollar Hong Kong worked out about eighty pounds and he quickly called out, before Ma Pang could withdraw the offer, "I say two thousand dollars, if I can walk with Anna in the street."

Ma Pang looked at him as though he was a toad. She was about to turn away, when he raised it again to three thousand dollars.

Ma Pang turned and faced him once again. Looking him straight in the eye, she said with a stern expression on her wrinkled face, "Is that all my daughter is worth to you? My husband gave me everything!" (What she didn't mention was her husband only had a cow when they lived in the country).

Thinking of how much he had in the Naval Bank Book and desperately wanting to save face in front of Anna, Sam smiled and held out his hand to her. Anna, taking it, moved closer to him as he said, "Ma Pang, I would give her the world if I could, but to marry Anna in an English church is worth far more than five thousand dollars, if you accept."

After Anna had explained what Sam had just said, beaming all over, Ma Pang came forward, kissed his hands, felt his face and said, "Honour her family."

Kissing Anna, she quietly left the laundry.

Taking Anna in his arms, they kissed each other and cuddled. Lee, her younger sister, who was standing close by, could not stop a tear falling down her pretty face for she did not understand what was going on.

"Don't worry little sister, I am not going away." comforted Anna.

Together, all three walked into the garden and the business in the laundry was forgotten for a moment, as the two sisters, one on each side, lay claim to one hand each of Sam's strong fingers.

Wilson had an embarrassing minute or two in Willies Willard's office, for Pierre's lady had phoned asking to speak to Teddy. Willie could hear someone else talking to the speaker, when the phone had gone dead. It rang again shortly afterwards, with Pierre asking to talk to Wilson.

Willie being rather curious, lingered as Wilson took up the phone to speak. Seeing Willie did not intend to leave, Wilson turned to him, saying, "Do you mind Petty Officer, but this is private."

Willie, in a huff left the office, muttering something about a private call on a service phone.

Yvonne was so excited being able to talk to Teddy, who could understand very little of what she said, apart from that she loved him and Pierre loved him and when were they going to see him again. With a promise to ring soon and saying, "I love you," he promised to ring again a little later when he was alone.

Every time Willie left his room and office, he always closed the outside window. It was a nice day outside and Wilson, with a book and a small chair from the mess, found a convenient spot on the lawn behind a tree from where he could watch Willie's office window.

It was almost lunch time before Willie made a move. Even then, he only appeared to be going to the Consul building to see Marcus.

Wasting no time after Willie had closed his window, he entered his office, picked up the phone and dialled Pierre.

Luckily, Pierre answered and speaking quickly into the phone he said, "Pierre, listen - listen. I must speak to you alone for I need your advice!"

"Of course, we can be alone in the house, there is no need for me to be in the workshop if Yvonne is there."

Pierre sounded anxious and before Teddy (Wilson) could speak again, Pierre began apologising, "I hope we have not offended you, my dear boy. You have brought us so much happiness. Please come to lunch and we can talk all afternoon, if it will make you happy."

With a promise to be there at one o'clock, Wilson thanked Pierre and then quickly rang off. Returning to his seat in the garden, he waited until he saw the office window open. Then he returned to the mess and dressed for lunch.

Tapping on the office door, he entered and asked for the leave book. Willie still curious as to what Wilson was up to, for he had heard of Wilson's previous all night stay at Pierre's on the night after the party.

Sarcastically he said to Wilson, "Sorting pearls with the girls again and staying all night. What about organising a few of those pearly dollies for us!"

Wilson quietly closed the door.

As Wilson was about to leave the mess, Sam came in from the kitchen and they chatted briefly, Wilson mentioning his having lunch with Pierre. They were rudely interrupted when Willie appeared at the mess door and addressing Wilson, he said, "Have you anyone to go with you to our friend Pierre? It's quite a long way, to be out on your own, in the French district."

Wilson had not expected this from Willie who had every right to apply the rules.

"Can I use the phone I will have to cancel the lunch?"

Sam butting in said, "What do you want the phone for, I'm going with him."

Before Willie could reply, he marched into his office, signed the leave book and quickly changing into a clean shirt, they marched out of the mess together, Wilson, happy to be rescued.

Together, they hurried to the gates and scrambling into the first rickshaw that came along, they headed for the Quai de France and into the French sector.

Wilson was sure Pierre wouldn't mind Weller coming along, for Weller too now had Chinese connections to the value of five thousand Hong Kong dollars. In any case any advice that Pierre might give, was equally of value to Sam, who like himself was liable to leave the Navy.

The rickshaw lad ran at a steady pace and Wilson who had done the trip two or three times, was able to keep the rickshaw on course.

Like London, this metropolis of the East with its millions of citizens was not a place for the faint-hearted.

Happily, sailors are pleased with the simple things of life and weaving in and out of the crowds and pedestrians, was as good as a chariot race to Wilson and Weller. On arrival, they thanked the rickshaw boy and tipped him generously.

The broken window of Pierre's workshop had been replaced and the outside of the premises, although now complete, looked even less prosperous than before.

This camouflage was all part of Pierre's strategy not to advertise his business in this sprawling city of crime and vice.

Refugees from the civil war between Communists and Nationalists continued to arrive in a steady stream as the Communists advanced.

Foreign businessmen were also on the move, not willing to risk the outcome of a Communist victory, although the vitality of Shanghai whatever happened, would maintain its importance as an industrial base and the largest sea port.

Their arrival must have been seen from inside the workshop, for as they were about to knock, the small wrinkled woman in charge of the girls appeared and conducted them through to the metal sliding doors leading to the private apartment in the next building.

There were no girls working today to tickle the fancies of Wilson or Weller.

Weller was more than surprised by the greeting given to Teddy (Wilson) as Pierre embraced Teddy, kissed him on both cheeks, then with another hug, passed him to his wife.

Pierre's lady was one of those rare women who are graceful in all they do. Looking at Teddy with adoring eyes, that Weller could see, she melted into Teddy's arms, saying softly, "Teddy my love, I've missed you so much." And clinging to him as though he would disappear any minute, her soft lips covered his mouth and face with kisses and whispering, "Love me," she placed his hand on her beautiful breast.

Weller embarrassed by what he saw, turned towards Pierre, who taking Sam's arm, led him into the magnificent drawing room of the apartment.

Teddy and Pierre's lady followed them in, still clinging to each other.

Pierre had moved to a small bar and poured four glasses of Chinese wine, whilst Weller, standing a little removed, waited to be introduced to Wilson's companion.

Pierre, handing round the drinks and then taking his wife's hand, led her over to Sam, saying to Wilson, "Introduce your friend, Teddy, to Yuen Fong, Yvonne I mean, - she is anxious to meet him."

Stepping forward and away from Teddy, Yvonne softly kissed Sam on each cheek as he in turn returned the kiss.

"You can call me Yvonne if you wish. I like that, it is more French."

Almost overcome by her expensive perfume, Sam Weller croaked, "Thanks Yvonne, my name is Sam." As he once again leaned forward and planted another kiss on each side of her perfumed face.

Pierre came forward and greeted Sam as men do in France, with a warm kiss on each cheek, saying, "Welcome to our home." And embraced Sam to his tall thin body.

Pierre then raising his glass toasted.

"Absent Comrades," they all repeated the toast.

Pierre then replaced his glass on the bar and embracing Teddy and Yvonne one in each arm said in an exuberant manner, "We are a beautiful family, are we not!" hugging Teddy and Yvonne to him.

The gaunt face of Pierre between the dark haired beautiful Yvonne and handsome Teddy glowed with happiness, as he announced, "I'm going to be a father."

Spontaneously everybody clapped, although no one knew for sure that such an announcement could be rather premature.

Kissing Pierre fondly, Yvonne left to supervise the lunch, while Sam and Teddy listened intently to what Pierre had to say.

Pierre because of his period in the P.O. War camp was a precise speaker and soon had Sam, rather a loner, talking to him as though Pierre was an understanding father.

Sam spoke of his girl friend Anna in affectionate terms and the bounty he had agreed for the privilege of walking out with Anna. Sam went even further, speaking of his ideas of settling in Hong Kong if this were possible having no desire to return to England.

Accepting that youth sees very little of the storms ahead and not wanting to discourage Sam in any way from talking, Pierre continued to listen, nodding and finally saying, "We must talk to Yvonne for she will be so interested to know about Anna, who I hope you will marry!"

A servant girl appeared at the door of the drawing room, indicating that lunch was ready.

With the guests in mind, a cold lunch followed the soup and it pleased Yvonne to see Teddy and Sam, who had practised hard with the chopsticks using them so naturally. Refusing mai tai and accepting another glass of wine instead, both men moved freely between dishes sampling everything on offer from prawns to cold chicken, and dishes of delicious salad with sauces and seasoned rice that tingled the tongue and tantalised the palate to be followed by fresh fruit and tea.

It had been a convivial meal with plenty of talk and appreciative guests enjoying the delights of the food on the table. Leaving the men to continue talking in the drawing room, Yvonne excused herself with a kiss blown to them all.

The difficulties that faced the young men contemplating living in China were explained by Pierre in a very disarming way, with emphasis on the language for the people he had found honest and charming although the language was hard but not impossible for an Englishman.

If you had a reason to speak in Chinese it would come in the end.

Honesty and respect for the Chinese and their customs, many of which were centuries old.

Pierre also dwelt on business dealings, particularly as foreigners dealing with customs and regulations. It all sounded rather intimidating at first, but Pierre added a sweetener, saying, "Even a Chinese looks English or French, if he speaks your language and the same applies to us."

Accepting the sense of Pierre's thinking, for after all he spoke Cantonese fluently, all he said demonstrated it was better still, to have a Chinese wife.

For Sam he advised that Hong Kong was a better starting base, particularly in import and export to England to begin with.

Pierre himself had already made provisional moves himself, to transfer his business to Hong Kong or alternatively Singapore, if the war looked like being lost by the Nationalists.

Many English and French businesses were withdrawing and the closure of a famous hotel Jinjang, used by the French Community, looked imminent.

Yvonne entered and the conversation changed, with her talking first to Sam she enquired, "When will you be seeing Anna again, Sam?"

Looking at his watch, he answered, "Usually about now, three o'clock."

"Will you be in trouble - she will miss you!" looking at Teddy with a meaningful look.

"If you would excuse me, I would like to see her, but we have an order about moving around in twos and I would spoil Teddy's day."

Wilson, however, was as keen as Sam for him to return on his own, but was reluctant to say so.

Pierre came to the rescue, "Use my boy, but do not pay him, he will be offended."

Pierre speaking to a maid, arranged for his rickshaw to be brought to the house and they all accompanied Sam into the hall. Pierre and Yuen Fong gave him a warm send off with a kiss and a hug.

Sam promised to bring Anna for an evening meal very soon, for her to meet Pierre, his beautiful wife and friend Teddy.

With a wave to them all, Sam was soon on his way and had no worries about where he was being taken.

Pierre had given the directions and the trip took far less time then when they had come. Not bothering to sign the liberty book, Sam headed for the rear door to the laundry, which he opened very quietly.

Anna was alone and standing at the table piled high with clean fresh washing from the line, which she was sorting.

Tip-toeing to be behind her, he touched her shoulder and as she turned, he took her in his arms. To see the welcoming sparkle in her dark brown eyes, her parted lips and pure white teeth, as she cooed, "Sam" and threw her arms around his neck and kissed him with such an impact, he trembled right down to his toes, as her soft parted lips and tongue caressed his lips.

Holding and caressing, they kissed each other, until a soft cough brought them apart.

Cuddling a pile of dry washing in their arms at the door, stood Ma Pang and Lee watching intently. Ma Pang was the first one to speak as the lovers drew apart. Speaking quite softly, she almost chanted, "I have never been kissed like that - is it nice?"

Placing her washing on the table, she held her face towards Sam to be kissed. Leaning forward, Sam kissed her pouted lips.

Lee not wanting to miss out on such things as kissing, smartly dumped her laundry basket and stood by her mother, fully expecting to be kissed too, It was not to be.

With a push and "tut-tutting" at Lee, Ma Pang scolded, "Don't be silly, kissing at your age could turn you into a street girl!"

Sam, with a wink at Lee, brought a smile back to her face, as Lee thought, "I will collect that kiss later."

Sam then helped the two girls with the sorting and folding, at the same time telling them of Pierre and his wife, also of the invitation for Anna and himself to go for a meal one evening for Anna to meet them both.

Ma Pang although understanding only a little of what Sam had been talking about, did not appear to object.

Later, as Anna discussed the invitation with her mother, there was a great deal of finger wagging by Ma Pang as she emphasised to Anna the way she should conduct herself, "Stay on the Bund near people and be back before dark."

Girls with foreigners were often stopped for the wrong reasons and were easy pickings for corrupt police. Muggers and a wide variety of petty thieves and pickpockets preyed on foreigners and servicemen like the 5th U.S. Fleet.

Shanghai was a sprawling mass of old large buildings and factories surrounded with overcrowded houses and slums with more migrants from the war ravaged countryside arriving every day, to swell the millions already living here.

For Sam to be given permission to walk with Anna, was a nice gesture by Ma Pang, who while distrusting all foreigners for they looked so funny except her laundryman pretty Sam.

Although the Pang family did not live far from the consul, Anna suggested that they meet at the Consul gates.

Sam was delighted when he first saw Anna in a dress. Anna's walk was almost athletic as she danced and swerved through the crowd towards him. They did not kiss as they met. Just took each other's hand and continued together towards the waterside to watch as they walked, the sampans, boats, junks, freighters, all finding a way somehow, up or down the Huangpu river.

Anna was radiant and insisted Sam wore the cap she had brought with her for him to wear. It was a bit too large for him and fitted down to his ears with a largish peak, It was quite a joke to Anna, who tended to laugh each time it dropped over his nose.

Anna claimed it made him look more Chinese, but it was doubtful that even a pigtail could have done that.

From the first moment they had seen each other and wanted to touch, they felt happy and carefree and very much in love. Reaching the Quai de France, they followed the bend of the river until Sam remarked he had been in this stretch of the river before.

Looking a bit further ahead, Sam could make out the bend in the river where the Kia Kia had been tied up.

Deciding this was far enough, they turned back, for the setting sun was getting low. Anna enjoyed being out, refused the offer of a rickshaw back, preferring to stroll back with their arms around each other.

They spoke about marriage and Sam explained about demob and what it meant. If he were to be discharged in Hong Kong and if possible she could join him there.

Anna smiled, saying to Sam, "With you, can I marry in Hong Kong?"

Sam nodded saying, "Yes, in church!"

It was a delightful evening with the sun still shining as Anna and Sam entered the Consul gardens. The flower beds were delightful at this time and they continued walking, admiring the flowers.

Sam offered to pick one, but Anna preferred the bloom to stay where it was. Anna did agree to hide behind a convenient shrub now and then for a kiss and a cuddle.

Arriving back at the small enclosed garden, they were both pleased to sit down on the garden bench.

It had been a wonderful day for them both, but Sam had something he wanted to do before they began looking for a rickshaw.

Taking a small box from his pocket, Sam invited Anna to open it. It contained a beautiful solitaire diamond ring, that had belonged to Sam's mother. Inviting Anna to open it, she exclaimed, "That is beautiful - can I try it on. I've only seen them in the shop windows."

Sam removed the ring and slipped it on to her finger saying, "Will you marry me Anna?"

Anna had not quite understood the significance of the ring and removing it from her finger she said, "My Sam, I will love you forever" and handed the ring back to Sam. Sam replacing the ring on her finger had then to explain the importance of the ring. Anna looked at the ring, her eyes dancing then moving away a little, she bowed gracefully, then waited for him to take her in his arms. They walked to the gates, oblivious of the patrol staring at them both as they passed the mess window.

Anna waved from the rickshaw as it disappeared into the traffic.

Pierre and Yvonne had been impressed by Sam's appearance and calm manner. It was obvious that he and Teddy (Wilson) got on well.

Pierre's own plans were well advanced for the opening of a branch in Hong Kong. During his internment in the colony, even as a P.O.W., he had survived largely because of the temperate climate and an extra ration of rice for working on burial graves.

Pierre accepted Teddy as a necessity for his wife's happiness. Her love for him, Teddy, was of another dimension, outside the spiritual harmony he and his wife shared.

With a healthy young lover, any child he would treat as his own if Yvonne was the mother. There was enough love between them for all to share.

Seeing her with Teddy on the settee holding hands, aroused no feelings other than enjoyment at seeing Yvonne happy.

Pierre had work to do in the office. Getting up and wanting to encourage them, he suggested: "Why don't you young lovers go to bed, for you performed very well the other night, for the first time. I couldn't do it. Forgive me for falling asleep, it was the brandy."

With a casual wave he headed for the office.

Yvonne and Teddy needed no prompting to go to bed and were soon in the shower, which they had both enjoyed like last night soaping and playfully fondling each other. Teddy was the only naked male Yvonne had ever seen apart from Pierre's emancipated body. Yvonne would never forget the look in his eyes, when he had first admired her beautiful bared breasts in the search room.

It had released her own desires and feminity. She could not ignore the passion she felt to be close to Teddy for she loved him deeply after the sterile relationship with her husband whom she loved in another way like a doting generous father.

Yvonne did not undress like Teddy in a hurry, but watched his lustful eyes as she tormented him by slowly and cleverly undressing to reveal her smooth skinned lightly tanned body.

She gave a little laugh of love, as Teddy seized her and carried her to the bed. Their kissing triggered off their loving with cries by both, as they slowly reached the climax of creation.

Later as they slept, Pierre entered and gently turned back the silken sheet to admire the sleeping postures of his wife and her lover. Teddy appeared limp and far away. Yvonne curled up as though cradling something, half smiling in her sleep. Pierre, covering the lovers, left the room, but still tip-toed over the thick Chinese carpet, with a happy smile all over his gaunt face.

Shortly afterwards the bedroom phone rang and as they stirred, it rang off.

Pierre and Teddy spent a considerable amount of time locked in the office after supper that evening. Any ambitions Teddy may have had of returning to work with the newspaper when he was demobbed were forgotten.

Pierre had offered him a job with them in Hong Kong, dealing mainly with advertising in trade journals, dispatch, insurance and registration etc. to which his literary skills could be adapted to fit in with the language and business studies he would have to undertake in any case.

The need for a uniform was gone forever.

What more could a young man want than to be taught by the beautiful Yvonne. The salary would be adequate initially, but the prospects were more than good, when the desire to serve your employers are someone you love.

Yvonne was always busy for a great deal of the business was under her control.

The secret of the pearl beds had been safely guarded by her when the Japanese had invaded, although she was then just the young wife of a foreigner. Pierre had suffered and been treated with contempt by the Japanese and survived only by doing the gruesome work of digging graves for fellow prisoners for a handful of rice and managed to leave the sign of the cross in footprints or scratches on every grave. France had been overrun, but he was treated as a P.O.W. for just being French.

Pierre also gave some thought to Marcus, who would have more information about the release of men like Wilson and Sam, who having served their country in war, were now in limbo on the other side of the world.

Perhaps the time had come for them all to be brought together, and what better way to introduce them all with their ladies, than by a party Yvonne and Pierre would love to give.

In the meantime, the rest of the patrol were finding plenty to occupy themselves except for Willie, the Petty Officer who now found his deputy, Leading Seaman Wilson had other interests. A woman, who had asked for Teddy on the phone and then rung off.

Willie unfortunately spent most of his time in uniform trying to stop the quarters turning into a holiday camp. It was very admirable, but even he, Willie, was getting a little fed up with the confines of the quarters. Deciding to act more like the others, he decided to splash out on buying a couple of shirts and cotton trousers.

If they could have a good time, why not him. It might do him good.

Out of uniform, he became a different person. The heel clicking and mess terror was gone.

Wilson was just sitting down to supper as Sam came into the mess. Am Ling had been expecting some late arrivals and they were soon tucking into chicken slices on aspic with a slice of boiled ham on a pile of fresh vegetables and rice.

Not wanting to get into conversation with anyone else, they conspired to concentrate on the food and keep their mouths full to avoid Wiggy's natural instinct to be nosey.

They did however, talk about learning some basic Chinese.

The Consul had a fairly comprehensive library and they felt certain that Marcus would support a request for the loan of books suitable for learning Chinese.

Wilson produced a simple book Pierre had given him with some comparative English - Chinese words and phrases. Am Ling, coming in to clear their plates, also saw the book and considering himself something of a linguist with pigeon English, offered to help. Wilson and Sam thanked him and when they were ready, they would ask for his help.

It looked as though the patrol were all going native, when Willie the Petty Officer entered the mess in a patterned shirt and drainpipe Chinese trousers without shouting.

Asking Wilson if he was in for the evening and getting 'yes' for an answer, handed the keys of his room plus office and said, "I'll be back before midnight" and departed without another word.

Wilson had half a mind to ask if he was going alone, against the orders of himself and Marcus the Officer, but thought better of it and kept his mouth shut.

A quiet evening with Sam without Willie was what they all needed. Wiggy, Bungy, Evans and Black were deeply engrossed in a sailors version of Mah Jong, hicking, bambooing and throwing dice with a lot of made up names and making a lot of noise as they called and laid down the pieces with a noisy click.

Ma Pang was so delighted when Anna showed her the ring, for she knew that all the ladies who were married wore them, two of whom were Chinese.

It was a great honour for the Pang family and with a grand gesture, she treated Anna to another day off from the laundry for they were no longer having to deal with uniforms.

It was a beautiful day and changing quickly into a dress, with a chiffon scarf to cover her face and a handbag, she was off to the laundry to tell Sam.

On arrival Anna had only to smile at Am Ling, for him to bring Sam running into the kitchen. With a kiss for Anna and hearing the news, he returned to the mess and changed while talking to Wilson and asking if it was all right for him to go out on his own with Anna.

Wilson ramming the cap Anna had given to Sam over Sam's head, said, "What are you waiting for," and with a friendly push, propelled Sam through the open door of the kitchen. Hand in hand, Anna and Sam headed for the Bund.

It was not too hot, so they decided to walk to the Quai de France, enjoying buying sweets and flowers from street vendors for the children who had befriended Sam after finding his knife on the junk.

Although Sam was not in uniform, the children of the junk recognised him at once and shouting, "Sam, Sam," they ran to meet him.

With a welcoming bow from all the children, Sam solemnly shook each one by the hand and handed them a bag of sweets. Clutching their sweets, the children, between the ages of four and ten years old, led the way up the gangplank.

Father, waving them on board from the deck, came forward to meet them. Anna a little nervous and excited, stood on the deck of a junk for the first time. Following Anna, she and Sam exchanged courtesies and bowed, each now speaking in Chinese as he gestured for Anna to enter the living quarters.

Met by his wife, a happy plump woman, who thought the gift of flowers was wonderful, departed into the kitchen to find a vase to display them in.

Anna, now speaking in English for Sam's benefit, told him the father's name was Chang and wife, Mai. Sam pleased them all by coming out with two phrases which must have sounded funny and hard to understand, when Sam said, "Chong-gwoa-ty-howla" and when they clapped, "Shiay-Shiay."

The children began falling round the floor as they prompted Sam to say "Ma" to their mother, for it meant different things for the different tones in which it was said.

The mother and Anna got as much fun out of it as the children, when Anna explained in a very forgiving way to Sam why the children were laughing.

"Sam, you have been tricked by the children into calling their mother an old horse!"

Sam, deciding that was enough Chinese for today became silent as tea was served and Anna interpreting for him, was able to keep him in the conversation.

Chang had been a marine engineer and earned foreign wages in many voyages, making it possible for him to buy a junk of his own. He had a crew of two young men who had their own cabin forward, but were part of the family for meals and celebrations.

Chang enjoyed his present work, chartering or carrying small cargoes around the China Sea. He said modestly, "I am always blessed with fair winds!"

Meaning of course he had sailed in all weathers.

Having finished tea, Chang beckoned Sam and Anna to follow him. Standing just for'ard of the after accommodation, were two cowlings, one on each side. With justifiable pride, for he was an engineer at heart, Chang slid an access hatch open to reveal one of the two powerful diesels that drove the junk through the water.

They were immaculate.

Turning on the fuel and pressing the starter, the whining diesel suddenly sprang into life and the throb of the powerful engine trembled its way throughout the hull of the junk. Switching off and closing the hatch, he then began talking of the rigging which appealed to Sam, a keen sailor. Gone were the old latticed sails and in their place, were sails of American cloth, with their original battens still in place in a modified form.

The hull at first sight, looked as though it needed a refit from the distance, but was in fact carefully camouflaged.

This was not missed by Sam, who found it hard not to believe the stories he had read and been told about pirates were true.

Sam had nicer things to talk about to Anna.

Mai Chang insisted they stayed to lunch and trouble broke out as soon as lunch was laid, as the children pushed and shoved to sit next to Sam.

Ignoring them completely, the grown-ups sat at the table and began the meal. Realising they were possibly losing out on the special tit-bits that had been served in honour of their guests, they seated themselves at their usual places and began using their chopsticks.

A large boned fish, rice, vegetable with sauces and fresh fruit to follow.

Chang having been abroad and quite used to westerners using knives and forks, thought to himself what a beautiful person this young lady was to find such a man using chopsticks.

The living quarters were quite spacious, because Chinese are experts at being economical with space. Even on board, much use was made of mosquito netting, to provide privacy.

A section, with a built-in double capacity bunk, was available to the parents and a separate section sleeping for the children. Additional bunks were built to fold up against the junk's shipside. The central table was the focal point for eating and social sports such as gambling. After lunch, Sam soon found himself tempted into a dice game with the eldest child.

Stoutly, defending his ten-dollar stake in chips, Sam slowly watched his chips disappear as Yang the boy named after his father's profession spun the dice with deadly expertise.

A big surprise was in store for Anna, for having confessed that she had never been on a boat of any kind, Chang had asked his crew to prepare for a little trip down the river, whilst they were at lunch.

The initial roar of the twin diesels and the bubbling throbbing of the exhaust made Anna cling to Sam, excited beyond belief that they were moving.

Slowly, the junk joined the flow of traffic going downstream heading for the sea.

Becoming more confident, Anna began to walk around the deck and turned many a sailor's head, as she waved happily to ships as they passed.

Sam was not jealous when they passed close to the anchored fleet, where Anna waving, could be seen on board through powerful binoculars. He knew it made many a duty sailor's life a lot happier.

It was now time to return and with the Captain's help on the wheel, Anna steered the boat for a while. Chang smiled happily as, unseen by his wife, Anna planted an appreciative kiss on his tanned cheek.

It had been a wonderfully exciting day for Anna. Her happiness had affected everyone aboard.

When the junk came alongside, helping hands took the bow and stern lines and the gangboard was soon in place. Short though the trip had been, it had given Anna something she would never forget. A taste of freedom.

If Anna had to travel to the end of the world, she felt she would not care if she could be with Sam.

After a little nudging by the eldest boy, Sam was coached into trying to say 'good-bye' (dzy-jen) in Chinese. Following it with his first success chong gwo-ty-howla. He was again applauded.

Promising to come again soon and with a grateful bow, Anna and Sam began the return walk home.

Every hour in Shanghai is a rush hour with its population over four millions. Sam could not help asking himself and Anna where they were all going.

Anna gave him an answer which seemed to satisfy his curiosity. Accommodation by Chinese standards is very small for the poorer families and to be confined within a small room or flat, was against the communal nature most of them had enjoyed before migrating into Shanghai's vast industrial areas in search of work and avoiding the compulsory methods of recruiting for the armies of the Nationalists and Communists, locked in battle across the North and West of vast areas of the countryside.

"It's not fireworks you can hear sometimes, but guns in the street," Anna emphasised very seriously.

Turning into the town to get away from the Bund, they continued along the Nanjing Road, with its beautiful shops and bazaars, now a little depleted of goods, but still swarming with crowds of people, just walking and looking, escaping from the confines of their small and crowded homes.

They now walked through the shopping area of the Nanjing Road towards the residential area in the northern sector of the city.

A little further down a particular street, Anna pointed into an arched entrance, saying with one of her smiles, "This is where I live with Ma and Pa."

Entering a courtyard, surrounded by flats on three levels, Anna pointed to one on the first floor with white curtains and said, "We live there."

Now taking his arm, she led him out of the courtyard. Anna spoke to a small boy, who ran away and quickly returned with a rickshaw. Anna sending him happily away with a few 'fen'.

Anna, rather sad that Sam would be returning to the quarters on his own did not want him out on the streets alone, for it was now getting towards evening. Retreating to the archway for a quick kiss, Sam, with a wave, sped away in the rickshaw after a wonderful day.

Entering the mess, he was surprised to see everything as it was the first day they had taken over the quarters.

Beds were tidy, towels on their rails, shoes and boots lined up under the bed and not a sign of a flashy summer shirt to be seen anywhere. No-one shouted medical advice like, "Go and have a bath" or cracked a joke, everyone appeared very glum.

Sam felt on top of the world, In an attempt to get a cheerful word from someone, he turned to Wilson his friend saying, "I've been down the river in a junk!" thinking that would get them all interested.

Wilson pointed to a note on Sam's pillow and replied, "You would have wished you kept going when you read that!"

The note read, "All leave cancelled and the wearing of civilian clothes is to be discontinued."

Sam felt really let down by this order and immediately reacted saying to everyone, "Has anybody requested to register a complaint?"

Still no one replied.

Even Wilson seemed reluctant to get involved, but did say in order to cool Sam down, "Take it easy, Sam - according to Willie it came direct from Marcus."

"In that case, why wasn't he man enough to tell us himself!"

Sam, normally the quiet member, began to simmer a little and white faced, headed for Willie's office.

Wilson, as the senior member of the mess, tried to stop Sam, but stepped back, as Sam in a steely voice, said, "Don't touch me, Leading Seaman or we both might get hurt. I don't belong to this bloody navy any more and neither you or Willie or anyone else, has the right to stop me talking or seeking justice instead of being locked in like a bunch of thugs without being told the reason why - I'm not a criminal and I've served my time during the war, I want out!"

Wilson was wise enough to let Sam have his way, but cautioned him, saying, "Be careful, Sam or you'll finish up in the Naval jail in Hong Kong instead of Civvy Street!"

White face but very determined, Sam was heard knocking on Willie's door.

The patrol stood up as one man, but Wilson, raising his hand said, "Don't, it would be mutiny!"

Not a sound could be heard through the thin wall that divided the two rooms. Slowly, the door of the mess opened again and Willie, white faced, and shaken, pinned a notice to the notice board and withdrew.

Sam returned to the mess, read the notice, then went to the kitchen, to enquire from Am Ling, "What time is supper?"

Willie had been resting on his bed, when Sam entered the office. Before he could properly open this eyes, he felt his testicles seized in a grip by a strong fist that was so excruciating that to call out, would have ruined his sex habits for life.

With his mouth open and speechless and terrified as the agony increased, he heard Sam say quite clearly, "Willie, I got engaged to Anna yesterday, aren't you going to congratulate me?"

Willie just nodded.

Sam, looking him straight in the eye, as he lay on his bed, saying quietly, "Being a married man you know how important these things are. You knew I was in the laundry that day, when you walked in, you asked Am Ling, didn't you?"

Again, Willie nodded.

"Were you jealous or just have a dirty mind!"

Again, Willie wincing, nodded his head.

Reaching over to the desk, Sam picked up a pencil and signal pad used by Willie for his nasty little orders and convinced Willie with a gentle agonizing tug to rescind the order, or give a good reason why Marcus had authorised it to be written.

With contempt in his voice, Sam snarled, "Repeal the order, Now." At the same time giving a gentle little twist.

Willie caught his breath, whimpered, then wrote the order.

"Now I'll put it up or they will come back in here and do the job for me!"

Willie did as he was told, with a final warning from Sam, that the war was over as far as they were concerned and so was Willie's pantomime of shouting orders.

Knowing Willie showed no marks of assault such as bruising, if he brought charges, Sam was prepared to say that they merely restrained him during a frantic period of self abuse, if Willie attempted to bring any charges at all. Sam was sure he could produce a witness or two.

There was complete silence in the mess when the new order was posted by Sam when he returned to the mess, even Wilson waited for Sam to say something, not knowing what had occurred in Willie's office. He should have stopped Sam, but thought wrongly that Sam was just going to apply to make a written permission to speak to his Senior Officer Marcus.

Even when asked by Wilson, Sam refused to comment, but stressed that Wilson keep out of it. It was settled.

At supper, things returned to normal more or less, although no one had changed out of their uniform singlets and trousers, making the meal a little more formal.

It did achieve one thing, the mess did not look like a Chinese bazaar any longer and concern for each other was as important as if they had been shipwrecked.

Willie, after the incident with Sam, was not only hurting a little downstairs, but feeling very sorry for himself having misjudged the mood of the patrol and respecting their rights with a little more understanding.

Thank goodness he had not to see a Chinese doctor, they do funny things out there.

Getting up from his single bed where he had been resting himself, Willie slowly began to shuffle around his room and feel better. Sam's assault had been painful, but these things don't last for ever. Sam promised to keep it quiet.

Willie, washing in the hand basin and changing into a shirt and trousers, was just about dressed, as Am Ling knocked on the door, with his supper on a tray. Having heard the sailors call Willie 'Chief', he gave his usual polite, "Ha, Chif-Chif your supper."

Willie nodded and Am Ling left.

Wilson, a little worried about Willie, asked Am Ling, as soon as he entered the mess, "Is the Chief all right?"

"Oh - I think so, he nodded like a donkey to me and I nodded like a cook to him - we always talk like that."

"Was he dressed?" enquired Wilson.

Am Ling nodded, then leaning over to whisper in Wilson's ear, he said helpfully. "I think he need woman, he stand like this all the time." demonstrating Willie's supportive posture before leaving the mess.

Wilson smiled to himself that Willie would get over it and taking a seat at the table next to Sam he muttered quietly, "I think he'll live."

Smiling at each other, they tucked into an Am Ling special, hot-sour soup, fried noodles, pork, rice and vegetables.

Wiggy always referred to the fried noodles and pork as Chinese fish and chips, but tonight he was in a sombre mood having jumped on his coolie hat in protest at the 'No Civilian Clothes' order. Slowly during the meal everyone came to realise that the crisis was over, added to which, Wilson made a special announcement with Sam's approval.

Tomorrow must be set aside by everyone, for Sam Weller was applying to the Consul himself for permission to hold a party here at the quarters to celebrate a very special occasion.

Everyone would be invited and guests, but no dodgy ladies from the dance halls

Wiggy piped up before Wilson had finished, saying, "Don't take a meeting to have a party."

Wilson shut him up saying, "It is not a children's party, so you are not needed to attend!"

Wiggy shut up.

What they were to celebrate would not be disclosed until the details were approved by Marcus, who, being the Officer in Charge of the patrol, would be ultimately responsible if anything were wrong. This was an official residence and it would be good for the ship if they conducted themselves with credit. At least, Wilson hoped so!

The idea of a party really took off, and that evening they all held their own little meeting, and came up with some good ideas.

One important detail came up that evening.

No one was to upset the cook, Am Ling, as a lot would rest on his co-operation.

Bungy emphasised and said, "Bow and bang your heads on the floor, if it keeps him happy, but happy he must be!"

Ma Pang would have to be treated gently for the men had already decided to move the beds out and stow them elsewhere to make more room.

The laundry was the most convenient.

The patrol would wear uniforms without medals, for these were probably still in the post somewhere.

Everyone, feeling a little guilty about Willie's incidental discomfort, whatever the cause, thought he would make an excellent toastmaster, if he could now cough with comfort. Sam received a polite congratulations from Willie in the form of a letter when Wilson offered him the chance to look after any members of the Consul staff who may put in an appearance and to propose a toast if needed for the engaged couple.

It took a couple of days to get things organised for the party. Everyone retired early the night before to allow the beds to be stacked early in the laundry to clear the mess.

All their grand ideas to have a party came to a standstill the next day as the Consulate suddenly closed all gates and outside doors ordering all personnel and the patrol into the main building. A raging riot of thousands filled the streets as the hungry mobs went on the rampage.

Rifle and machine gun fire was heard as the soldiers fought to get control. Rifle fire had shattered the quarters' windows where Wiggy's hat had been visible for all to take a pot shot at. It was some party, but not the one the patrol expected.

Forlornly Willie held his shattered hat, thinking at least he could say he had been wearing it on active service, the little fibber.

CHAPTER 7

Unexpected flowers arrived from the gardeners, no doubt instructed by a member of the Consul staff, many of them knowing Miss Anna Pang from the days she attended school with the other children in the Consul.

Willie was at his best organising the setting out of the mess, although he was still upset and said to Wilson, "Are they laughing about me out there?"

Thinking quickly, Wilson had replied, "What do you mean, Chief - they all thought it was pretty clever of you to get the mess cleaned up - after all, it had become a pigsty."

Wilson went on, "Sorry, I let you down Chief. It won't happen again."

Still a little apprehensive, Willie nodded his head towards Sam Weller and said, "Did he have anything to say?"

Looking as glum as he could, Wilson lied a little saying, "God, you must have given him a hell of a telling off he's hardly spoken to anyone since he left your office."

Willie smiled weakly as Wilson said smartly, "Is that all Chief!" and closed the door.

Thinking it better to let him and Sam get over their differences, Wilson picked up the newly delivered daily paper printed in English, 'China News' and just as he settled down Willie called him from the doorway saying he was required on the phone. Willie also excused himself and waited in the passage until Wilson had finished.

Yvonne and Pierre had both missed him, although it was hours, not weeks, since Yvonne and her Teddy had been romping in her bed.

Yvonne, speaking in a less excited way, implored him to bring Sam and Anna to supper and drinks. Thinking also in terms of her own relationship with Teddy Wilson, she said they could stay the night if they wished. The guest room was available. Wilson excused himself because of Willie and rang off.

Thanking Willie for allowing him to use the phone, Willie answered, "That's OK - anytime!"

Although it was not yet lunchtime, Wilson knew where to find Sam these days. Am Ling, busy in the kitchen on the stove, waved him through and with a knock, he entered the laundry.

Sam had apparently just burnt his finger slightly while testing the iron he was using. Now seated on a chair, with Anna and her beautiful younger sister Lee, fussing and holding his hand, he looked up at Wilson with a sweet contented smile. He said, as though he was wounded as badly as Nelson at the Battle of Trafalgar, "Don't kiss me Wilson, I'm in good hands" and allowed his head to slump sideways with his eyes closed. Lee, always quick to practice her kissing on Sam, seized his head and lining up his mouth and chanting briefly in Chinese, kissed him passionately like any girl of fifteen enjoying a game of making love.

"I thought I could revive him," she said with a grin as the others watched Sam's rather embarrassed recovery.

Wilson now had a chance to tell Anna and Sam about the invitation to supper from Pierre and Yvonne.

Anna was delighted and at the same time anxious about Ma Pang's reactions to her being out at night with adults. Sam assured Anna they would be dressed in civilian clothes and would be safe in the care of Wilson and himself.

Speaking to Willie in the office, who just completed his lunch, Wilson informed Willie of the invitation they had received from Pierre to supper that night and asked if he had any objections.

Much to Wilson's surprise Willie said, "Why don't you use the jeep, if you can find Chung, Marcus isn't using it tonight."

Wilson gratefully said, "Thank you, Chief, that's very kind of you - I promise we won't be too late and Chung knows the way."

Bowing out Chinese style Wilson left the office.

Anna and Sam still a little apprehensive about getting there, cheered up when Wilson mentioned the jeep. This again was a new experience for Anna who had never travelled in anything but a rickshaw. Having seen the jeep, with Chung driving it, Anna had thought it very smart indeed and she would enjoy that with Sam sitting beside her.

It would not be dark at that time and with a promise that she would be brought home under escort by Sam at not later than 11pm in her rain cape and with her face covered. Ma Pang also felt she should wear the Chinese dress which she, her Mother had spent months on the embroidery.

Am Ling cycled regularly to the large house on minor errands to do with the kitchen and was able to give a message to Chung that he was needed to take Wilson and Sam to the jewellers that evening.

There was nothing he liked better than driving and as usual Chung was already waiting outside the mess door when the time came for Wilson and Sam to leave.

For a moment Sam did not recognise Anna as she stepped from the rickshaw, shrouded in a drab rain cape and a drooping hood. Nervously, Anna assisted by Sam, climbed into the rear of the jeep and held on to his hand until they arrived.

Wilson rang and the steel doors opened and they were greeted by Yvonne and Pierre in the hall on the inside and taken to the private quarters.

Yvonne leaving the men, took Anna into her room and was very impressed by her young guest who shedding the drab rain cape and hood, turned her beautiful face to Yvonne and bowed.

Dressed in a traditional Chinese style of Jade Green with a Mandarin collar in black, her pretty legs and neat fitting green shoes showed Anna off to perfection. Fingering a small lotus brooch placed by her neck her hand displayed the engagement ring she was wearing.

Anna bowed graciously to her host.

Sam had never seen Anna look more beautiful as when she bowed with Yvonne as they entered the room. Yvonne soon had them all seated and the meal served by her two house girls, was soon on the table. Anna radiated happiness talking to Yvonne on one side and Sam on the other. Pierre too enjoyed her, for he had always had an eye for a pretty face.

Pierre, being French, also had a great interest in what was provided at the table and invariably suggested and presented to his guests, titbits and sauced pieces he thought had special merit. His knowledge of Chinese sauces was extensive, being able to tell each taste and smell, even when he was blindfolded.

It was a game Yvonne would not allow tonight, for the serving girl was already displaying the Peking duck before returning it to the kitchen for slicing and serving

A rich variety of vegetables and sauces were served and Wilson, from past experience cautiously tasted each of the sauces, having been caught by a hot pepper variety of Am Ling's making.

Yvonne, besides being beautiful, was also the power behind the throne when it came to business and for a change began to talk to Anna of her work in the laundry, for it was obvious to Yvonne, being a successful business woman, that Anna had a great deal of potential with her looks, good English and business sense and was wasted in the family business of running a laundry.

Admiring Anna's engagement ring, she asked, "When you and Sam are married, do you intend to live in Shanghai?"

Without hesitation, Anna replied, "I shall live with my husband, wherever it takes me."

They then got lost in the intricacies of a wedding, old and new, Chinese and Christian, a mixture of each in a church.

Yvonne then turned to Sam and with a serious look on her face, she said, "You can be married tonight, if you wish, for we have a beautiful love nest in there, and you are free to use it tonight if you wish."

Sam thought quietly to himself, it would be a dream come true, but no thanks, Anna was worth waiting for in the near future.

Hearing Yvonne talking so freely about marriage and going to bed was not quite what Anna had been used to, but she responded in the same spirit, and looking at Sam for support, she answered, "Thank you Yvonne, Sam and I will think about that when we are married - I dread the thought of having a child and so much want to be a bride like the ladies at the Consul."

Looking at her fiance she stated, "We have plenty of time to have a little 'Sam, Sam'."

Sam in support and quite enthusiastic about having a family, said quite blithely, "Once we're settled in Hong Kong, we'll have two or three!"

Yvonne's hand gently moved across her stomach and with a dreamy look in her eyes, she said softly, "Pierre would like a little girl too!"

No one seemed inclined to move from the table after the Peking duck and tasty vegetables, followed by fresh fruit. Sam, always fond of good food, could only manage to nibble a grape or two, before coffee was served. Pierre as usual had an excellent wine served after the meal, for he loved to toast his guests with a flourish in the French manner, with a "Vive" here and there.

Leaving the men at the table, Yvonne and Anna retired to the bedroom, whilst the men turned their minds to the increasing difficulties of staying in China under a Communist Government. Pierre showed great interest in Sam's friend the junk owner and skipper, who chartered down to Hong Kong. It might be of use to them all as a group of friends, to all evacuate together by sea.

Difficulty with all forms of transport were already under threat and used by both sides, Nationalists and Communists, to herd refugees towards Shanghai.

Pierre, a worldly man and living in what used to be the French concession, was well aware of the dangers around him.

Gunfire was commonplace and the meat wagons, as they were called by the Americans, were nightly going around picking up the dead left like the garbage in the street.

To make a point how serious the situation was becoming, Pierre getting up from the table, took them into the study and showed them a number of boxes which they recognized as gun crates.

Opening them up, each of them contained machine guns, revolvers or rifles and boxes of ammunition stacked in a corner. Pierre really believed it was coming to this and he was prepared to fight. It made Wilson and Sam think what a cocooned existence they lived within the Consul grounds. Perhaps the feel of a gun in their hands might stir up the blood.

Each of them tried their hands with a sub machine gun, rifle and revolver, first checking they were unloaded, although they were still packed and greasy.

Sam noting the cases were marked U.S. asked, "Where would a Frenchman get hold of American small arms?"

Pierre smiling, answered, "The Chinese black market."

Businessmen came to Shanghai and did secret deals and were expected to leave the same way.

Pierre going to a safe in the wall, withdrow an envelope and handed it to Sam, saying, "Can you trust your friend Chang the junk captain?"

Telling him the story of the knife, Sam confirmed it by saying, "Yes, I would trust Chang!"

On Sam's word Pierre gave him the envelope and said, "Book his boat for a charter to Hong Kong with our families, on a day to be agreed and at the same time, make an appointment for us to see the boat, it might be useful in transferring some of our equipment to Hong Kong."

The envelope contained one thousand dollars (American). Sam thinking a receipt in these circumstances a pretty futile gesture, suggested it should be retained until he collected it on his next visit to the junk.

Pierre agreed, but Yvonne asked if he could bring the beautiful Anna with him.

It was soon time for Anna to leave to keep in Ma Pang's good books. It had been a comfortable, almost family evening with friends coming together in a bond of friendship in uncertain times. Even their farewells and goodbyes had turned into 'Shaiy Shaiy' and 'dzy jen' as Anna shrouded in her cape said warm goodbyes, to their charming hosts.

Sam with his oversize cap and Anna, shrouded in her cape, were inconspicuous, as they walked round the corner from the jeep to the entrance to the flats.

A single long kiss in the shadows had to do and waiting to see Anna enter the flat safely, Sam sprinted back to the jeep.

There was quite a noise going on as Sam entered the mess, but it was nothing more than a rowdy game of Mah Jong with small yuen notes and fen scattered all over the table like some low-down gambling joint.

If you had scooped up the lot, it would not have made a ten dollar (HK) bill, but it created a hell of an atmosphere with a few bottles of Chinese beer.

Reporting to Willie in the office that they were back, Willie had been having a night-cap from a bottle of rum he had brought from the ship. It was pretty strong stuff if not taken as grog with a measure of water.

He invited them to join him, saying. "It's me birthday and I'd like someone to sing and wish me 'Happy Birthday'."

Sam and Willie shook hands and the sound of 'Happy Birthday' rang throughout the quarters.

Together half drunk after a tot of rum each, they were all discussing seriously the changing mood of this vast city and came to the conclusion after hearing Pierre talking, they should think soon about making their own way home via Hong Kong. It was only a thousand miles, and no distance at all when you have had a tot of rum. Marcus and Joe came to a similar conclusion whilst chatting in the restaurant about the news that Joe had received on advances by Communists in the North and skirmishes going on to the North and West between Nationalists and Communists, were causing a greater refugee problem for the Municipal Government which the Police found more difficult to control.

The growth of the slum areas on the outskirts and the increased activity by crime gangs fighting over the pickings from prostitution, drugs, looting and murder throughout the city kept the meat wagons busy as they picked up the corpses like garbage in the morning.

Marcus had for the first time managed to speak by phone to the duty staff officer in Hong Kong on the Admiral's staff.

He got rather short shift from him, who treated Marcus's situation as a huge joke and told him to catch the next ferry as though he were phoning from the Isle of Wight with a short trip to Portsmouth.

Before Marcus could explain China had a little war going on and the ship had sailed without them, a thousand miles and an out of date telephone line were quite enough to worry about without some fool joking about it. Marcus now felt he had a free hand to get back to base whatever way he chose.

One of Marcus' heroes was Captain Bligh of the Bounty and he wondered what he would have done in these circumstances? Bligh crossed an ocean!

At least he, Marcus, had a willing crew and could try.

Because Pierre asked them, Wilson and Sam were having a busy day, stripping and cleaning Pierre's brand new guns, practising loading and misfires as though they were still in the Navy on active service instead of nearly civilians once again.

Wilson had other benefits too, for Yvonne never missed an opportunity to take her lover Teddy Wilson into the bedroom to practice having a baby. There was nothing better than trying and so many ways of trying to succeed.

Willie had now decided to give hourly sessions each day in such things as first aid, resuscitation and fire fighting just to keep his hand in.

Wiggy and Bungy catching on with the spirit that something was on, began playing with odd pieces of string tying knots and splices, while Black the stoker, coveting Chung's possession of the jeep had his nose under the bonnet at every opportunity to do a bit of tuning.

Kemp the signalman used up two batteries reviving his morse code and flashing for help in some imagined emergency as he walked round the Consul grounds.

Marcus, in the reference library, neglected to phone Lita on one occasion. Driving up to the Consul, she was conducted to his room, where Lita spent a pleasant hour just using her long slender fingers to massage his more sensitive spots as he pondered over numerous coastal charts of China seas.

It was almost as though they all expected to go to sea again, although there was no news of the ship or that she had even been sighted.

Sam and Anna, with Wilson, who had previously met the Chang family aboard the junk, arranged to call.

Pierre's plan were already well advanced for a move from Shanghai and his chance meeting with Marcus and the patrol had seemed heaven sent. The horrors of the P.O.W camp in Hong Kong had receded, but his gratitude to those who had released him was still strong. He placed a lot of faith in the fact that the British would again be on his side.

Chang and his family were all on deck when Sam, Anna and Wilson arrived alongside and dismounted from the rickshaws. They had been told by the eldest boy who had spotted them almost as far away as the Quai de France and had raced them home, proud to have beaten the rickshaw.

Their meeting was Chinese and it delighted the Chang family that Wilson and Sam got their greeting correct, although the children found something funny in Sam's pronunciation and all broke out in fits of giggling when, once again for their amusement Sam repeated his 'hello' as 'Nee Hoowy' instead of 'Nee how'. It was a bit of Dorset asserting itself too strongly.

It was tea time of course and once again, they all gathered round the table with Anna acting as helper to everyone, particularly Sam and Wilson anxious to try out what they had attempted to learn of Chinese since they last met.

The children sang for their amusement, the first line of, "What shall we do with a drunken sailor" which the children repeated three times.

Anna, who had brought a bag of sweets for each of them and each repeat performance was sung much louder, in return for the sweets.

After the entertainment, the Chang children with a polite bow and seeking a suitable spot on the midship deck, had a sweet party.

Anna, having been briefed on the charter of the junk, put it together fluently in Chinese for Captain and Mai Chang to consider. It would be a dangerous trip, particularly with women aboard as beautiful as Yvonne and Anna. It was coolie suits for them, not that Anna cared.

His guns were all serviced for him and his crew could out-sail and outfight most junks that threatened or tried to board.

Pierre and Yvonne both held British passports and visas for some of his girls. He hoped that Yvonne would take most of the girls for whom he had obtained visas for those he wanted to go.

Anna no doubt would be looked after by Sam, whether they had married or not by the time they had arranged and hoped to leave.

Mr Chang was much keener on the trip when Wilson told him of Pierre's Hong Kong connections. To be taking illegal immigrants into Hong Kong would be putting his junk at risk. To impound a junk brought good prices if sold on the black market.

Mr Chang was rather pleased about Pierre's guns. With a bunch of ex-naval gunners onboard, he could leave it to them, whilst he sailed and looked after his beloved engines.

The greatest peril of all when sailing down the coast of China were the vast fleets of fishing boats that spread for miles and miles across the North to South Sea routes. Special lookout has to be kept day and night for some, without navigation lights completely ignored the rules of the sea. A collision at sea is the last thing any mariner wants and to keep a good lookout and steer clear of trouble is the only safe way of reaching your destination.

Naturally, Mrs Chang would be on board, leaving the children with her sister. Mrs Chang was the one who cooked and in port finally negotiated the price of any trip.

It was important to Mr Chang that his junk was properly sailed and handled. Anna was considered as part of the crew interpreting Chinese terms into naval ones was a bit of a tongue twister, but the crew were not exactly landlubbers and had done a certain amount of sailing, even in the Navy.

As an afterthought, Wilson through Anna, asked Mr Chang how he would feel if one or two of his shipmates came along too. Chang turned to his wife, who would have to do the cooking and she grinned and then answered, "If they pay another hundred dollars and work hard!"

Wilson laughed as he thought of Marcus and Willie scrubbing the decks with holystones.

Mr Chang would need some help in preparing for the trip and suggested that coolie clothes for work would be best for all on board.

Embarkation must be done at night and all luggage was to be in sacks, not cases. No pretty dresses for the women. Chinese working clothes only. Womens' toilet over stern on lee side, men only, weather side. Carry your own cloth.

Everyone burn one candle when we sail. Everyone burn one candle when we arrive but one candle for the junk 'Petihoo' to keep junk's spirit happy and give us a good wind each day was to be lit at least once a day.

They went on discussing things for a while, with a constant supply of tea.

Accommodation and sleeping arrangements would be done by Mrs Chang, for it was better to accept her allocation of berths for she had made special provision for the women.

Any man found in their section would be horse whipped by her, for she believed hanky panky upset the junk's spirit when at sea.

Mr Chang tried it once and got a beating, but he was younger then and Mai had been caught with him.

They had all talked for much longer than they had first thought. Already some were stirring and anxious to get to sea for they were homeward bound. It would be a voyage whatever the weather they were confident of reaching a friendly home port even if they had to fight to get there. The children were very quiet when Sam, Anna and Wilson had to leave. Even though they were invited to share a meal, Anna thought it was time to say dzy-jen, for Wilson had to talk to Pierre about the cost of the charter.

To make it up to the children, he challenged Yang the eldest, to a throw of the dice. Best of three, Yang won the first two and collected the ten Yuan with a smile and another Chinese chorus of, "what do we do with a drunken sailor" from the children, a hand shake from Sam and Wilson to Mr Chang and a bow from them all to the Chang family, they climbed once again into the waiting rickshaws and led by Wilson, made for the home of Pierre.

Chinese are not normally demonstrative, but Yvonne was so delighted to see Anna, embraced her with affection, for there were few women she had met and had no sisters.

Whatever was to happen from now on they would share together and clinging to the arm of the beautiful Anna, she led her safely away to her room, to talk women's talk.

Pierre was very pleased with the deal so far and considered they had done well in the negotiations. It was half he had been expecting to pay, with the assurance that Wilson, whatever happened he agreed to stay with him. If Sam and Anna could make it too he would be forever grateful.

The idea of sailing back to Hong Kong in a junk was taken as a joke at first by the rest of the patrol, as Wilson and Weller, in a joking mood at the supper table, began offering berths for a thousand dollars, first class or five hundred as steerage.

Taffy, not too keen on sailing and quite happy where he was until the ship came in, had better things to do with the miserable pay packet he would get, whenever that would be. Black the stoker having heard Sam speak of the immaculate diesels on the junk, couldn't wait to get aboard. He, like Mr Chang was hooked on the throb of a diesel.

Kemp was not too keen to be left behind at all, for he read everything he could get hold of from the Consul papers and more than most, understood their predicament better than most if the war suddenly erupted in the streets of Shanghai. He would rather like a trip in a junk, it could be something he could write up in his journal.

Wiggy, who had not yet slept with a Chinese girl, felt he would have better luck in Hong Kong with all these Yanks around in Shanghai. It was a bit uncivilised in Shanghai for dancing and Hong Kong sounded romantic as him. Wiggy settled for trying to work his passage if there were any girls on board and little did he know, but that is exactly what he would do.

CHAPTER 8

Marcus and Lita were having a quiet meal at the Jung's restaurant, when who should walk in but Pierre and his wife Yvonne.

They were all delighted to see each other and were invited to join Lita and Marcus at the table. Pierre and Yvonne had already had a meal.

It came as a bit of a bombshell to Marcus and Lita to hear about Pierre's plans for leaving in a junk manned by his sailors. To think his own men were involved with Pierre was hard to believe and showed how much he had got out of touch and neglected their welfare.

Pierre told them of his chartering of a junk and evacuating his wife and staff to Hong Kong, with the help of Wilson and a few shipmates as crew and passengers to sail and safeguard the family during the voyage.

Pierre, thought it a marvellous idea. He would make sure the boys were looked after during the trip. Pierre also had plans for Wilson and Weller, who were keen to leave his Majesty's Navy and work in Hong Kong. It was something to do with their being demobbed now the war was over.

Pierre then addressed Marcus directly, "Yvonne told me that Mrs Jung was also actively thinking on the same lines, if the war and troubles actually begin here in Shanghai."

Marcus looked at Pierre, but could not come up with a reply. Things were happening all around him and he was so besotted with Lita, he did not even know what his own men were doing.

The duty staff officer in Hong Kong had told him to catch a ferry. His own men were manning a junk and he would be left here in Shanghai, waiting patiently for his ship to pick him up. Not exactly the Captain Bligh spirit. Wouldn't look very nice on his record.

Thinking to himself it's about time I spoke to the men and found out what the hell is going on, he got up from the table, excused himself and Lita and left by the private door.

Pierre thought nothing of Marcus excusing himself so soon and put it down to being in love with a pretty girl.

Marcus and Lita retiring early, found the door of their room did not appear to open easily and they were horrified to find the room had been ransacked with the contents of drawers and cupboards scattered all over the floor.

Pictures had been ripped from the walls, searching for a safe. Everything that glittered had been taken, including his officer's naval cap with the distinctive crown on the front.

Fortunately all the family jewellery was in the family safe and Lita had been wearing the precious pearls she treasured, given to her by Marcus.

All the same, although Lita appeared calm, she was quite distraught and clung to Marcus for comfort and protection.

Together, they went downstairs to tell her parents. Marcus had to admire the calm manner in which Mr Jung took the news of the burglary, Lita, at the same time hugged her mother who calmly shed a tear. Marcus waited to help if necessary.

Mr Jung, rising from his chair, rang the buzzer on the wall for the head houseboy and all together, they inspected the room where the entrance and robbery had taken place. The bathroom window was still open and broken.

Mr Jung did not phone the police but instead phoned friends and put the phone down. Embracing his wife, they slowly made their way to bed.

Marcus and Lita, sitting together on the settee, quietly talked over the events of the evening. Surprisingly enough it was Marcus's cap that had angered her father and she explained, "He was furious that a guest in this house had been left naked."

Marcus, not particularly worried about the cap then asked, "Are you insured?"

Lita replied, "Yes and no - because we insure to comply with the law, but it is rare that the claims are ever considered, the rich should take of such things themselves! There are other ways of getting your goods back, by offering a good price for their return or calling in the collectors - they not only get your goods back, but punished the thief for operating in their area."

Marcus cuddled Lita a little tighter and she then asked. "You will be staying the night?"

Not answering, Marcus took her to bed.

When Joe and Una came home that night from a party, they were surprised to see the headboy still waiting up for them. He quickly told them of the burglary knowing that they would want to know. He also informed them that the bathroom window had been repaired. With a polite "goodnight" he returned to his room.

The next morning at breakfast there was plenty to talk about. They all agreed that nothing much had been taken except Marcus's cap. To Mr Jung to lose such an irreplaceable object was terrible in Chinese eyes, because he was a guest in Mr Jung's home. Joe would deal with the security of the premises and promised Mr Jung that he would find Marcus's cap.

Marcus then brought up the subject of Pierre's plans to evacuate his family with the aid of the sailors by sailing to Hong Kong in a junk. To Joe it seemed a crazy idea being a soldier to sail a thousand miles in pirate infested waters, but it was not so, when seen through the eyes of a sailor. Allowing for reasonable weather it would only take a matter of two or three weeks. Even less, if the junk was well founded with a good auxiliary engine.

Joe had to mention the worst danger. "What about pirates and boat gangs down the coast, Marcus? - They are a bit of a threat," just to keep the topic going.

Marcus had to admit he didn't know much about what his men were letting themselves in for and he was jolly well going to find out this morning.

Marcus changed his mind about getting into uniform to visit the mess and phoning Willie first, found out that he also knew nothing of the junk story.

Telling him to get everyone into the mess now, he would be down in five minutes to get a few answers.

Dead on time he arrived looking very stern. No one seemed very disturbed by his appearance in civilian clothes, although they all stood up as he entered the mess. Telling them to be seated and speaking in a friendly voice, he said, "Would someone kindly tell me what is going on?"

Everyone looked blankly at one another, but no one had any suggestions to make.

Marcus then addressed Wilson, "I met Pierre yesterday and he tells you are planning to take him and his family to Hong Kong in a junk - is that true?"

Wilson feeling no obligation to tell Marcus although he was still their commanding officer said bluntly, "Well Sir, it is one way of getting back to base in Hong Kong for our demob and we are awaiting to see if you have a better offer!"

In normal circumstances this would have been treated as insubordination, but these were not normal times with nothing being done and just sitting on their backsides waiting for something to happen was getting nowhere.

We are all civilians separated from our families and halfway round the world, thought Wilson.

Marcus was not used to being spoken to by a rating like this, but accepted he had not given this matter the attention it deserved, with the ship expected to return any time. When that was going to happen he had not the faintest idea, for up to now he had been thoroughly enjoying being ashore.

He then warned them, "Whatever plans you may cook up you are all my responsibility. Furthermore, you are all still bound by the Naval Disciplinary Act, and any desertion, under any pretext, will be treated as mutiny when you arrive in Hong Kong unless you have plans to land on a little island, like the crew of the famous Bounty and live on rice for the rest of your lives."

Wilson did not back down and said bluntly once again, "Marcus, we have been thinking about getting to Hong Kong for a few days, since it was first mentioned to us by Pierre. So far these are only ideas, but at least it is one way of rejoining our ship and I don't see why our motives should be questioned in this way. After all, you told us that someone had told you to catch a ferry when you phoned Hong Kong!"

Marcus, a bit embarrassed by the way the talks were going, closed the meeting and told Willie he would see Wilson and Weller in the office now.

In the office, Marcus demanded the whole story and in return told them of what Pierre had said to Wilson.

Without jumping to conclusions, Marcus considered this matter much too serious to be treated lightly and offered to hold a meeting today with Pierre to get this thing thrashed out. Marcus understood very well the growing unrest in Shanghai for it was affecting the Jung family also, with a lot of activity in the Consulate of which he had no knowledge.

Telling them to be ready to attend a meeting, he asked them to leave while he made a telephone call. Knowing Pierre's number he rang him from Willie's office. Pierre was surprised to have Marcus on the phone and more surprised still at what Marcus wanted to talk about.

Pierre insisted that the meeting was held at his home and everyone was invited who may wish to travel with him, Pierre was sorry that Marcus had not been told by Wilson, but pointed out that he,

Marcus, spent a lot of time with Lita. Why not bring her along too, she could tell her family.

It was not the meeting Marcus had in mind, but if they all got together everything would be out in the open and a common objective achieved Marcus and Pierre agreed they were both on the same side and in the same boat.

An early start at six in the evening was fine and agreed. Putting down the phone Marcus called Wilson into the office and told him to invite anyone interested.

In the mess Wilson got the lads together and told them all about Pierre's plans to leave Shanghai by junk and his hopes of going along with him to Hong Kong. From Wilson's point of view it would be a bit of an adventure, sailing a junk in the China Sea. That would be a tale to tell the children. If things got worse in Shanghai, they may not even get out of harbour. From a service point of view, they were only trying to rejoin their ship.

It may have been the thoughts of a buffet, or just getting out of the mess, but everyone wanted to dress up and attend.

That evening you would have thought they were all going out to a banyan party in their bright shirts and cheery good humour.

Willie a changed man was enjoying himself as one of the lads, watching them pile into rickshaws and took off singularly like planes from an aircraft carrier, for Pierre's home in the old French settlement.

Willie, using the jeep with Marcus's permission was only too pleased to take Anna. Sitting in the rear, Willie, Wilson, Anna and Sam all sat together. Sitting opposite Willie, Anna bowed her head, he could not take his eyes from this very stunning girl.

When the engine started she tensed a little and reached for Sam's hand whilst the rest of them clung on for dear life as Chung began honking their way through the evening traffic.

It was noisy in the jeep but Willie insisted on being friendly and asked Anna, "Is that your engagement ring?"

Anna showed him the ring. It was a fine solitaire. Sam then introduced Willie in the bumping jeep, "Anna, meet the Petty Officer Willie."

Anna nodded her head and Willie feeling one of the family now said, as they bumped along, "What do you want for a wedding present?" looking at Anna and thinking what a beautiful bride she would be. Anna turned to Sam, not quite understanding what he meant, and whispered into Sam's ear. Not whispering because of the noise, Sam said for a laugh, "A pram!"

Anna's beautiful eyes opened wide and with a smack on his hand she cried, "You mustn't say that or my mother will think I have been naughty!"

Willie cringed a little but it gave him an idea.

They were now drawing close to Pierre's home and with a 'toot, toot' at the racing rickshaw just drawing up to the house, they waited until the entrance was cleared.

Now whether the patrol knew of the engagement or had heard a rumour was not quite clear, but they manned the entrance to Pierre's house like a guard of honour at a wedding and began singing, "Here comes the bride" for Anna.

Wilson needed no introduction and his greeting from Yvonne was as passionate as ever as she kissed and hugged him, causing raised eyebrows.

It was a large room and they all fitted comfortably inside, all they needed was for Marcus and Lita to arrive and the whole party would be assembled. Drinks were quickly served by Yvonne's girls and it became noisy by the time Marcus and Lita arrived.

The older or more senior people present occupied the armchairs, whilst the rest sat happily around listening to Pierre's opening remarks on his planned trip to Hong Kong and how he needed their help.

Now that looting had begun and rioting made it dangerous to stay. The actual voyage would take not more than a fortnight in Mr. Chang's junk. He was an experienced Chinese skipper who had sailed his boat many times to Hong Kong. It was the calm season with no typhoons expected.

His final point was, "We shall all be safe if the sailors come along too."

During a break in Pierre's address, one of the Chinese girls asked about the threat of pirates to the junk. Pierre really put on a show about the Navy and spoke of his rescue from the war camp by the British. According to Pierre they had enough gunners and guns to sweep the seas clear and that was the least of his worries. He didn't want to mention anything about Mrs Chang's views on Hanky Panky aboard, although he did mention the burning of joss sticks by everyone for a safe passage and a good harbour.

It would be helpful in these troubled times if the time came for them to sail or even before, if all luggage could be put into sacks to look like cargo being loaded. Everyone would be dressed in coolie suits and sandals and no jewellery was to be shown at any time on board, even when embarking aboard. Luggage would be loaded at night or late evening. Don't speak to anyone about where you are going. If you must, mention a dying relative or fevering Petihoo. That should keep them quiet.

Bring plenty of things to read although there will be lots to do, we're all in this together. Women must not wave to passing strangers, even in boats. Go below decks or into the poop until they have passed. Fishing is fun and the few days the trip will take will be over as soon as a dragon's day.

It was now time for a break and the drinks were soon underway again. Yvonne was a wonderful hostess with her beauty and charm. All the sailors fell for her, hoping she would give them the same treatment she had showered on Wilson when she greeted him at the door.

Yvonne, Lita and Anna all had interest in the men who might sail away into the distant sunset in the near future and were in a serious conversation until Pierre made them circulate a little.

Willie waited on Anna like a queen, whilst Bungy, Taffy, Evans and Wiggy monopolised the pearly girls who were part of Yvonne's staff.

Marcus and Wilson with Pierre got their heads together and Marcus himself began thinking about Lita. Would she take the plunge and go, if Marcus was to propose it. It was worth a try.

It appeared there was a general agreement among the three principal people in charge of the assembled guests. Pierre invited Marcus or Wilson to speak after he addressed them once again on minor things like getting through customs and health checks. Both preferred to talk back at the quarters.

The buffet was a great success as they all sat round a great communal table of warm and cold dishes served Chinese style.

The girls were feeding the sailors with all the known titbits, whilst Wiggy always a bit of a clown, gave a demonstration of tying knots in noodles.

The wail of a police siren sounded and the sound of a distant gunshot or two brought the meeting to a close for it was now time to go. Anna felt quite safe with three escorts, Chung, Willie and Sam. Lita was safe with Marcus and Pierre and Yvonne needed Teddy Wilson.

The next morning Marcus was on the phone to Willie the Petty Officer, to have all the patrol in the mess for a meeting when they had finished their duties.

Marcus also tried to phone Hong Kong but it was a wasted effort phoning from the Consul switchboard. Next he phoned Joe at his office in the U.S. Military Police Headquarters and was answered by Sergeant Borkowski. As usual, the sergeant was full of goodwill and asked if he wanted anything. Marcus appreciated Borkowski's generous spirit, but declined the offer and asked to speak to Joe.

When Joe came on, you would have thought Marcus had been on the moon, as Joe bawled, "Hey, Marcus, where you been? - Thought you'd gone back to sea or something - are you OK?"

If anyone could get anything in Shanghai it was Joe and Marcus having usually phoned with his begging bowl in his hand asked, "Where can I get an Admiralty chart or the U.S. equivalent, to cover the coast to Hong Kong?"

"Hell," said Joe, "You're not leaving us are you? - thought you'd had enough of the sea during the war!"

Marcus then went on to tell Joe of Pierre's planned move to Hong Kong and taking some or all of the patrol with him for protection who wanted to get them back to base in Hong Kong.

Joe said in reply, like any service officer, "Can they do that in the Royal Navy, I thought you still had hanging over there for mutineers?"

Marcus told him about their demob being due, as civilians and being unable to get in touch with the ship or response from Hong Kong, apart from that glib message, "Catch the ferry."

He had half a mind to join Pierre, but did not want to lose Lita. Joe personally didn't want to lose either of them, he rather liked the idea of Marcus as his brother-in-law. Marcus may have lost his heart to Lita, but as a regular serving officer, his chances of leaving the service just like that, may not be easy.

Hesitating before he said it, he then asked Joe, "Do you think Lita would be prepared to travel with me on the junk to Hong Kong - Pierre is a good friend and Yvonne and Lita have a lot in common."

Joe answered bluntly, "You want me to ask her!"

Marcus equally forthright answered. "Well, you're one of the family and understand them better than I. I could be off to sea tomorrow if the ship turned up and it may be my only chance of taking the woman I love from this war-ravaged country for ever."

Marcus went on, "Hong Kong is British and we can survive there and get married. I might even get a transfer to the Canadian Navy and we could all be neighbours if I was posted to Vancouver. I have a Canadian passport!"

Joe, hanging on to the phone and thinking, suddenly said enthusiastically, "Gee, that would be great. We could drive over at weekends or meet in Miami for a roasting on the beach. Yes, I'll tell her Marcus, but I can't make her mind up for her."

Marcus agreed to that and more settled in his mind that the situation in which he found himself might have a happy ending, with a cheerful goodbye to Joe, he replaced the phone and headed for the mess. They were all in uniform when he arrived, but there was no saluting for he was without a cap.

It helped to make the meeting informal and they all took seats, waiting for Marcus to begin. First of all he asked for a show of hands of those who wished to escort Pierre and his family in the junk to Hong Kong.

Taffy was the only dissenter, but made a valid point. He was a married man although not a good marriage. Taffy had obligations just the same, and felt that before he took part in any hair brained scheme, he wanted his next of kin informed, in case they never made it. At least, she may get a widow's pension. He was a Catholic and wanted a Christian burial not joss sticks.

Taffy was also fed up with Chinese food and thought it was about time someone bought or found a few tins of corned beef.

Marcus, in complete sympathy for a Welsh Catholic who liked corned beef, asked if these conditions were met would he be prepared to join the others?

Taffy agreed saying, "It's not that really, I'm just a rotten sailor, I'll spend half the day spewing me bloody dinner up!"

Marcus sympathised with him and agreed, "I'm not so good myself in destroyers."

Now all his men had agreed to go, Marcus confident they could make it pirates or no pirates he was prepared to give it a go.

If Taffy had stayed behind, he would have had to do so too.

That night there was a riot as people fled before an armed skirmish that took place on the outskirts of the town. It was some way from the Consul but left them with a nasty feeling of being vulnerable and not being able to do anything about it. Between themselves they talked about boarding up the windows, although the drill for emergency was to retreat to the main building in the Consul.

Having spent that night with the others in the quarters, Wilson thought he would ring Pierre to see that everything was all right. It was as well he had rung. The riot had been nearer to Pierre's place and Yvonne was rather upset.

What Pierre wanted Wilson to do was to see how soon they could begin loading some of the workshop gear and other items on to the junk and he would pay the lads anything they wanted just to help. Wilson scoffed at that from Pierre, and told him any more of that and he would destroy the "Entente Cordiale."

Pierre laughed at Wilson's French and said he would leave it to Wilson.

Captain Chang as they now called him, agreed with Wilson when they met about being cautious when the boat was loaded. Anyway, there were rumours of some funny looking coolies working overtime at night, with some foul smelling sacks marked Danger - Poison, keeping people away. It may be illegal dumping, but no one cared.

Over the next few days the patrol were introduced to the Chang family in twos and threes and seen playing with the children. It spoilt the children who were showered with little presents from these funny pale coolies. They were not pale so much as brown and dirty. The children were most obedient and disappeared when any strangers were seen nosing about, although the crew were always on the watch and very threatening to anyone loitering near the craft.

Ma Pang adopted Taffy for some reason, being a married man. He spent most of his time in the living quarters setting up bunks, helping her to hang mosquito net curtains and partitioning the living section into small cubicles.

The dining area was sacrosanct and a washing cupboard for the women, with buckets outside on deck for the crew had to suffice.

The men were used to it, and if all went well, it would only be for a few days.

Action stations for fighting the ship were left to Marcus and you would have thought it was an armed raider the way he resolved arcs of fire so that no one would fire at each other, day or night. Spare ammunition, proper cover for the women, fire and abandon ship drill. They may now be a bunch of civvies, but he was leaving nothing to chance. The Navy hadn't trained them for nothing and they would be at sea again and precautions were always essential.

Mrs Chang was most proud of her efforts for the girls, although Bungy jokingly said in the mess as they were skylarking about, "It looked like a sheik's harem."

At least the girls they were taking with them were a damned sight better looking than any Wrens he met in the Navy.

Black, the stoker, was in his second heaven polishing and tending the diesel engines. Clean as they were, Black added that bit of spit and polish found in all ships' engine rooms in the Navy and applied it equally well to Captain Chang's beautiful engines.

Captain Chang was so pleased by Black's enthusiasm that he gave him an old engineering cap to wear.

Kemp, the signalman, had been quietly active and from his own pocket had made a white ensign to fly from the masthead in addition to a quarantine flag and Union Jack. He also thought of torches and batteries and a pair of hand flags in case they needed to signal or call someone up.

The patrol, were like bees coming and going to the hive. There was a great urgency in what they did, for after all, this could be the first leg of their journey home.

A flash point for riots seemed to occur in the poorer slum areas of the old French concession area. It was as well that Pierre had that armoured section in the house next door to the workshops, for looters, part of a rioting mob, knowing that it had been a jeweller's workshop, broke in and ransacked the workshops hoping to find loot. Furious at finding nothing, they set the place alight. Pierre and Wilson, who were at home behind the steel section, were able to extinguish the flames after the mob had passed. It still left a terrible mess to clear up. The time to leave was getting very close.

It was a good thing that Pierre had the foresight to clear out the workshops when he did, for many specialised pieces of equipment now in the hold aboard were priceless and would have been smashed or stolen by the looters not knowing their worth.

It had been hard work to re-establish the business after Pierre returned to the firm after his P.O.W. experiences and for him it was all happening again like a bad dream.

Yvonne was no longer her usual exuberant self and her lifestyle with other changes in the last few weeks appeared to have brought about a change. Pierre himself, not a strong man, had noticed a change also, they must get away now and he decided as soon as Wilson came into the room and told him of his decision.

Looking around the beautiful room he said, "Don't bother with any of this," and waved his arms to embrace everything. Near to tears he asked Wilson, "Just get on to Mr Chang and ask him when we can come aboard and set sail for Hong Kong."

Wilson, also concerned for Yvonne, wasted no time in phoning Marcus, with Pierre's message.

Marcus, having already given attention to most things since he realised the trip was on, had received an up to date chart (U.S.Navy Dept.) from Joe with a message that Lita would not be coming, deciding to stay for the sake of her elderly parent, although she would keep in touch because she loved him. Marcus kept this feelings to himself and put all his energy into getting to sea.

Calling for Chung the jeep driver, he headed for Pierre's house to pick up Wilson and Pierre. Together they all went aboard for a meeting with Captain Chang who wanted to clear the Huangpu river by 2100 (9pm) and the Yangtse estuary by midnight to be free of the fishing fleets for the first part of the trip. For his leg of the passage he would be using the junk's diesels. This would get everyone familiar with the hum of the engines and also allow the passengers to see the magnificent spread of the lights of the town and ships which, together, would make a pleasant memory for them all to go to sleep on.

He needed and got, two lookouts for each watch of four hours in coastal waters at night with a general lookout during the day. His two Chinese crewmen would helm or steer the junk, under normal running by diesel and under sail.

It was agreed that all sail handling and deck work after the first day could be done by Marcus's men under the mate and Marcus would act as the Captain's relief and deal with any emergencies, man overboard and other seaman like activities coming naturally to a trained officer.

Marcus had not forgotten a splendid first aid box (U.S.) that Joe had given to them during their shore activities. Marcus and Wilson would be arriving on board from different places, but to make it convenient for Pierre and his party to get to the junk. Wilson would arrive early and get settled in before Willie arrived with the patrol travelling from the Consulate in rickshaws.

Marcus would be at the restaurant saying goodbye to Lita and the Jung family. The jeep would also be returned to Joe with a farewell gift from the patrol.

Marcus said his farewell to the Consul secretary in the absence of the Consul and left a written report to be forwarded to his Captain aboard H.M.S. Battener with a copy for H.M.S. Tamar, Hong Kong.

Having already cleared his room, he then got Chung to drive him to the men's quarters. All the men seemed in good heart and were busy tucking into Peking roast duck which Am Ling had laid on as a treat.

Marcus did not hang around but thanked Am Ling personally for looking after his men.

The laundry was silent and empty as the Pang family all at home said a tearful farewell to Anna and Sam where they shared a final meal.

Anna too shed a tear as the sound of a distant explosion shook the windows of her parents' flat as they were about to leave.

Once more in her unsightly cape, Anna waved to her family as she and Sam in a rickshaw moved off and merged with the passing traffic. Holding hands, Anna continued to shed a tear as they jogged steadily to the waterfront.

Putting his arm around her, Sam spoke softly of his love and her great courage for coming with him. Sam spoke of their wedding, as if it were tomorrow. Hong Kong to him was no more than a bus ride with the church just round the corner. By the time they arrived her tears had ceased, as she turned her head for Sam to kiss her before she stepped aboard.

Approaching the jetty, her eyes lit up once again at the sight of the junk and her memory of the short trip down the river. The journey of her dreams was about to begin.

Marcus and Lita dined quietly together in a corner of the Jung restaurant. Marcus had already said his farewells to Mrs Jung who was still in bed and unwell.

Una was with her, but rather anxious because Joe had not appeared at his usual time and there had been minor riots throughout the city with some casualties amongst U.S. personnel.

Marcus was finding saying goodbye to Lita very difficult. Marcus loved this woman and if it had not been for the troubles raging through Shanghai he was certain Lita would have been on the boat with him.

Lita, whatever happened was going back to the U.S. with her sister Una, so there was no reason for the romance to end.

His first destination was Canada to see his only living relative, his father, when Lita, who was returning to the U.S. with her sister, and Joe, her brother-in-law could cross by ferry to Vancouver to meet him. They could be married the next day. They were merely going about it the long way round the world before they got to the altar. Lita did not want a shot gun wedding, but was fairly certain she was pregnant.

CHAPTER 9

It was better for Marcus to save his career and get his men home safely to Hong Kong than worrying about an unborn child in the middle of a civil war in which he had no part to play. To Lita, he was the most devoted and exciting man she had ever known, he was a gentleman also and always thought of his men.

Above all, she loved him passionately and did not intend to give him up easily.

Lita, to Marcus, would always be the most elegant and beautiful woman he would ever meet. There could not be anyone quite so adorable anywhere.

Marcus intended to make her the mother of his child one day although little did he know but she already was.

Joe arrived in a hurry, but had to return to duty at once. He and Marcus gave each other a hearty hug and goodbye, promising to meet up in Canada. Joe, always generous, promised to find a job for Chung, Marcus's driver, then he was gone.

Lita insisted on driving Marcus down to the junk in the Chevrolet, even though it meant her changing into old clothes to see Marcus off. For her to drive at all on her own was dangerous, but the old 'Chev' was much better for kissing someone goodbye.

Not a lot was seen on the darkened junk as they drew up alongside. In the dark they kissed a passionate goodbye.

Watching him as he disappeared into the darkness of the junk, Lita allowed herself a few tears of regret before she drove off.

Standing in the dark by the gangboard were Sam and Anna to take Marcus aft and up to the small wheelhouse where the Captain was preparing for sea, poring over an old chart.

With a polite bow to each other they then shook hands, with Anna acting as an interpreter for them both. Marcus then produced his brand new chart of the China Sea and handed it to Captain Chang and saying to himself, "Obligate thy brother first."

Captain Chang, accepting the gift, beamed as he opened it, laying it carefully on top of the older one on the chart table, under which was his sea bunk with clean covers that the Captain used at sea when he was in bad weather always on watch.

The Captain called for Anna and she repeated to Marcus what he just said, "Marcus that is your bunk for the trip, my wife has said I can sleep with her for this trip!"

Smiling to each other, they dismissed Sam and Anna and began to examine the chart for channels and buoys.

The name of the junk was Petihoo, but it was not used often because it reminded Mrs Chang of the black coal area from which she came.

Everything had to be clean and tidy on board and that is exactly how she had made the sleeping and eating arrangements for them all within the confines of the after poop living quarters.

Pierre and Yvonne had the double bed aft on the starboard side, with the girls in shipside bunks on the same side, draped in dyed mosquito netting to give some privacy, these were normally used by the children. Compartments were separated by the colour of their curtains. The men slept on a heavy straw mattress between the table and the bunks but further forward to keep the gangway clear around the table.

The Changs' bunk was next to the galley with curtains, with another heavy mattress on the floor with sheets and coverings and made up like twin beds, with shipside bunks for Willie and the mate who would be on watch more than the rest.

Hammocks too were available, but prove rather a nuisance on a crowded mess-deck. Sleeping on deck was comfortable when it was fine but with showery weather or wind borne spray wet bedding left you without a bed for the night

Two hammocks and a further two camp beds on the deck for two more. Other camp beds were available, for sleeping on deck was more comfortable in fine weather, but sailing hard and sea spray could make a wet bed for the night. Everyone seemed happy with the arrangement and getting on board and settling down had come easily for them, with Mrs Chang treating everyone as though they were in a hotel on dry land.

After all, they were all in the same boat together!

The Captain had asked them to all assemble and pray for the ship's spirit and a safe journey. The Captain lighting a candle, bowed to the shrine with a brief prayer, followed by each in turn with their own candle. It was a delightful touch of faith. Mrs Chang then appeared from the kitchen with a tray of small tin mugs and two large flagons of wine.

With a toast from the captain for a good wind with, "A friendly and a welcome harbour," a strong chorus of, "Gan-Bay, Gan-bay and Shiay - Shiay" rang out and they all drank to each other.

Looking at his watch, the captain then asked the women not to appear on the upper deck until his Mate, Marcus, had given them the signal. It would then be safe for them to enjoy the lights and night sky of the China Sea.

Every seaman had a job with Willie in charge. Kemp was on the poop with the Captain and Marcus and Black the engineer, hovering with his oiling can, ready to press the starter button to those magnificent diesels.

The whole crew with dirty faces, scruffy coolie suits looked a seedy bunch. With a wave from the wheelhouse, they let go aft and let the stern swing out a little, then let go forward as the junk swung out into midstream with the pull of the current, moving quietly away from the berth. The throaty bubble when the diesels fired and settled down to a silenced healthy throb was not too loud. On came the steaming light as the junk responded to the engines and they steadily made their way down the Wangpou river and into the open expanse of the Yangtse estuary.

All around lights were blinking and twinkling from shore, with ships and craft large and small all going somewhere or doing something. It was now time to invite the girls to enjoy the view.

Holding hands, they came out in twos and threes happy and expectant to see something they had lived with, but never seen. Even at night the vast expanse of water covered by twinkling lights added to which the powerful bubbling noise of the exhaust as the Petihoo, with increased speed, raising waves of white and phosphorous foam on either side of the junk as it surged ahead towards the open sea.

Everyone was on deck now and being well clear of the harbour, deck lights made faces recognisable and excited talking and laughter gave a feeling of adventure as people reacted to the gentle rolling of the Petihoo.

The air was warm and as people found their sea legs and couples began to move around and explore their little world for the next two weeks. Sam and Anna were already laying claim to one shady corner on a coil of thick rope under the after poop, while Bungy and Wiggy, wasting no time, began chatting to Cheng Sui, Mai Ling and Li Ann, who between them knew a few phrases of English but all had lots of charm and cheerful giggles.

Pierre and Yvonne bravely climbed the few steps to the poop and talked to Marcus and the Captain. Yvonne seemed to have recovered some of her old vitality and the sea air had returned the colour to her beautiful face. Speaking to the Captain in Chinese, Yvonne spoke of her gratitude to him and how she was looking forward already to arriving in Hong Kong where she and Pierre could repay Mrs Chang and himself for rescuing them from some dreadful fate it would have been as foreigner's under the Communists.

In order to be sure of clearing the busy sea lanes leading to Shanghai, the Captain set course to the west and seaward. Remaining on watch himself until they were well clear of sea traffic, he called a Chinese crewman to take over.

The sea was still calm and the wind light. There was plenty of time to set sail after breakfast. Going to bed was a noisy affair with the girls having fits of giggles at the noises coming from behind the crew's curtains as they tried to say good night in Chinese to the girls.

Mrs Chang's voice soon put a stop to that, by telling the girls that any Hanky Panky would upset the junk's spirit and they would be horse whipped like the crew if they were naughty.

Yvonne and Pierre, considering all things and enjoying a feeling of being on holiday were amused by the banter between the girls and the sailors and pleased the noise ceased, after the arrival of Mrs Chang. It was easy to sleep in the hum of the diesels and holding hands they fell asleep. Nothing stirred when the Captain came off watch and half undressing, slid quietly into bed to cuddle his ample wife

The morning sun was already rising over the starboard quarter and a freshening breeze from the north west could not be ignored.

With a call from Willie, "All hands on deck!" the seaman now the crew, formed a line on the midships deck and guided by the two Chinese crewmen began unlashing the fore and mainsail, checking the main and gaff halyards and reeving the sheets through the running blocks on the gunwale.

Anna became involved to curb the enthusiasm of the crew, who were used to handling all things as being expendable.

On board the junk every piece of string or rope was valuable and you could not go to the bosun's locker and grab a new one as if you were still in the Navy.

The sail rig, refitted by the Captain with American sail cloth, set nice and tight against the mast and gaff, with good lashings at the tack and clew. The down-haul on the boom was a Chinese puzzle but

Marcus soon modified that and when the sail was fully set and pulling, the Petihoo picked up her bow and sailed like a thoroughbred.

The Captain's pride when sailing the Petihoo under sail showed in his face when, with the foresail set, she was handsome indeed.

Now running with the wind on the quarter, the Captain set course for a long haul south, handing her over to the duty Chinese helmsman, when he and Marcus went down for breakfast.

A meal of rice with syrup, crusty bread and fruit was available with plenty of fresh tea.

Wiggy lingering at the breakfast table trying to talk to the pretty Cheng Sui. It did not do him much good for the sharp eye of Mrs Chang soon had him fixed and quickly handed him a bucket of dirty crocks and pointed to the kitchen. Cheng Sui, fearing the horse whip she had heard about, quickly left the table and hid behind her curtains.

Throughout the day the Petihoo made a marvellous run just east of south, not bothered by fishing fleets, or in sight of many vessels. All the passengers were eating well and Pierre, not one for sitting in the sun, had developed a reddish glow on his cheeks from the sea and wind. The women soon lost interest in looking over the side and were now gathering around the table, listening to Anna and Yvonne talking in English and demonstrating English manners and habits. This little get together proved most popular and lasted daily for most of the trip.

Mrs Chang learned to use the orders,"stop," "shut up" and "sailor boy", to keep the men in order, but spoilt it by chuckling every time she tried to give an order.

It was just before dusk, with the sun low in the west, Marcus spotted two sails close in shore to the east, with the sun reflecting briefly on their white sails. They were a long way off and passed quickly out of sight as the sun dipped below the distant cloudy horizon. Marcus wondered briefly who they were.

If they had been a little closer and flying a flag, he thought a race to the Formosa Straits may test the Petihoo's speed through the water. Normally ships pass their name and destination in return for a similar reply followed by "bon voyage" or some other friendly message, in the vast oceans of the world. It keeps ships in touch and is a useful piece of information for other ships to have knowledge of your whereabouts even if you were as big as the fated 'Titanic'.

Anna was a good companion for Yvonne and loved doing little things for her. Yvonne couldn't bear staying in a coolie suit. Mrs Chang took a lot on convincing that for Yvonne to put on a dress was more important than a meal. Reluctantly conceding to Yvonne's wishes, Mrs Chang allowed the midship hold to be opened by Wilson and Sam to permit one of Yvonne's sack covered cases to be removed and a dress or two unpacked with a pair of shoes. Yvonne quickly put on a dress as soon as she could.

With her voluptuous figure, she soon brought appreciative comments from the men, for Yvonne now mixed much more freely and was happier. Mrs Chang had never seen such a dress, let alone wear one. Her four children had kept her busy and she was now quite a plump, cuddly woman. For young attractive women to be seen on a junk was enough to provoke an attack from raiders and this worried Mrs Chang who had suffered such an experience, when young and pretty but suffering with chicken pox at the time. It had saved her from coastal pirates who had thought it something much more unpleasant. In her opinion Yvonne was pregnant and she should know as a mother of four. Her cooking was clean and wholesome and the sea calm. Why should Yvonne try to be sick early this morning, the sea was quite calm.

Mrs Chang had been pregnant herself and knew the signs when she was pregnant. It is a pity Yvonne wants to dress up, for it won't be long before she is unable to squeeze into that frock she was wearing today. If they did have trouble, poor Yvonne would be the first one to be raped. Feeling a little sad, Mrs Chang worried a little more about her large family.

Up in the wheelhouse where Marcus had slept quite soundly last night, the Captain and Marcus were quite content with their eyes on the sails, a glance at the old magnetic compass and looking at the new chart. It had many up to date corrections and amendments that had not been shown on Captain Chang's old one, and in order to save time on this voyage, Captain Chang had already plotted a fresh course closer inshore on his next leg, provided the weather remained good with a fair breeze.

The reefs and rocks on the old chart were merely estimated by his father on the coastal run with occasional wrecks here and there on the chart of those that ran ashore.

The Formosa Strait was always busy and only two days away if they maintained their present speed. Marcus had the watch tonight and the Captain was to be called for a change of course about 0400 (4am) unless there was a change in the weather or wind.

The sun was again low in the west and Marcus, out of curiosity, looked once more to the coast on the beam to the east to see if the two sails were still to be seen. They were there all right, but a little closer and more ahead. At least we are keeping up with them, Marcus thought and went down to get his supper.

It was a beautiful romantic night with the half moon glistening sparkling white on the now small choppy sea. The wind in the rigging and sail kept up a steady chatter as little eddies blew the reef tails.

Yvonne with Pierre and Wilson looked quite stunning in the moonlight, whilst Anna and Sam, arms round each other's waist, walked up and down the midship deck wobbling from side to side in the slight rolling movement of the junk. Black, not moving far from the diesels, was joined by two of Yvonne's girls, Mai Ling and Lay Hua, sitting on the engine housing.

They didn't talk, they just seemed to like his company and quiet manner. Black's eyes gave him away, for he looked from one to the other with a lot of feeling for both of them.

Wiggy was sitting on the other engine housing on the port side with Siew Choo and they were giggling as Wiggy, unable to keep his fingers from touching her thighs and saying something in English which Siew would never understand, but at the same time she was enjoying the attention,

Li Ann and Kemp were untangling the rules of Ludo at the dining table. They contrasted a great deal in their looks, he thin in the face and fair, whilst Li Ann had a broad face with a great big smile. They were very happy as they struggled to throw sixes and their compatibility was obvious as they praised each other and touched each other in moments of great harmony.

Mrs Chang toiled endlessly, cooking, tidying and generally managing everything like a contented mother hen.

Tomorrow was to be a busy day, for Marcus, not wanting them to be unhappy, for these were early days, had duties to perform in the interest of everyone's safety. Tomorrow, with the Captain's approval, they were to test the guns whilst well out to sea.

The guns Pierre had brought with him were still boxed and Marcus suggested that it was about time they were assembled and made ready for firing. Wilson and Weller were gunnery trained. Wiggy and Bungy had been trained in close range weapons.

Given the job they quickly had the guns out of their boxes and assembled. The heavy machine guns were sited one forward and one aft to give them as much height as possible and with a good arc of fire clear of the sails. The gun stands were easily lashed down with plenty of ring bolts and cleats on the fore poop and on the stern deck aft of the wheelhouse. The positions were a bit exposed but there were plenty of old sails in the hold to cover the guns and hide the gunners.

The six submachine guns were allocated to Marcus and Willie aft on the poop deck close to the wheelhouse. The Captain and Chinese crew each had a pistol and knives, but gladly accepted the additional submachine gun as their principal weapon. Mrs Chang not only had a pistol in a holster on her hip, but a horse whip slung on her pistol belt.

The Captain altered course to allow an empty box that was thrown over the side to drift away and pass the ship, as each gun in turn opened fire with a few single shots then a burst or two. Mrs Chang fired a submachine gun but the rest of the women remained under cover.

It had been a useful exercise with further instruction from Marcus on sighting important targets before blasting off and wasting ammunition.

Willie gave an excellent demonstration of single shot shooting at a piece of flotsam floating by the junk and followed this by spoiling a pleasant lazy afternoon by suddenly shouting in an alarming way. "Action Stations! Action Stations!" and making the gun crews rush to their weapons, uncover, load and apply safety catches. This repeated drill achieved one thing - on the last run they all avoided the many obstacles in their way aboard an unfamiliar vessel as they rushed to man their guns. It was a worth while exercise and a greater awareness of their vulnerability in the case of a surprise attack.

The alteration to the course they were steering came late in the afternoon and they were now ahead of the two sails that had been sighted in the evening on the previous day. That he had not dropped astern of those vessels pleased the Captain for under sail alone he had covered a good two hundred miles in the first two days approximately and was standing out well into the East of the China Sea.

If the weather held and the wind blew, this course would take them within sight of the northern Isles of Formosa and a straight run through the Formosa Strait.

Happy with the day's run, the Captain turned the ship over to Marcus and his Chinese mate and went down to supper with his wife and the girls. Almost everyone was seated when the Captain took his chair at the head of the table. Mrs Chang came from the kitchen, touched his cheek and whispered something in his ear.

The Captain beamed a huge smile and nodded his head for having made such a fine run today, a little glass of wine was not out of place. The Captain had become rather a father figure to the girls and all of them wanted to talk to him at once.

Pierre, sitting next to the Captain became worried that his girls were becoming tiresome and asked, "Are the girls being a nuisance?"

Shaking his head, the Captain beckoned one of the girls to sit on his lap.

Without hesitation the girl Cheng Sui accepted and seating herself on his ample lap, cuddled his thick neck. Entering with the wine, Mrs Chang saw the girl and putting the wine on the table, began laughing as though something very funny had happened. Her laughter was very infectious and soon everyone was laughing. Intimidated by the laughter, the girl slipped from the Captain's lap and took her place at the table.

Mrs Chang, still chuckling, then began to serve the wine. Serving the Captain last of all, Mrs Chang then plomped her broad buttocks squarely in his lap and began to drink his wine. The idea of the Captain's wife sitting on his lap came as a bit of a surprise after the talk of Mrs Chang's strong views on behaviour.

Wiggy was quick to take advantage of the slightest excuse to get his hands around Cheng Sui who was seated next to him at the table. With a tickle and a wink he conveyed what he wanted. Sliding sideways onto his lap and putting her arms around his neck, there were cat calls from all the others for her to kiss him and she duly obliged to the roar of all the crew.

Deciding enough was enough, Cheng Sui slipped back to her own seat but was interested in Wiggy enough to wipe her lipstick from his face. Mrs Chang, struggling out of her husband's lap, thanked the young Cheng Sui, saying, "He hasn't done that to me for years!" and returned to the kitchen to serve up the meal.

Considering the numbers she had to cater, for the supper of sweet and sour vegetables and rice with sauces satisfied them all. The fruit also kept well in the nets hung outside on deck. Tea was available at any time and very popular. The girls were now not quite so scared of Mrs Chang after the display of cuddling with her Captain and helping her in the kitchen was welcomed when they washed up the bowls and dishes.

Yvonne. still feeling better for wearing a dress and looking after Pierre, for he was a poor sailor and unaware her condition could make her perhaps a little seasick.

Marcus, now standing in the wheelhouse, had felt the surge of the waves as the Petihoo responded to a stronger blow of the wind and heaving a little on the sheets she listed a little as the junk increased her speed. More spray from the stubby bow frothed its way down the junk's side, on this course, there were many hours to go before another change of course was needed and the exhilaration of racing and the lean of the mast made them all want to go on deck and be part of being excited at racing, it was a wonderful feeling.

Competitive by nature, Marcus eased the main sail sheets a little as though he was sailing some grand yacht at Cowes, to get that extra pull from the Petihoo's driving canvas. Looking to starboard he still maintained his position relative to the other craft sailing inshore, although he should be dropping behind. The thrill of racing under sail on a moonlight night in a frothy sea, excited them all and most of the passengers forsook the comfort of the poop to stand on deck amidships and play at dodging the spray on the weather side.

Sam and Anna came on the bridge for a while and shouting to Marcus, Anna called, "Are you enjoying this?"

As the wind blew her dress tightly around her beautiful figure, he thought of Lita as he looked at Anna and shouted back, "Yes - but I wish that Lita could have come!"

Anna, feeling sorry for his lonely heart, said brightly, "At this speed, you're going quick enough to go back and collect her."

It was windy on the poop and Sam and Anna did not stay long chatting to Marcus who had things to do.

Every time he looked at the set of the sails Marcus could not help admiring the skill of Mr Chang who had supervised and built this larger than usual junk from his earnings at sea. The engines which were his pride and joy were also his own work being first an engineer. The Petihoo handled more like a schooner than a junk and was a great thrill to sail her under these conditions. Again, thinking of Lita, what a joy it would have been for them both to be here together.

It was 0200 (2am) when the Captain returned to take over the watch and he was followed up the ladder by the relief helmsman carrying a large jug of hot tea and Chinese cake, not unlike bread pudding. Eating cake and drinking tea. They all agreed the Petihoo was going well, although the Captain couldn't agree they could do it in a week.

Marcus was soon in his bunk, when the Captain took over the watch. He slept like a log for four hours to be woken by a soft female voice saying, "Tea, tea, Mr Marcus."

Standing by his bunk was the cheeky Cheng Sui. Sitting outside on a bench seat, with a broad grin on his face, sat the Captain puffing a long stemmed pipe. With a distinct wiggle, she swayed her way back to the Captain when they had finished their tea, kissed him on the cheek and disappeared down the ladder.

The Captain, smiling, made Marcus understand by slapping his thigh. Punishment - punishment! He mimed. Marcus wondered what she had been up to.

This morning the first for three days that the sun had not greeted them early as the clouds rose high to the east on the mainland of China.

The exhilarating breeze that had driven them so well for the last three days had turned to a variable 3 to 4 coming from the south west. There was little purpose in exhausting the crew chasing each little puff as the wind changed, so the Captain settled for a mean course although it meant they would be going rather slower. Visibility had also dropped and no longer was the shoreline clearly visible on the horizon. Marcus as usual looked for the two other boats or junks that had been on the same course but closer inland and in the worsening visibility were still to be seen and getting much closer.

Hidden by a sudden rainy squall, Marcus lost interest for a while and concentrated on sailing safely.

Wiggy and Evans had to be relieved from lookout duty in the bows, being soaked to the skin by the heavy shower. Whilst they were already wet, Marcus made them check the guns were well wrapped and securely lashed. The change in weather did not entirely dampen their spirit.

The language class turned into a riot as Yvonne and Anna decided to try a bit of Chinese drama which consisted of a lot of make up for the girls and after a bit of coaxing, Sam and Wiggy allowed themselves to be given hideous faces. Having got over the hysterics by the girls as they daubed lipstick over Sam and Wiggy. The girls insisted the men should be given oriental eyes. Lines were made up for them to say in Chinese and English.

Wiggy and Cheng Sui were given a dramatic line to say, "I love you" scene in Chinese restaurant which Wiggy said quite well and even looked the part of a Chinese 'Gigolo'. Everyone clapped, for a repeat performance and as Wiggy had finished his line in Chinese, Mrs Chang looking through the galley hatch to see what all the noise was about, came running out of the galley with her horse whip shouting in Chinese, "I give you play Hanky Panky you dirty man!" and gave Wiggy a right crack across the buttocks. Cheng, raced through the door and got rather wet.

Sam, in the excitement, snatched a kiss from Anna, forgetting the layers of make up on his face. Realising what Sam had done, Anna quickly shouted in Chinese "Hanky Panky" and before Sam realised what Anna had shouted, Mrs Chang swung into action and cracked Sam's backside.

Pierre, who had been resting on his bed and half asleep, came from behind the curtains and placed his arm around Yvonne as if to protect her. Looking around to see if there were any more bottoms to whip, Mrs Chang half raised her arm, then lowered it when she realised it was Pierre doing the cuddling. Smiling sweetly, Mrs Chang called out, "Good man, now is the time to look after your wife, when she is pregnant!"

Mrs Chang returned to the galley.

The girls sitting at the table all began whispering and wondered how long she had known. None of them would have dreamed for a moment that Yvonne could have been that way. Yvonne had such a perfect figure.

Wilson had slipped out of the mess to get his breath back on the deck. It was their love child.

Wilson returned to the mess, calling "Pierre."

The curtains parted and the family now united could see the love and tenderness in Yvonne's face, as Pierre touched her on the place where the child was growing.

Yvonne looked at Wilson loving him with every fibre in her body. Trying hard not to show too much of how she really felt, and repeatedly kissed Pierre, wiping away the occasional tear. Deep in her heart, she loved him too, for he had been a kind, generous and loving husband. To let her have this child after all the pain and misery he had suffered as a POW was the gift from a saint, not a man.

Wilson, putting his arms around Pierre as they sat on the side of the bed said, "Papa, would you mind if I asked Mrs Chang to pass the wine at lunch? After all, it's not everyday one becomes a godfather!"

Pierre smiled, saying, "Teddy, for us I have something better," and reaching under the bunk bed he brought out a jeweller's leather case. Inside lay two litre bottles of champagne of which he withdrew one.

In the excitement created by the announcement of Yvonne being pregnant, no one seemed to have noticed the rougher conditions now prevailing on deck. The wind had gone more to the south and the Captain had sheeted the sails hard on the same tack to keep the bow into the wind to hold the same course. Instead of slicing through the waves the Petihoo was taking the sea square on the stem with showers of spray over the bow.

The Captain and Marcus were not wearing oilskin coats and everything on deck was getting pretty soaked as the lowering clouds raced in and opened up with heavy showers and bursts of rain. There was no point in keeping the lookouts in the bows and sending them down to get dried out, the Captain on the poop kept a sharp lookout, although the visibility was not much better.

The worst hazard was still the fishing boats, but the Captain kept a cool head and ran one or two very close before they gave way.

There were occasional breaks in the clouds and the sun shone briefly before being snuffed out by the passing clouds. It was during one of these short spells of clear sky that the Captain saw and pointed to the two sailing craft that had been on a similar course, but hugging the shoreline. They were now much closer to the Petihoo and steering a similar course.

They appeared to be unable to point into the wind as well as Petihoo. On this course it would mean that the three ships would come together later in the day.

The Captain was not a fool and all those craft needed was to reduce sail by taking down the extra foresail they were carrying.

Captain Chang, handing his binoculars to Marcus, asked for an opinion. Marcus was pretty explicit in his sign language, drawing his hand across his throat. He had spotted a large crew, far too many for a junk, hauling on the sheets as they were again trimming the sails.

Maintaining his course, the Captain ordered the lookout to fetch Mrs Chang and Anna. They arrived very quickly, Anna having to try hard to keep up with Mrs Chang who ran up the poop ladder. Quickly, the Captain explained and pointed to the two suspicious craft now to be seen clearly on the starboard side.

His wife understood perfectly as Anna translated what he said for Marcus to understand. Everything below decks must be tied down and more hand ropes fitted for people to hold on to when moving about. It was safer for the women to lie down using the bunks. We have enough guns to frighten anyone off, and not worry if we fire them.

Mrs Chang asked if they wanted tea now. They both said "Yes," because Confucius could not say when the next one would be offered until this matter was over. Whether they were friendly or not the Captain and Marcus had the guns loaded and safety catches on.

Marcus checked his machine gun and placed it in the wheelhouse, with plenty of ammunition. The captain had enough to do manoeuvring the Petihoo.

Food for the gun crews was served out and stuffed in their pockets to eat when they could, and surrounded with old sails was all the shelter they would get until the suspicious craft had declared their intentions.

Every time the Petihoo was going to be turned or tacked the Captain kicked a loose panel in the wheelhouse which banged down in the kitchen and Mrs Chang banged her gong, the signal for everyone to hold on tight.

Mrs Chang also had cotton wool for the ears of the girls, if they wanted it, for having been in this situation before, understood most of what was going on.

Anna spoke to the women as soon as she came down from the briefing in the wheelhouse, to comfort those already wondering what was going on, particularly Yvonne who fortunately was fast asleep.

Ten minutes later, with all spare hands on deck, the Captain kicked the plank and heard the gong. At the same time Marcus called, "Ease main sheets," and the bow slewed to starboard, the Petihoo immediately gathering speed, heading straight for the other craft.

It took about twenty minutes for the Petihoo to pass through the wake of both vessels. Everyone was under cover, but for the Captain and his helmsman. Marcus watching from the wheelhouse and the Captain, both had a good look at the raiders motley crew gathered aft, some of whom were armed. Some were seen to be carrying guns.

The helmsman became excited when he saw the 'crews' shirts and calling to the Captain to come, he explained that before the kidnap of Una, the Major's wife, that three shirts worn by members of the other boat had been hanging in the same order on the clothes line of a craft moored alongside the Kia Kia in Shanghai. They looked so bright and expensive he coveted the lot. He would recognise them anywhere.

It was enough to convince the Captain, particularly when as they sheered off, as was a bullet that thumped into the woodwork of the wheelhouse.

Nothing better than a bullet could be found to stir Marcus into action, being a gunnery officer. Telling the Captain to stay on that course he kept kicking the plank to make Mrs Chang bang the gong, and the gun crews appeared on the upper deck and manned their guns.

In a few brief words he told them of the raiders opening fire. He wanted all guns on the forecastle deck pointing forward. All guns would fire at the same target and continue firing until cease fire was ordered. If the gun jammed continue firing with the sub machine guns.

The gong had brought Pierre to the bridge and after a few words explaining what was going on, Marcus asked him to tell the Captain to repeat the last tack and cross the stern again, but this time with the diesels running to give the other craft a push if possible. After Pierre got a positive reply from the Captain of what Marcus wanted him to do, he left to look after the women. Captain and Marcus now using a bit of the old chart and a bit of mime, agreed the way they were going to fight the raiders. The Captain knew his ship and would do the manoeuvring for Marcus to use the guns to the greatest effect.

Visibility was getting a little clearer as the Petihoo appeared to make two false tacks in feeble attempts to escape, much to the amused contempt of the jeering crews of the raiders, already armed and preparing to board.

The Petihoo made another pointless tack like a frightened duck, until her course took her once again towards the wake of the two raiders. It was too late for the raiders to respond when, with increased power from the warmed up diesels and the altering of the helm, the Petihoo gunners now faced the enemy with the precise order, "Open Fire!"

CHAPTER 10

The combined roar of the massed machine guns as the bullets thundered into the wheelhouse of the raider and motley crew of killers created havoc.

Not stopping but closing very fast the sturdy Petihoo under the hand of the Captain came alongside with a powerful push on the already careening hull of the first raider and she keeled over.

The second raider turned tail and scudded down wind, using sail and power in the opposite direction, to get away from the Petihoo who by dawn was well into the busy waters of the Formosa Strait.

The concentration of the guns for'ard had made a considerable less noise in the accommodation area in the poop with the bulkhead door closed. The bumping alongside was a bit uncomfortable but no one fell out of bed and the noise was lost in the breeze.

The women had been calm and brave with Mrs Chang firing a burst or two at the enemy and called for a glass of wine all round when the noise of the fight was over. The fishing fleets of both Formosa and China were busy in the Formosa Strait and again a good lookout was needed for the winds were still fresh. The anxiety of the last twenty four hours was soon over as the women, grateful for the protection made a fuss of the men.

Sam and Anna joined Pierre and Yvonne with Wilson to celebrate with a jug of Mrs Chang's special wine. Wiggy and the others sitting on the girls' bunks made a lot of noise over a little wine. Yvonne seemed to have slept soundly, through the brief but noisy action that had taken place.

All on board were sworn to say nothing once ashore for their own sakes, for idle talk can cost lives.

Mrs Chang thought they made a lot of noise just to frighten someone off, but she did like bashing the gong.

Early the sun was awake and warming the decks, drying the sails. The women once again after breakfast were sitting around with the sailors, smiling and looking pleasant to watch.

A large merchantman with passengers cruised by quite close. More than one pair of binoculars were lifted as Yvonne paraded on the poop in a glorious red frock with Pierre and the Captain posing with her for Wilson, who still had some film in his camera.

Wiggy now showing more respect for pretty Cheng Sui could be seen walking with her up and down the deck, like an old married couple.

Marcus thanked the men for the way they had conducted themselves during the brief action. He had written a report on the incident in which he exonerated the crew from any blame should anything ever come under investigation and reports required.

The arms would be dumped in the sea as soon as it was prudent for Pierre and Captain Chang to do so. With the weather improving as they sailed south, the Captain decided to change the appearance of the junk as a precaution in case the second raider decided to seek revenge.

The American cloth sail was quite unusual on a junk and with all the crew to help, the Chinese mate brought the spare sail from the hold and with a good shake-out, it was laid out for inspection. Many of the patches it showed had been sewn on with loving care, but basically it was sound and strong. Keeping the foresail up to keep her into the wind, the mainsail was quickly unlaced from the gaff and lowered to the deck and neatly folded ready to go into the sail locker.

The old sail by comparison looked more like a patchwork quilt, but it still did the job, but completely changed the look of the Petihoo and more so when the rusty coloured jib of indeterminable age was added to confuse anyone looking for a sleek junk sailing well.

For a good measure the faint word 'Petihoo' on the stern was quickly painted over by Bungy Edwards hanging over the stern in a boatswain's chair and with a large brush and pot of black bottom colour quickly covered the name of Petihoo forever.

Kemp, the signalman, having made a couple of nice flags for use on the trip showed them to the Captain and asked if he could hoist them. One flag was much the same as another in the Captain's book and being an engineer by profession, saw nothing wrong with flying the white and red ensigns together, after all the crew were technically still R.N. sailors.

Petihoo, now looking like a sedate old lady in her patchy old sails still made good headway in a fresh breeze.

The Captain and his wife that evening joined them for the evening meal and with the help of a glass of Mrs Chang's wine, he told the girls stories of his great adventures on the China Seas.

Like all sea dogs, he spiced it up a little when he fell in love with a beautiful girl in Petihoo whom he smuggled on board in the dead of night and sailed before her angry parents discovered she had eloped with a junk's captain. Mrs Chang made an excuse to go to the galley.

Cheng Sui, cheeky as ever, again sat on the Captain's lap, saying, "Oh my beautiful Captain, how nice of you to have waited for me." Kissing on the cheek.

Wiggy, a little jealous, scowled at the lucky old man as Cheng sat on his lap, but smiled again when Cheng taking her seat again as Mrs Chang appeared, sat next to Wiggy and turned her attention to Wiggy.

Cheng was like that, preferring men's company to girls. Her own father she did not know, having been born in Macau of Portuguese and Chinese parents which accounted for her keen outgoing character for she was part European.

Wiggy and Cheng wanted to be alone and as usual, they made for the privacy of a corner on the midship deck. It was blowing enough to drive them back to the mess until Wiggy spotted a flapping corner on the hold cover had now come loose.

Untying the lashing, Wiggy lowered himself into the hold. Standing on the sails that had been stowed below earlier, he held out his hand for Cheng to join him. First sitting on the combing she slid through his arms around her legs as he gently dropped to the bundled canvas below. It was dark, warm and soft to the feet.

Moving further into the hold, away from the hatch, they snuggled down. Wiggy did not, as usual, fantasise in the dark about all that had gone on during the previous twenty four hours. Imagining he were a pirate or raider, he would have dragged her by the hair down the hold and she would no longer have been a virgin. It was then that Cheng cuddled closer and feeling something hard in his pocket, she put her hand inside and withdrew his seaman's knife. The blade glinted in flecks of light around the hatch as Wiggy opened the blade.

Wiggy felt her tense but could understand her fear of the shiny blade. Placing it to one side, he took a little courage from the dark and placed her hand on his hip and waited for something to happen. Nothing did, and again he moved her hand a little closer to between his legs saying, "Cheng, hold me."

Cheng, no virgin and liking what she felt, whispered in his ear, "Lovely Wiggy, me not want like Yvonne, baby!"

Quickly he dived into his pocket and produced a French letter. Together in the dark, giggling and feeling one another they tried to get the elusive thing on in the dark. Giggling a little as she finally dressed it, they gradually sank into the pile of sails as they tried to do it.

A little out of breath with trying, they finally made it and lay panting and exhausted until they fell asleep cuddled up in the canvas.

They were not missed until breakfast when the gong was heard by Cheng in the sail hold. It was still dark in the hold and they just had time to get their clothes on when the corner of the hold cover was removed and the glaring brightness of the morning lit up the two confused lovers and hauled them into the daylight.

Wiggy seemed to have grown up overnight as he sat down to breakfast without his usual chatter.

It was Sam's turn to feel envious, although he and Anna were more serious about each other. A child would complicate things for them both however strong the tide of passion was between them.

Their love would be shared fully, very soon.

The following evening Li Ann and Kemp, the quiet ones who spent each evening at Ludo, were missing from their usual spot with the Ludo board untouched.

The others didn't comment too much, for fear of giving a false alarm.

Smiling happily, Kemp and Li Ann reappeared from the hold with Wiggy helping with a lift and the hold covers. Poor Bungy, still missing his mum, unfortunately tried his luck on a Saturday night with Li Ann. All he wanted was a kiss and cuddle, but it took longer than that and missed their supper.

Mrs Chang suspected something and putting two and two together, met them coming up from the hold with her 'Hanky Panky' whip. A chase round the decks got Mrs Chang nowhere, as the youngsters Kemp and Lay Mua kept well ahead shouting their innocence and only wanting to be alone. The Captain thought Mrs Chang was a spoilsport, after all they had their share of 'Hanky Panky' once they had got aboard.

The wind, now north westerly was still a healthy breeze and kept the Petihoo steadily eating up the miles. With lights of Penghu clearly seen to port and many old steamships using coal, had spirals of black smoke coming from their funnels. Many seemed to be still as the Petihoo sailed on.

Each meal now became a social occasion for they had all shared with each other the joys and fears of living together in the confines of a junk in dangerous waters.

Friendships formed in adversity, last a long time and the intimate way they talked about each other was more like a large friendly family. Pierre spoke of Wilson and Sam more like his sons, although Wilson had a special affinity in both Pierre and Yvonne's heart as one of their own.

The expertise of his trade as a jeweller was garnered over the many years and he was confident that Sam and Wilson were clever enough to learn to be partners in the business and taking care of him in his old age. Wilson, to all intents and purposes, was a blood member of the family. Pierre already had plans for Anna too.

Her skills at learning languages was amazing. Although it was but a short time she had been working in a laundry in Shanghai. Since she had been aboard the junk, Anna was already able to converse with Pierre and Yvonne in a mixture of French and Chinese quite fluently.

Pierre had been keenly aware of Anna's intelligence and good looks which matched Yvonne's for beauty. Yvonne also had been impressed and Anna was an asset they would embrace in the business. They would be the envy of Hong Kong with Anna running the showroom.

It happened just off Swatoo as they were on the last leg of some two hundred miles on a straight course to Hong Kong that the wind increased and spiralled round to the south east. It was not like a local front causing the change of wind, but as though some great big force from God had swept his hand across the whole area and flattened the seas from the Philippines to the South China Sea.

Like a scythe over the wheat, it left behind small regular waves all dancing and frothing in the same direction. North east. For the first time Marcus heard the Captain lose his temper as he raised his fists and cursed the heavens.

Having got it out of his system, he tacked the Petihoo to accept the wind from the new direction and, shouting at Marcus, mimed that he was tying a knot. Marcus got the message, they were to reef down the sail as quick as God would let them.

The cry, "All hands on deck!" in Chinese and English brought them all out fast. With no wireless it was instinct that warned the Captain it was a typhoon on the way.

Every bit of lashing that could be found was brought into use to hold things down. With the main reefed down, the jib furled, the foresail was lashed to the fore gaff, ready as a standby sail. The small mizzen would be left for as long as it lasted to give a little steerage.

Marcus, using the binoculars to follow the weather front and studying the new chart, gave the Captain new heart as he showed on the chart they were much closer to Hong Kong than the Captain had thought. With a bit of luck, if they took a chance, they could just make it.

Marcus ordered two of the crew to unfurl the foresail and reset it, whilst the Captain in the wheelhouse pressed the bridge starter button in the wheelhouse to start the diesels.

They started the first time and were soon running at full throttle. With the combined pull of the small mizzen and foresail and with the thrust of the engines, the Petihoo picked up speed, running freely before the wind and sea she rode the growing swell like some great duck trying to take flight, surging forward and almost lifting off.

It was not the sea so much to begin with, but the steady increase in the wind, blowing through the bamboo battens on the sails, making a mournful sound of wind and seas rising and falling each time a gust of wind hit the sail.

The speed of the Petihoo seemed incredible and trying to the crew, holding on grimly to the lifelines, sheltered by the poop as waves coasting past faster than the junk, crashed aboard amidships and spewed over the other side.

Members of the crew were sometimes excited, sometimes scared, as they rode on the back of one wave after another, surging forward in great rushes over the foaming seas all round.

The screams of some of the girls could not be heard in their bunks clinging on for dear life, for it sounded as if all hell was going on outside.

CHAPTER 11

Ahead, the Captain and Marcus could see the welcoming open width of Hong Kong harbour with many ships and junks straining at their anchor cables, in the increasing force of the typhoon as it built up to force eleven and beyond.

Easing the power of the engines to a turn-over speed, immediately snapped the foremast.

The only vacant space to tie up was the reserved berths for R.N. vessels only and the only chance of stopping was with the help of sailors at the base being ready to take a hawser or two no matter what the weather.

Without hesitation, Marcus ordered the helmsman to go alongside with the Captain on the throttles of the roaring heavy diesels.

The Petihoo shook like an angry dog as they went astern on one engine then ahead as they turned in the lee of the harbour jetty. Sailors struggling to stand up straight, secured lines and wires whilst the engines still going ahead held their station safely alongside until more hawsers were passed to secure them alongside.

Thank God, the duty watch on the jetty had spotted Kemp's home made White Ensign, flying on the main mast halyards and tossed a "Ready to use" heaving line aboard to take the first of many hawsers to the bollards on the jetty. Slowly, with lethal ferocity the typhoon built up tearing away anything lose, but Petihoo held firm. Men now unable to stand on deck, took shelter with the women. Everyone needed someone to cuddle, except Mrs Chang whose husband with Marcus kept watch in the wheelhouse.

There was a great deal of damage to boats in the harbour by the typhoon which finally blew itself out by midnight.

Mrs Chang, that dauntless spirit of a woman, was soon in action with cups of tea and jugs of hot soup and bread. The shock of the last few hours began to disappear with the soup now being served by Mrs Chang.

The fact that they were filling the most prestigious berth in the Naval base was of no consequence as they all bundled into their beds and bunks and fell asleep.

The duty O.O. Watch the next morning, smart in his clean white uniform, turned up to order them to clear the jetty and anchor elsewhere, until a scruffy individual surprised him by wearing a naval cap and saluting, reported crew mustered and correct as a bunch of coolies in sailors caps all sprung to attention by the gangway.

They looked an odd bunch not sailors at all, but he let them stay until he had reported to the Commander.

Marcus changed into uniform and, wearing a spare cap of Willie's about three sizes too small, met the now amused Officer of the Watch and took him to see the Commander who ordered an officer to make the Petihoo's crew welcome. Baths were made available and emergency clothing was on hand and anything else they required.

Quarantine and Customs were to be informed. The Commander shook Marcus by the hand and thought it was a damned good show. The Commanding Officer of the base, formally met Marcus in his office and listened keenly to Marcus's account of their activities in Shanghai and the subsequent voyage back to base in a junk.

Captain Llewelyn Byers, D.S.O., R.N. not committing himself by approving or disapproving of Marcus's actions, showed concern for the women aboard the junk and detailed the Commander to provide an officer to deal with any problems of housing the women and the billeting of the ratings in a suitable mess at the base.

The Gunner of the base was chosen as the liaison officer, being of similar rank. Marcus and Freddie Simms knew each other from the Gunnery School, Whale Island. It was just a question of renewing old ties and being gunners there was little between them that their long experience in the services could not provide.

Pierre had most to do and Freddie Simms soon put a phone in his office at Pierre's disposal to call his agent Mr Quan to inform him of their safe arrival. That he was at the Naval base was considered very important. Pierre was under no circumstances to leave the base until Mr Quan arrived there to greet him.

There were advantages to being involved with the British Forces. It could speed up lots of things, particularly using the Chinese lawyers who represented the Navy in certain circumstances.

Pierre's circumstances, he felt sure, fell into that category.

Freddie Simms, as Liaison Officer, soon got things moving to provide a little more comfort for the crew and passengers of the Petihoo. First he had them towed to a berth for small craft in a basin used for small R.N. vessels. On the jetty alongside were toilet and washing facilities. There was also access for vehicles to drive up alongside for deliveries.

The status of the Petihoo was still unknown, having been unofficially seconded for service purposes. To keep this misconception alive, Kemp, borrowing a slightly larger White Ensign, hoisted it for all to see.

Not many people went around challenging one's right to fly a certain flag, even if it was the R.N.'s distinctive colours.

Freddie Simms had already contacted Customs and Excise and advised that it was better for the main luggage to remain in the hold in the sacks for the Customs to rummage about if they wished. The women had already recovered, with the help of the crew, all the clothes they needed to make them respectable once more, had been rescued from the hold.

The showers were in use by the men as soon as the Petihoo was finally secured, but the second block of showers for the women would be ready very soon.

Freddie advised it was better if the women kept out of sight from prying eyes. Women were not allowed in the base, under normal conditions.

Even before the Customs and Excise people arrived, a taxi bringing Mr Quan drew up alongside, carrying a briefcase and requested to see Monsieur Pierre.

Now that they had arrived in Hong Kong and were finally back in the Navy, the crew all seemed a little lost. The junk in the time they had been on board, had become like a home to them.

The memories, traumatic, passionate and personal were all precious. They just did not want it to end They were safe and on their way home. It was the real world and Shanghai a long way off, as it had always been.

Willie, the Petty Officer, had been busy. He had arranged beds and billets for them in the base. He handed out passes for them to use when going ashore and leave, until midnight for men aboard (in base; married men in quarters 7am and 8am for senior rates).

Willie thought he had done a good job, sorting that lot out and was a little disappointed to see their glum faces. Even Willie was not that hard hearted, but the girls also may have to leave the junk today if Pierre completed his business with the Customs and Immigration Officers.

Willie had one other bit of good news. They would all be paid a fortnight's pay and any back pay they were due. He also reminded them that the girls who had brought them so much pleasure had never been in Hong Kong, which was another world to them. At least it is as safe as London and there are some beautiful shops and sights to see.

Having slopped about in coolie suits for almost a fortnight, seemed to have robbed them of any desire to get back into uniform. Two sailors from the base passed and looking over the junk and crew said, "Scruffy bloody lot, aren't they - need a good scrub if you ask me!"

One turned, looked at the boat and said, "Can't see any girls, can you?" and walked on.

Pierre with the Captain's permission used the wheelhouse as an office to talk over their business arrangements.

Yvonne had complete faith in Mr Quan who had worked for her father, now deceased, and a partner of her husband Pierre. The girls were her chief concern.

Producing work permits, residential qualifications, passport applications and other documents, Yvonne seemed to have covered every department in the Chinese Embassy and Municipality offices in Shanghai to produce the mass of paper dealing with the entry of the girls for work of a specialised kind in Hong Kong.

Mr Quan was delighted, for the job had almost been done. Still unsmiling and serious, he studied each piece of paper in sequence, to see all was in order. Mr Quan did not want to lose face that everything was not in order.

The goods were Pierre's concern and his transfer of stock had already taken place. There was the little matter of smuggling half a million dollars' worth of pearls, but that had already reached a point of no return and he could not bother anyone with that responsibility.

Pierre had already written off the cost of the guns that were now deep in the South China Sea sunk by Captain Chang in a suitable place.

Pierre wanted a nice small flat for the girls who were new staff joining the firm here in Hong Kong. Mr Quan smiled, his brother had just the place. Mr Quan was not so cool when Pierre said that his personal bedroom was needed as a nursery.

Dumbfounded, Mr Quan said, "Why?"

Pierre, sticking out his thin chest, announced in a very expressive French manner, "I am to be a pa-pa!"

The team of three Customs and Excise Officers who arrived to pass the Petihoo through the customs procedure, two English and one

Chinese, were escorted by Freddie Simms, who had already given them an account of the escape of the stranded sailors from Shanghai.

Already overworked they saw no international band of smugglers in the assorted bunch of half dressed sailors and Chinese girls holding up a tottering Frenchman, who looked half dead.

An English member set up his portable table and invited Marcus to be the first to present himself. Marcus said briefly, "Nothing to declare."

Like a penny slot machine, the customs officer recited a list of dutiable goods, "No jewellery, drugs, watches, cameras, booze?"

With a smile, Marcus replied, "I've got a couple of used Shanghai shirts."

Without a change of expression, the customs officer waved him on and waited for Willie, the Petty Officer, to present himself. With a click of his heels he shouted, "Nothing to declare, Sir!"

Wincing from the noise of Willie's shout, he waved him on. Each in turn declared their simple purchases and were charged a nominal duty of a couple of Hong Kong dollars in return for their clearance chit and it was all over. The two Chinese were a little more diligent and climbed into the hold and searched through a couple of sacks, but there was nothing there except rather well used items of personal clothing.

"Where are your guns?"

Captain Chang handed him a certificate for his own two guns and also the key to the gun cupboard, and invited the Customs Officer to enter the poop and inspect the guns. Their eyes met and the officer returned the key.

Pierre was the last to be seen by the Customs Officer. Hard-bitten though he may be, looking at Pierre he could not help being touched by this frail old man wearing the badge of an ex-P.O.W. on his lapel, who offered him a modest tin of cultured pearls he wanted to declare.

Pierre emphasised illogically that they were real pearls. Without hesitation, the Customs Officer opened the tin and taking a small handful, quickly examined them. They were a mixture of cultured pearls and of no real value, but to please the old man he charged him. Looking at Pierre with a grinning face of a Japanese guard he snapped, "You're quite right, sir. That will cost you twenty dollars." Giving Pierre the weakest of winks and, shaking his hand as the last customer, handed him his customs clearance form and altered it to pearls.

There was nothing to stop Pierre and his girls going ashore now, but with Wilson's help, Mr Quan unloaded a crate of Champagne from the taxi with an assortment of hors d'oeuvres boxed and freshly made. The Customs Officers, although invited, were too busy to attend, although they thought Shanghai girls for looks, were something special.

Yvonne almost cried when she saw the hors d'oeuvres and handed them around for every one to taste. It was a happy little party with everyone kissing someone, for all the natural reserve of the Chinese seemed to have disappeared.

Pierre and Yvonne with things to do, left early with Wilson and Sam carrying Pierre to the car in their arms in a fireman's lift.

Sam commented as the car drove off, "Stone me! He's heavy for a thin man!"

Wilson, with Pierre's welfare always close to the surface, asked Yvonne if Pierre needed any help as he looked very pale. Yvonne smiled as though he had given her a bunch of flowers and said, patting the empty rear seat beside her turned her pretty face and said, "I couldn't possibly undress him myself, he has put on so much weight during the voyage!"

Running back on board and collecting his leave pass and cap, they were soon on their way to their new Hong Kong home.

On board everyone began asking if Pierre was all right, for without him there was no future. Sam with Anna on his arm and a fresh glass of champagne in his hand, replied confidentially, "Pierre's all right. He's put on as much weight as Yvonne since he heard she was pregnant."

With Mrs Chang's wine and the champagne, the party got quite lively. Freddie, who had dropped in at Marcus's invitation to celebrate their safe arrival, kept the party pretty quiet just by being there, it was a naval base.

Marcus, over a glass or two, was able to talk about the demob of his men with Freddie who was more in touch with the men passing through the base on their way home. An aircraft carrier was due and there would be plenty of accommodation for those being demobbed. Her destination was Portsmouth, to pay off and give leave.

Freddie unattached and living with a Chinese housekeeper in a neat little flat, informed Marcus that accommodation was not difficult if you lived like others on the island. The service was already making provision for married service families in all the services. Many, like himself, lived in private flats which freed the service accommodation for those who wanted it.

Freddie had news about the Ship, H.M.S. Battener. She, the ship was in Australia acting as safety ship for the carriers dumping surplus aircraft now the war was over. Marcus will have to find something to do. He will have to do duty officer in the base eventually, but a week or two leave will do him some good thought the Commander.

Marcus wishing Lita was here.

Getting Pierre up the steps of the business premises was a struggle until Wilson was able to dump him into an armchair. Even the pleasure of carrying Yvonne over the threshold like a bride was denied him when Yvonne insisted on walking slowly from the car and up a few stairs to the commodious accommodation for Hong Kong over the business premises.

Wilson followed Yvonne up the steps and thought to himself that she had put on weight because he could no longer see the form of her shapely waistline. Once inside, Yvonne wasted no time in serving champagne and toasted the success of the mission. Pierre, as he drank, seemed to have a problem raising his glass until unable to stand any more, he asked Wilson to lift a weight from his shoulders.

Wilson was in for a shock as he removed Pierre's jacket and shirt from his thin scraggy body.

Around his neck and shoulders hung a yoke from which dangled strings of pearls, back and front, almost two metres long, hanging from his shoulders down inside his trousers down to his ankles. No wonder Pierre had been a problem to carry up the stairs.

One by one they gently detached each string and lowered it to the carpet. Each long string was safety clipped into sections and while Yvonne and Wilson did the unclipping and sorting, Pierre filled the glasses as they all celebrated. Standing together with their arms around each other admiring the groups of assorted pearls on the carpets, they quietly toasted the crew of the Petihoo. Handing her glass to Pierre, Yvonne turned to Wilson saying, "Now you've got to undress me."

Pierre mumbled to him, "That's one little lot the Communists will not get their hands on!"

Wilson too stunned for words to think they had just committed a major crime, smuggling that amount of jewellery into Hong Kong without declaring it.

Pierre, however, had no conscience at all after how he had suffered here as a P.O.W.

Each of the strings of pearls that Pierre had carried were two metres in length and there were very many of them. For Pierre to carry ten Kilos in weight must have reminded him of his P.O.W. days.

Teddy, for Yvonne would call him nothing else, now had the job of removing the skirt, which he looked forward to with some pleasure. Knowing that Yvonne was ticklish, he first of all asked her, "Where do you want me to start?"

Yvonne found it difficult not to laugh, for everything to do with Teddy had a sexy implication. With a sweep of her hand she said, "We need a sheet, of course."

Once the sheet was in place over the carpet, Yvonne began easing the shoulder strap on her slip to tease him with a show of her breast.

Teddy, not knowing what to expect for they had not been to bed together for over a fortnight, looked at Pierre still sipping his champagne in an armchair and said half-heartedly to Yvonne, "Not here, in front of Pierre."

Yvonne proudly held up her head, "Why not - he always watches us, you know that."

Teddy, still not sure that Yvonne was not teasing him, said defensively, "What in that thing?" Pointing to the bulging skirt.

With her head held high, in a sexy whimsical way, she said, "Oh Teddy, you've no imagination - just think of me floating under you in a sea of pearls!"

The mood passed and Yvonne's mind turned back to business. Placing Teddy at one end of the long carpet, she handed him a cord she had taken from the top front of the skirt. This was attached to the end of a zip clip.

Yvonne eased herself a little away from him then said, quite seriously, "I am going to twirl my way to the other end of the carpet, and you will see a wide band of pearls rotate from my waist. Lower them gently to the floor and once they are in the safe, I will deal with them in the morning."

Yvonne now turning in the skirt of pearls, gently un-wrapped a continuous length of rows and rows of pearls and lowered them to the carpet. Yvonne in her slip was a delight to see with her shapely legs exposed and perfect little feet.

She let Teddy admire them and then together they folded the skirt of pearls and locked it in a large safe.

Pierre, having finished off the champagne, was dozing in the chair.

Their love making began with holding each other in a soft embrace and just thinking about the young being inside. Teddy nervously touched her stomach saying in all seriousness, "I cannot feel anything."

Loving her gentle Teddy, she pulled him to her naked breast and said, "You better kiss them while you can, they will belong to somebody else soon!"

Now in his arms in the comfort of the new bed, they made love with passion and aroused Pierre's interest talking about the baby.

Slipping into a comfortable chair just inside the bedroom, Pierre watched their naked bodies with the pleasure of feeling he was taking part in the creation of a child.

It was early days, but their separation they should have been in each other's arms after the fighting, had been hard to bear.

Tenderly he loved her and she cried with happiness and praised the Gods for bringing her loved ones safely to their home in Hong Kong.

The morning after the party, Willie was up early and had already washed, shaved and dressed in a clean uniform before anyone, apart from Mrs Chang, stirred.

He would like to call, "Wakey, Wakey, Wakey," but did not want to scare the girls. Mrs Chang brought him a cup of tea and waving her hand and holding her head, indicated to Willie she had drunk too much.

With a cup of tea she woke the Captain, who first lit a candle and prayed at the shrine. His mind was already thinking of the trip home to Shanghai. Fuel for the diesels, food and water, presents for the children and maybe a passenger or two with a little cargo thrown in.

Dressed only in his shorts with soap and towel, he was about to go ashore to the wash-house when Mrs Chang shouted to him to cover himself and make himself decent in front of the girls. Captain Chang was not quite himself this morning, and draping himself in a waterproof cape, headed for the washroom and toilets on the jetty.

Unbeknown to him, Mrs Chang's shout had aroused the girls, who slipping on something over their shoulders, all did likewise and followed the Captain, one by one.

A group of sailors, returning to base after a night's shore leave, all stopped, to allow the Captain and the girls to cross in front of them. One of the sailors noting the drooping white ensign flying on the main mast said, "Look mates" pointing to the white ensign. "That dirty old man, has got a ship full of wrens."

Another laughed and answered, "They don't have Chinese Wrens, but if they did, I wouldn't mind any one of those sharing my bunk."

Watching them disappear into the wash-house, another wished aloud, "I'd love to scrub her back," as the last girl ran into the washhouse.

The crew now beginning to stir and suddenly realised the girls had gone, and instinctively reverting to sailors, they got up grabbed their towel, toilet gear, and in their underpants, which barely covered their backsides they staggered, half naked, over to the washrooms.

There were no signs saying Men or Women, and in their sleepy state entered the first door they came to with Bungy leading.

Bungy had reached a washbowl by the time a scream raised the roof and the other sailors bolted.

Bungy had three sisters and was used to fighting over the bathroom. He thought nothing of the girls being there and continued to hold on to his wash basin filling it with warm water. He didn't understand what all the fuss was about and continued to wash himself vigorously.

Cheng said something to the other girls, and there was complete silence. As Bungy began to dry his face they grabbed him from the rear, pulled the towel over his head, ripped off his underpants and pushed him out of the door.

Bungy's first instinct was to run back on board, but catching sight of Mrs Chang as he stepped on board, he changed his mind and scampered back to where Wiggy was frantically waving from the other washroom doorway.

Panic over, Wiggy recovered Bungy's toilet gear, now in the road outside.

Things were pretty cool between the men and women aboard the Petihoo, although the women had a giggle or two as they pointed at Wiggy and wiggled their little fingers, saying naughty things in Chinese.

Wilson had a lot to think about this morning as he sat down to breakfast with Pierre and Yvonne. First there was Pierre's equipment and luggage to be collected and brought home which he had arranged with Mr Quan.

Also the flat to be occupied by the girls, was now vacant and furnished ready for immediate use. A covered van for the girls should not enlist any of the sailors to travel with them, or help with the luggage. Pierre did not want the neighbours thinking they were the other sort of girl, setting up shop.

It was a tearful farewell as Captain and Mrs Chang with all the crew waved goodbye to their pretty passengers. They took with them the hearts of the whole family and crew.

Something had left the Petihoo too, for a total emptiness had filled the once crowded curtained mess and it would never be the same again. Already Marcus and Willie were accommodated in the wardroom and Petty Officers' mess with their luggage.

The crew too had gone their separate way, and billeted with those lucky members already holding their demob notices and were idling away their time waiting for the first ship homeward bound to transport them home. This was one of the other things that Wilson had on his mind. He must get Marcus to let him see the base Commander with Weller. They had every right to be demobbed where they wanted and treated fairly.

Marcus having already been approached by Weller on behalf of them both about his own and Wilson's demob or discharge and he decided to see them in the morning.

They were both seen together, at the Commander's table for requestmen at 9am. Jointly they put their case well and in the absence of the ship their case was considered favourably for the documents for their discharge, were already here at the base. Any personal kit that the ship may hold could be landed at the base whenever the ship returned to harbour.

The Commander in any case had already granted two weeks local leave for the patrol to recover from their ordeal in Shanghai and the journey home. The Commander was a little puzzled at Marcus's grim face, when he gave notice of the leave granted. Maybe he did not approve or expecting rather more, he thought.

Marcus who had spent more time than anyone with Captain Chang on the trip, was very grateful to all the Chang family, for putting their home at risk to save them. It was difficult to repay them without giving offence.

He had a sudden inspiration and knew the crew felt like he did. It would give the crew an interest, until their ship came in to take them home. When he mentioned it, they all rallied round to refit and repaint the Petihoo for the Chang family at Navy expense, there was tons of gear around that no one would miss.

Mr Chang was in no particular hurry to get back to Shanghai, except for their children and a good refit would do for the next five years.

Somehow the press had made up a typical story for public consumption, of brave Chinese captain, rescues British navy men!

It brought him a lucrative order and cargo, for whenever he made a return trip, but he resented the publicity, there were pirates out there who wanted his blood.

Now that names had been added to the list of name and group members for demob, Wilson and Weller had only to await for a confirming approval before they became citizens of Hong Kong. The Master at Arms of the base who controlled leave did not seem interested in whether they returned from leave or not. It was wiser to play by the rules and they had to help with refitting the Petihoo anyway.

Losing the girls so quickly after their arrival in Hong Kong had left Bungy, Wiggy and Kemp, rather unhappy. They did not know where the girls had gone or if they would ever see them again.

Anna and Sam already had a flat and that they were getting married anyway. Wiggy knew that for sure, because he had heard and seen Willie the Petty Officer talking to the base Chaplain about it.

Anna's example had been the ladies at the Consul and she had attended Christian services with the other mixed children and wanted to be baptised.

Anna prayed every night to God to keep Sam safe for her to love. Anna knew that Sam prayed, because every night he said, "God bless you" and that meant he prayed for her when he said, "Goodnight Anna".

Yvonne arranged the flat and Anna was thrilled. It had a view of the sea from a small side window which reminded her of the Chang family and the Petihoo. There was one bedroom, also a small room with a built-in bed, but she knew what Sam would want that for!

Padre Walters of the base and his wife were kept very busy, but he found time to consider Sam's case, brought to him by Marcus.

It was not just a case of a sailor falling in love with one of the many pretty girls in Hong Kong with little or no idea of the cultural and religious differences they faced here.

Sam's case was quite unique, he was already a civilian although still in uniform. His future was here in Hong Kong, working for a reputable firm of jewellers and he had no family to return to in England. His fiance had been employed and educated in the British Consul in Shanghai in a class of bilingual children.

An invitation to tea from the Reverend and Mrs Walters gave them the chance to judge this exceptional girl.

Anna was not only extremely attractive, her speech in both English and Chinese was excellent. The references from the Consul spoke highly of her as a person with intelligence and gifted.

What most impressed Reverend and Mrs Walters was her Christian beliefs. Her recital of the Lord's prayer, the Creed, were beyond reproach and freely recited from memory, when asked. Anna and Sam had been in love from the moment they met and both wanted a Christian marriage.

The following day, Padre Walters a compassionate man after hearing the story of her brave flight from Shanghai, promised to expedite the banns.

Captain Chang was having a good day too. Marcus had been given a Captain's uniform from the base 'Scran Bag', where lost and found items are kept from survivors. A cap also that had floated around a while, was given a cap badge and he was proud of them both.

To think his boat was to be painted and refitted by the crew pleased Mr and Mrs Chang very much, particularly as Bungy who had been in the furniture business said he would restore the shrine and paint it as it was painted originally.

Freddie Simms, the fellow officer of Marcus Beatty, was helpful too. A sailing man, he had made additional shrouds and stays for Petihoo to strengthen the mast.

A good strong forcsail that had been thrown out was added to the rig of the junk. With new sheets and cleats, it would help the junk to point better into the wind.

After the last attack, Marcus now suggested new positions for the machine guns.

Captain Chang, at heart an engineer, gave Marcus a free hand, for nothing Marcus did was visible.

After working on board the sailors always spent some time with the Changs. The tea pot was always in use after they had painted, scraped and spliced. Mrs Chang having gone to all the trouble to make the curtains up for the girls wanted to keep them up for the colours were so bright.

Taffy, good at splicing made her some fancy knotted sashes to drape the curtains, for he knew Mrs Chang hoped she would again see the girls.

It was nearly 2300 one evening, when the Chinese steward at H.M.S. Tamar called Marcus by telephone.

There was heavy interference at first, but then the line cleared and Marcus heard the lovely voice of Lita on the line. Almost in tears with happiness, Lita spoke quickly of how much she loved and missed him.

They were all pleased that the junk Petihoo had made it, and gave him a telephone number via a U.S. P.X. exchange at Joe's Headquarters.

The line went dead after that, but Marcus had been thrilled to hear her voice again and that she was well. Now they had established contact Marcus felt they were not that far apart after all.

Wasting no time he called the number Lita had given in the hope of speaking to Joe. The call was answered loud and clear, but Joe was not available, "Would Sergeant Borkowski do." Happy to speak to anyone, particularly Borkowski, he answered, "Put him on."

"Hey Ya Marcus", boomed from the earpiece, Marcus spoke briefly then asked, "How are things in Shanghai?"

It was important.

Borkowski mentioned there were more squatters riots as hundreds camped in streets on the outskirts, but it did not affect the waterfront area. Marcus asked about Pierre's premises and Borkowski said he would find out.

Thinking it would be sensible for Borkowski to have the number of the mess here in H.M.S. Tamar. Marcus gave it, with good wishes to them all.

Talking to Lita and Borkowski did wonders for his appetite. He just caught the mess bar for a night-cap before a night of dreaming about Lita. Now that Lita had managed to get through to Marcus on the telephone, Marcus wasted no time the next evening on returning the call to Lita and was on the line at 6pm. They talked of happy days together and how much they missed each other with Lita almost confessing, that she wished she, too, had been able to come with him to Hong Kong.

There had been a minor incident at the restaurant last night with the food and dustbins at the back, being stolen and tipped on an open site as beggars searched for food. Thank goodness, they were unable to break into the kitchen. There really wasn't much more news, but both were happy just to chat.

The bar in the mess was open at six and Freddie and Marcus were just about to taste the pleasure of drinking a John Collins, when Marcus was called to the phone again, this time by Pierre.

Marcus, wondering what this was all about, answered Pierre cheerfully. "Hello, Pierre and how are you and your pretty wife-all settled in?"

Pierre seemed nervous and a little upset and replied that they were alright, but would he care to go round that evening for a drink and a meal, Pierre was sorry for the short notice.

Marcus with nothing on in particular tonight apart from a nightcap later with Freddie, said "OK where is it?"

Pierre gave him the address and suggested 7.30pm. Mr Quan would pick him up a little before that time.

Marcus still enjoyed his Shanghai suit and was glad to be going out for part of the evening. Marcus arrived and was greeted warmly by Pierre and affectionately by Yvonne with a kiss. Marcus was not surprised to see Wilson (Teddy) there, who also was in civvies.

Now that Wilson had almost left the Navy, apart from a piece of paper, and without a uniform, reacted in a very natural way. That he was in love with Yvonne was obvious, but it did not intrude into the relationship of Pierre and his wife, for they all shared a common bond like a loving family.

Already one could see Pierre's dependence on Wilson in many ways, for he appeared to Marcus thinner than when he had last seen him. In fact, he looked ill.

The meal was perfect, marinated pork basted and served with selected Chinese vegetables, with individual dishes of spicy sauces. Fresh fruit was always interesting. Everyone seemed to discover or use a different way to peel an orange, or discard the unwanted stone of a peach.

It was Mai Ling, whom Yvonne had brought from Shanghai, that waited on the table. Each time she looked at Marcus, she tugged at her tunic to make sure she was smart. Marcus was the man who could find her a sailor.

Pierre had eaten very little, and during tea which followed the meal, he was like a greyhound, straining in the trap, to tell Marcus about his problem.

When he lifted his head and spoke, Yvonne's mouth opened, her eyes opened wide and Wilson said, "I cannot believe it!" while Marcus speaking to himself said, "You forgot to clear the safe!"

Pierre looking over his glasses, with a long drawn face, repeated. "I have forgotten the safe!"

Yvonne rose from the chair, moved to the head of the table and hugged her fragile husband. "Pierre my love", she crooned, "What does it matter, there are only a few baubles of mine in there, for you took the diamonds out on the morning we left. I saw you darling!"

Pierre looked mournful, "The bag you saw was not the diamonds, Cherie, that bag contained the garnets and semi-precious stone of little value."

Wilson looked from Pierre to Marcus and finally at Yvonne and said, with all the nonchalance in the world, "I'll have to go back and collect them Pierre, you wouldn't like those to go to Communist Party funds would you?"

Pierre couldn't really take it in, but Marcus, supporting Wilson's enterprise said, "Why not, you're a civilian now, why not take Weller with you, Captain Chang's looking for a crew."

Wilson shook his head. "I don't think Sam would be interested, he is getting married!"

Pierre now showed more interest and said in a stronger voice, "Teddy, you will not go unrewarded, if you took this risk for us, we are family - The same goes for Sam, too, every young man needs money to start up with and we have our children as they will one day."

Yvonne joined in. "Now we're here, it didn't take very long at all although I shall be worried sick all the time Teddy is out there, with those dreadful pirates!"

Wilson took that part of it as protecting the firm's interest.

Pierre had already promised him a partnership, when he thought Wilson was able to take over some responsibilities of running the firm.

The prize was worth any risk, for Pierre confided the safe held valuable documents and priceless diamonds.

The subject became a little one sided when Pierre began talking about cash. Marcus the most senior of the Navy present, was only receiving the paltry sum of seven hundred pounds a year (gross) in salary for his present rank.

Marcus' war gratuity of £86 U.K. after fighting for five years wasn't very much.

Marcus, thinking to himself that this was the only chance he would ever have of making something above his naval salary enquired, "How much would you pay me if I came along too Wilson, I'm a good navigator and sailor!"

Wilson jokingly added, "You'll have to scrub the deck as well!"

Pierre, a businessman, could see some advantage in this and without hesitation suggested, "First of all, I want you all to return safely. Secondly, what ever we agree will be credited now to personal accounts. Thirdly, it doesn't matter if you do not get the diamonds, although it would be a beautiful present to the mother of my child." "Gentlemen, would two thousand pounds each, be a suitable reward?"

They both nodded.

"To my friends and for calm seas."

Marcus and Wilson had never had such personal wealth, but they still had to earn it.

It was like joining the Petihoo all over again. They continued talking and covering every detail from the safe key to the food, guns and an interpreter.

Yvonne had suggested Cheng Sui, who spoke English, better than the other girls and that was agreed if the girl was willing.

Guns had played such an important part in the last voyage. Maybe Freddie Simms could help, he controlled the armoury at the base.

Pierre surprised them all by saying, "Captain Chang approached me about buying two sub machine guns on the way into Hong Kong, when we were about to dispose of them over the side. They were no use to us and I told him to help himself."

Wilson who had helped to drop the boxes containing the guns over the side, remarked, "All the boxes felt loaded to me, they were too heavy to be empty when we dropped them over the side!"

Pierre smiled and answered, "You should check Captain Chang's sand locker. It was usually full, but I don't think it is any more, unless he has refilled it."

Yvonne came up with a suggestion, that took the men by surprise, when she said, "You have got to take Cheng Sui as your interpreter, you will be in trouble once you are ashore and have to explain what you are doing in Shanghai. You are now citizens of Hong Kong and could be shot as spies - This is common practice for getting rid of unwanted foreigners. You might get away with it if you took your uniforms, for Major Joe O'Brien, Lita's brother-in-law, could give you some support if you get into Chinese trouble."

Yvonne threatened, "I shall kill myself, if anything happened to Teddy!"

CHAPTER 12

Yvonne, standing behind Pierre, with her hands on his shoulders, said quite seriously, "I think you need women with you, should one of you die. In any case, it will give you something to fight for, the diamonds would not count for one life lost."

Yvonne then brought up the position of Weller, who already on the company's books, would have to be fully consulted. Yvonne, always pragmatic, could see no difference between men and women. Again she came out with a bombshell, "If Sam wants to take Anna he can do so, she will be able to see her family at the same time."

Turning to Wilson, she said: "Teddy, promise me, you will put it to Anna, for it will be another month before the wedding is fixed. What does it matter if she loses her virginity, they can treat the trip as a practice honeymoon." "I would" she added, looking at Teddy, then adding, "I know that Mrs Chang is keeping the bed!"

Pierre, looking over his glasses, with a cheeky smirk on his face, said, "I think it is time to find the brandy." As Pierre rose to get up, Wilson began to speak, but Pierre raising his hand, spoke first, "I know exactly what you are thinking, Teddy, but I just couldn't spare the girls, I've a business to run."

Yvonne smiled and remembered how happy and fulfilled all her girls had been.

It was the next morning, when Marcus and Wilson called on Captain Chang, to ask if he would consider one more round trip to Shanghai and back, for the same price.

Captain Chang was very fair, for he already held an export manifest and delivery notes for the cargo due on board any day. He had been well paid. Now he had a captain's cap like Marcus, with a captain's coat, they could all travel as his family, free but hard working.

Wilson would like Sam to go but whether or not Anna would permit it raised a problem for the wedding arrangements had already begun.

Sam and Anna needed the money for a nursery. Anna with a superior look at them both told them firmly. "If Sam is going to Shanghai, I am going too, you will need more than one girl to help Mrs Chang who is not a servant. I require money too, I need clothes and presents to buy in Hong Kong for the family."

Sam cuddled her and said, "Anna, if we achieve nothing else, I promise you will see your family."

With that the men left to contact Captain Chang and prepare for the return trip.

Anna, staying with the girls at the moment, was not lacking for company, for they all took a great interest in the flat and spent half their time helping to make curtains and one major project was a patchwork bedspread. Sitting on the bed, they sewed and talked, giggled and sewed a little more, always happy with their memories of the Petihoo.

They talked crazy things for a laugh, like kidnapping Bungy, Wiggy and their quiet friend Kemp to seduce them until they promised to marry.

Money was needed too, for the shops here were magnificent, to a Chinese girl from the mainland China. Everything a girl had ever dreamed of ever owning was on display and you could walk in and try them on and smell real scent for nothing.

Pierre had always been a good master and they would soon know how much they were to be paid. It had crossed all their minds and been spoken about between themselves, that the street girls all seemed well dressed.

"We will all do better than that," said Mai Ling, with a far away look in her eyes, "Do you think Yvonne would let me hold her baby, when it is born, I have never had a baby brother or sister."

Cheng immediately teased Mai, saying, "You're not feeling like that already, you're just broody - Marry your sailor."

When Wilson met Sam at the base the next day, they both had lots to talk about. Wilson got in first by telling Sam about having Marcus round for supper, with Pierre talking about business, of all things.

Sam thought Wilson meant the Navy, when he spoke to Marcus about business and before Wilson could continue, Sam bubbled over, talking about Anna, the flat, the wedding, getting some furniture and that it was all going to cost a lot of money.

"Hang on a bit, Sam. You didn't let me finish," said Wilson, butting in himself. "This is about our part of the business now we are working for Pierre. You haven't got to discuss it with anybody except Anna, but listen to what I have to say first."

Sam, now very interested, said half jokingly, "Any money in it for me?"

Wilson replied, "There will be if we are business like!"

Wilson then went on to quietly tell Sam of Pierre's misfortune of leaving a bag full of diamonds in the safe at Shanghai and the proposed attempt to get them back, before the squatters now invading any empty property in Shanghai, move in on Pierre's home.

Wilson thought that Sam was too starry-eyed about Anna to volunteer. Thinking of their sparsely furnished flat and picturing Anna beautifully dressed, wearing her pearls at their wedding, he couldn't wait to say, "How much is he paying us to make the trip in Petihoo?"

Wilson then said, "Yvonne wants Anna to see her family, to make sure they are all right. You could double what you are offered, if Anna goes with you to act as interpreter with Captain Chang or in any situation ashore, remember Pierre will not be with us."

"Come on" said Sam excitedly, "How much!"

"Two thousand each, including Anna, if she is willing to go."

Sam could not take it in and queried, "Do you mean Hong Kong dollars?"

"No, pounds Hong Kong, you fool. We're on civvy rates of pay now!"

"I cannot wait to tell Anna, she'll come like a shot, I know, she said so, providing we get back for the wedding in time."

Wilson said, "I did not believe what she said in the flat. You've got to wait for the banns to be posted and that takes three weeks. Then the wedding service, the bride's dress, God knows how long that will take. Anyway, who's the best man - you can't get married without a best man!" "If I were you, this trip could be your honeymoon, South China Sea, moonlit nights followed by the Hong Kong wedding of the year."

Sam, a little overcome with Wilson's enthusiasm, said hopefully, "Would you be my best man, Teddy?"

Smiling, Wilson put his arm around Sam's shoulder and said, "I thought you would never ask me!"

Together they walked to the fleet canteen to celebrate with a pint or two.

Later, sitting in the flat and drinking tea with Anna, Sam mentioned the proposed trip to Shanghai in the Petihoo and would she like to go as an interpreter.

Anna could not bear the thought of parting and overjoyed to be with Sam and seeing the family she asked with a twinkle in her eye, "Can we have Yvonne's bed?"

There were no complications in preparing for this trip and apart from Marcus, no one was bound by King's rules and regulations.

A bit of fiddling went on, when it came to ship's stores and convenient loan of two good rifles and ammunition, for Marcus to maintain his Bisley standard of marksmanship whilst on leave. All it needed was a signature, between two understanding gunners, Freddie and Marcus.

The stores contained tinned salmon, baked beans, milk, fruit, all in tins, suited the palates of Wilson and Sam who were corned beef men. What Mrs Chang could do with corned beef, was out of this world.

Captain Chang was pleased that the cargo arrived by lorry, it was manageable and well boxed to a standard size. This made work a lot easier in the hold and when finished, still left an even walking surface for securing the cargo down to the lower ring bolts.

There was an anxious moment or two when two Chinese customs officers appeared, checked the consignment notes, and opened one or two crates. Satisfied, they chatted cheerfully with Captain Chang. It was as well that Captain Chang had been paid in advance, for this consignment was destined for the Municipality, who rarely paid any accounts for months. Sometimes not at all. Things were even worse according to the rumours from ships the customs men had searched arriving from Hong Kong.

Captain Chang with his cargo now stowed, fuelled, victualed and with a smart ship, Petihoo, was ready to sail. The weather was set fair with a good breeze to get them on their way. The Captain was keen for the Petihoo to show her paces after her refit.

Everyone was on board, including a stowaway, for everyone had been aboard to say farewell.

Pierre had handed the house and safe keys to Wilson and Marcus with a small pistol and shells that Yvonne had kept for her personal protection. Yvonne wanted Anna to have it.

It would appear that everyone in Hong Kong was in the Naval base to see the Petihoo sail. There were loud cheers from the sailors and a few tears from the girls.

Running on her diesels, Petihoo was quickly out of sight of the base, steering East by South and altering to a more East by North and picking up a steady breeze and was running strongly before the wind. Just to see how she would really go, running free, they goose winged the main with a pair of jibs on the port side and she sped along, leaving a wake, white and foaming, a delight to see.

Captain Chang, standing on the poop was still wearing the Captain's cap and jacket Marcus had obtained with four plain bands of gold lace similar to that worn by captains of great ocean liners and large tankers. His R.N. cap did not quite match the gold on his sleeve, but Captain Chang's stubbly beard made up for that.

They were about to have their evening meal before Marcus took over for the first watch, when Mrs Chang, coming from the galley to the table, suddenly held up her hand for silence.

There, it sounded again, as if someone sneezed. Miming to make them all talk, Mrs Chang, collecting her horse whip, approached the bunks where the girls had slept during the previous voyage.

Raising her whip ready to spank whoever was there, she gaped at the pretty face of Cheng, who had before sneezed at the smell of the cooking.

"Don't hit me." Cheng Sui cried, before she sneezed again then covered her face with the bedclothes.

Mrs Chang, drawing the curtains around the girls bunks, told Cheng Sui to get out. Cheng still dressed in a pretty frock, climbed from the bunk showing her beautiful legs and brushing down her dress.

Bowing humbly to Mrs Chang, she raised her eyes which now began to weep tears down her cheeks. Almost in a whisper, she said softly, to Mrs Chang, "Yvonne told me to come because Anna might be lonely."

Wiping her tears with the end of her apron, Mrs Chang gave her a cuddle, saying, "Come on my pretty flower, let us have some supper."

Drawing the curtain to one side, Cheng looked at the astonished faces of the assembled crew around the table. Anna seeing Cheng, almost jumped from her seat to reach Cheng and embrace her. Their pretty faces touching, the girls clung to each other.

The rattle of plates indicated there were hungry mouths to feed and everyone had something to say to someone until the food was served.

The arrival of Cheng was made more unusual by the news that Yvonne had overruled Pierre in sending another girl.

The Chinese are not superstitious about women being on board ship and as for the crew, Cheng with her lively personality was a welcome addition and would join in everything. She had always been the Captain's favourite on the last voyage.

There was ample sleeping accommodation for all. Once out of dresses and into their coolie suits, the girls would very soon become just members of the crew as they hoisted sails, manned the halyards and sheets to adjust and trim the sails.

If a vote had been taken to name a suitable stowaway, Cheng would have been a popular choice from the Captain down. It came as no surprise to the Captain when he took over the watch from Marcus who reported that Cheng was on board having stowed away before they sailed.

The Captain's face beamed at the thought of pretty Cheng being on board. Perhaps she might sit on his knee a little more often this trip.

A change of wind shortly after Marcus had taken over the watch gave Marcus the chance of resetting the sails to get a little more speed from them. Petihoo was answering the wheel very quickly and this showed the cargo was well balanced.

Satisfied the Petihoo was sailing at her best, Marcus with a contented feeling searched the horizon once more, settled down to the surge of the sea and the sight of the sails pulling well, joined the helmsman in the wheelhouse and took over the steering for an hour.

There was little activity on deck, although he knew Sam and Anna in the shadow of the poop, were kissing and cuddling in their own little world.

Wilson, cornered Cheng Sui as soon as he was able, to find out if all was well with Yvonne and real reason for despatching Cheng, for the diamonds were now his responsibility, he tended to suspect everything that was out of the ordinary.

Liking her too much to really suspect Cheng of anything he was puzzled as to why she wanted to come at all.

Sitting together quite closely on the engine cowling after supper he said for a joke, "Cheng, the Captain could have punished you for coming aboard like that. Mrs Chang could have whipped your bottom!"

With a giggle, Cheng slipped off the cowling, turned away and wiggling her hips as she slapped her own bottom replied, "Captain Chang would never hurt me, he likes by bottom!" With that she walked away and entered the galley to help Mrs Chang.

Ahead lay a vast number of fishing boats, each with a twinkling oily light, stretching endlessly as far as the eye could look into the distant sea. It was hard work for Marcus for there were boats to starboard of which he had to keep clear. That he managed an hour without running anyone down was a miracle.

The Chinese helmsman chuckled and shouted Chinese warnings as boat after boat refused to give way until the very last second, knowing the ships on passage could not afford to collide.

It was like a continuous game of Russian roulette and Marcus was glad to hand the wheel over to his grinning crewman. That he had not thrown anyone out of their bunks was commendable, otherwise the dinner gong would have been ringing.

Captain Chang seemed delighted and made a point, letting Marcus know how pleased he was to have Marcus sailing the ship with him.

At breakfast, Captain Chang gave quite a speech, for a quiet man as he got Anna and Cheng to extol Marcus' command of the wind and sea in Chinese as he rode on the back of a sea-dragon, to conquer all the seas ahead.

It was a little embarrassing for Marcus, as he stood up to accept the praise, but his bow was dignified. To receive such an accolade so early in the trip was great honour, from a Chinese, it was noticed that when they had eggs from that day, Marcus was always given two. That really meant that Marcus had gone up in the world, aboard the Petihoo.

By dawn, the number of fishing boats were beginning to diminish as boats returned to land their catches.

With the seas clearer ahead the next morning and sailing well clear of the traffic lanes, after breakfast Marcus began a period of practice for all the crew to learn and practice using the guns. There were ample boxes of ammunition to let everyone get used to their selected weapon. The Captain's regular crew had their own guns and four sub-machine guns were allocated to Marcus, Mrs Chang, Weller and Wilson, who were also manning the heavy machine gun. Ten U.S steel helmets that had appeared on board, were a prudent reminder from Freddie that a headache is better than a bullet.

Marcus gave an entertaining display of shooting using the rifles. It was Marcus's favourite weapon. He was deadly accurate with a rifle.

Mrs Chang, Anna and Cheng all had some practice with a revolver. Mrs Chang was as good as any man, whilst the girls taking it very seriously were soon able to load and fire without closing their eyes when they pulled the trigger.

Marcus had made it quite fun, with his patience and floating targets, encouraging everyone to join in the fun, for using them in anger may never happen. Cheng got a kiss from Marcus for hitting a floating target, but Wilson complained it was Marcus that got the prize and that was unfair.

The next two or three days would take them through dangerous waters. The Captain said he wanted every pair of eyes in the Petihoo to be on duty. No matter what you may see, a puff of smoke, a flare, coloured lights, anything floating, call one of the crew.

To please the Captain, everyone burnt a candle at the shrine that night, to the Spirit of the Ship Petihoo, praying for calm seas and a welcoming harbour.

The Chinese crew's mess and bunks had been specially built in the fo'c's'le of the Petihoo to accommodate a crew of three.

With one extra crew that Captain Chang had taken on before the Pierre contract, it was accepted that with one on watch, it was adequate for them for one trip to Shanghai.

Normally it was filled by the children, who loved to gamble with their distant cousin, Captain Chang's mate.

It was also a comfortable arrangement for the crew who like Chinese everywhere, love to gamble. Chinese gambling can be noisy.

After the noisy day of firing all the guns, it was a breezy evening with the wheel in the hands of the mate, the Petihoo was making good headway. If he had not been on watch, the argument between the two crew would never have happened. Chang's other crewman had never experienced anything like this with a large knife being drawn and held perilously close to the throat by another player.

There was murder in the eyes of the man who had recently joined the ship for a single trip to Shanghai. Everyone cheated all the time on the Petihoo particularly when you were playing with the children.

If he had been playing for money he felt certain the other man would have killed the other man. Not wanting to play after what he had just seen, he quietly left the fo'c's'le and went up to the wheelhouse to tell the Captain's mate.

The Captain, in having sailed the deep seas himself, had not been too strict when he signed the new crewman who only wanted to work a passage to Shanghai.

When the mate was at breakfast, and knowing what had happened the night before, he spoke to the crew man who had the knife as though he was a wise sailor, "You have sailed in the big ships and been paid a lot of money, could I get a job in a big ship and sail to America like you? - I have no papers."

One crewman was Captains Chang's cousin and had sailed outside Chinese waters.

The new crew man boasted, "You can always get papers, you knife a drunk!" and threw two pieces of paper on the table and said, "You can have those, if you do a watch for me when I ask you."

Chang's cousin picked up the papers and said, "Don't you want them?"

"No, I am staying ashore for a while, there are plenty of papers where they came from."

And he laughed in a demented way.

He and the man he had threatened had never been shipmates or served together in an ocean going freighter.

The man with the knife had told him he knew the Captain of Petihoo and took his discharge papers to show the Captain the name of the ship on which he had been serving. He was not sure, but he thought the Captain had believed they were both from the same ship.

He had been terrified by the look of the other man's face when he suggested that he was not playing fair. At that moment, he knew he was going to die.

The crewman who had done the threatening became most humble when the mate, seeing that he had no knife, questioned him about it.

Cringing, bowing and apologetic, he grovelled in front of the mate, saying it would never happen again.

Having never served in a large vessel or holding any certificates himself, the mate was easily impressed by the papers he was shown. Unfortunately, he failed to realise that these were the papers of the man that had just threatened.

There was no further gambling in the fo'c's'le and the aggressive crewman had become servile and snivelling, fetching the meals from the galley and being very friendly, particularly to the man he had tried to cheat. Not wanting to make a hawser out of a piece of string. the mate let the matter drop.

Tomorrow would see the half-way mark, if they continued to be favoured with the wind they had had so far. The sun had shone most of the day, with everyone on deck enjoying the pleasure of sailing. Friendly fishing boats were still to be seen occasionally, with waving crews holding up fish with the hope of selling a few.

It was at dawn that Marcus spotted that the Petihoo had company. It was miles away, but the habit of always watching for the following submarines taking a last visual sight before the visibility favoured the enemy.

The vessel Marcus sighted was dead astern, her sails clearly in sight in the growing light of the sun. The vessel on the horizon had done nothing suspicious, Marcus had just had that feeling, that they were being followed.

Staying on the same course for another two hours, Marcus could see little or no difference in their positions from when he had first seen the vessel astern.

Petihoo had eased sails during the night to give everyone a comfortable night.

The Captain took over the ship at 0800 and with the help of the chart, Marcus denoted the relative position of Petihoo and the following vessel, sailing in the same course.

Together, they agreed to take a more westerly course to close nearer to the centre of the Pharmacy Strait, which would allow the following vessel to continue her present course, if she had no interest in the Petihoo.

It took about half an hour before the ship astern responded to Petihoo's change of course and once again, was in a position of following astern.

The Captain called for Anna who with Sam, appeared on the bridge instantly.

Marcus explained their joint suspicions on the following vessel which may be a junk, but whatever it was, they were interested in the Petihoo's solitary course.

It did not take long for Anna to understand what the Captain intended to do, which she conveyed accurately to Marcus.

Sam and Wilson were to prepare all guns for action, with the heavy machine gun for'ard. All the automatic guns to be dispersed mainly on the poop.

Marcus, clearing the chart table, was able to lay prone upon it and aim either to port or starboard, using his favourite weapon, a rifle. It was about as high as he could get, without lying outside on the top.

It was in the midst of these preparations on a sunny afternoon, that the traitor in their midst struck. Unaware of the incident in the crew's mess last night, the girls were taking the tea jug and mugs to where the men were working, approaching the fo'c's'le, Anna called, 'tea'. The door opened. It was dark inside and a hand reached out and took the jug. With the mugs on her fingers of the other hand, she reached in, turning her face in case anyone was undressed.

Before she could scream, a smelly hand spread like a dirty pad over her mouth and she was grabbed by the waist and dragged through the door. In shock and unable to speak, she could smell the foul breathing of the person who shouted, "If you scream, I will slit your skinny throat, you Chinese whore."

The hard steel of his knife rested coldly against the side of her face. In fear she froze, but there were no tears.

In a matter of seconds, the crew were at the door, but the voice in Chinese, stopped them from entering, as it screamed in a maniacal voice, "I'll slit her throat and breasts now, if you move that door - fetch the Captain, now!" In a manic half scream, he kept shouting, "Get away f.../ scum - get away!"

Pricking Anna's arm, she screamed hysterically.

Sam had to be held back by Marcus and Wilson, as he gritted his teeth and swore with anger in not being able to smash in the head of the evil maniac holding his beloved Anna.

The deck was cleared of all except the Captain, who standing close to the door, made himself heard and asked for the girl to be released.

Ignoring the Captain's wishes, the manic crewman screamed in his ungodly heathen voice. "Take me and the girl to the poop deck where we can be seen by everyone, or I'll slit her throat!"

The Captain backed away from the door and Anna with a large wicked knife held to her throat appeared with blood streaming down her arm in the grip of a killer and walking crab like with the killer toward the poop.

The sight of blood stopped anyone from trying anything foolish. They reached the wheelhouse and with a vicious slash at the mate's arm, he kicked him bleeding down the short ladder to the midship deck.

Screaming again for the Captain to come forward he ordered the sheets of the fore and mainsail to be let go, bringing the bows of the

Petihoo into the wind and stop her sailing. Petihoo wallowed helplessly in the constant running swell of the strait for anyone to see.

Already the vessel astern was closing fast as though signalled. It was a raider with the clear insignia of the Kia Tong flying at the main. The letting go of the sheets on the sails was a pre-arranged signal for the raider to commence it's attack which now appeared to be closing very fast on the Petihoo.

The sight of Cheng climbing the ladder to the poop dressed in a pretty frock stunned everyone. A chorus of warning cries went out, "Go back. Go back," but that did not stop her from climbing the short ladder and calling, "Kia Kia - Kia Kia" and waving a colourful scarf over her head.

At the sight of Cheng Sui, Anna fainted, causing the maniac crew member to stagger towards Cheng at the same time he raised his knife. As he raised his arm, Cheng lowered hers and shot him three times in the face. Anna screaming and dragged to the floor by the bloody corpse was pulled clear by Cheng as Sam rushed the poop and threw the body over the side.

Cheng handing the pistol still in the folds of the scarf to Marcus leaned over the junk's side to be violently sick.

Sam now took Anna in his arms and helped her down to the mess followed by Cheng feeling better close behind.

The Captain shouted orders, for the raider was barely two miles away, Mrs Chang was banging the gong in the kitchen as the Captain pressed the starter button to fire the two diesels.

The crewmen, grabbing the sheets, set the sails in time for the mate to bring the bows around on a course away from the raider. The raider got within about a thousand yards before the Petihoo really got the feel of the wind, and the thrust from her diesels.

Marcus ordered all guns aft on the poop, using old sails as ground sheets to give a bit of grip and camouflage the gun position a little and to break the line of the poop from the enemy. Marcus and Sam, using the rifles, began a steady stream of single shots aimed accurately at deck level and the wheelhouse of the following ship, a very modified junk with very little poop aft.

Marcus did not intend to use the heavy machine guns all the time he was able to get accurate shots into the raider by rifle.

The Captain felt he had a bit of an edge over the raider, as he altered course to the West and pitched into the wind. His diesels were ticking over and the raider gained no water. Mrs Chang and Cheng were busy bringing tea around in jugs with mugs, with corned beef in thick wads of crusty bread. The whine of the occasional bullet did not deter them.

It was another two to three hours before sunset and the chance for Petihoo to slip away in the dark and avoid a fight.

Not that the raiders would give up. They wanted revenge. Marcus wanted victory.

A brief word with the Captain and Marcus was once again playing Navy games. Leaving the rifles with Wilson who was now manning the heavy machine gun, Marcus and Sam joined up with the others handling the sails. Knowing that the Petihoo had had a damn good refit at Navy expense, Captain Chang was now about to test whether the raider could take the weather.

The wind was getting up and swinging northwesterly which suited Petihoo. Her extra strong wire shrouds and stays began to sing a little, as the Captain, seeing the raider tack, immediately tacked and returned to his original course.

This went on for an hour or more, before the raider now wasting his ammunition, blasted away at the out of range Petihoo each time she tacked again. The women had retired to their bunks, whilst this tacking match went on.

The Captain then gave a wave to Marcus, who shifted all his guns back to the fo'c's'le. It was very wet forward with the wind and spray, but Wilson and Sam had no concern for the weather, but just wanted to blast those bastards to hell.

The Captain, standing outside the wheelhouse, spoke briefly to the mate at the wheel, that they were now to 'wear', which meant they were turning stern into the wind. With a wave to Marcus, he began hauling the sheets carefully, for a wear was a difficult manoeuvre if the wind and waves were misjudged.

With a bit more on the wheel, the poop began to slew sideways over the tossing sea, whilst the bow went the other way. With a sound like a clap of thunder the sail filled like a balloon until sheeted hard in by the struggling crew to get the sail under control. The gunners all ready to fire their guns on the fo'c's'le had all barrels pointing forward over the bow and at the enemy.

Aimed like an arrow, Captain Chang steered Petihoo with increasing speed straight at the raider with every gun firing and smashing the wheelhouse to pieces. With every gun still blazing they raked the decks from stem to stern as they sailed round her stern. The raider careened badly as her mast with a sail snapped and went over the side.

There was nothing to be gained by showing mercy to the boat load of cut-throats and Marcus ordered short bursts at anything that moved or looked like a cut-throat, if it was within range.

A fire started aboard the raider and the Petihoo kept her distance in case of an explosion.

The sea was now becoming rougher as the night drew in. The blaze seemed to be taking hold and there was little that Petihoo could do, but to get back on course and let the sea and wind be the grave stones of the damned.

Captain Chang ordered candles to be burnt to the spirit of Petihoo for his protection and a welcome harbour.

On board Petihoo there were no celebrations or regrets for the outcome of the fight against the raider. The Captain had asked for candles to the spirit of the Petihoo and that was all.

With the wind blowing harder from the north-west, the Captain reefed down, for the Petihoo was bludgeoning her way through a very gusty rain squall. Everyone apart from those on watch, were in their bunks. It was a rough night, but the morning brought clear skies and a warming sun which soon dried the sails. Whatever the shower had done, it had made the Petihoo as clean as a freshly built junk.

Breakfast was a family meal, with Mrs Chang herself sitting at the table with her happy brood. Everybody wanted to kiss Cheng, because she was a true heroine, brave as well as beautiful to face a manic killer. Cheng had to admit to Anna she liked being kissed by the bearded Captain Chang because he tickled her with his whiskers.

The kiss that really turned her on, came from Wilson, who, hungry for her lips, kissed her as though he had something to say.

The Mate's watch had been a stressful time for him, having never carried out the sailing tactic of a 'wear' before. He really felt a mariner after the last few hours and he could speak of pirates he had outsailed if he ever became the Captain of the Petihoo like his Uncle.

That evening as the sun was going down, Cheng and Wilson found a quiet spot on the fo'c's'le and poured out the torment each felt over the killings. Remorse was inevitable, as they sat together, holding hands swearing they would never do such a thing again!

That night, unable to sleep, Cheng crept behind the curtains to sit on the side of Wilson's bunk, just to look at his handsome face. He stirred and opened his eyes to see the beautiful face of Cheng leaning over him as though she wanted to be kissed. Thinking he was dreaming, he took her slowly into his arms, kissing her passionately for she was a beautiful sexy woman. Drawing the mosquito net curtain they snuggled up together.

With the trauma of the last two days still with them, Sam and Anna had fallen asleep in Sam's arms, comforted and reassured by his tenderness and understanding.

Sitting on the bed, Anna dreaming of making love began to undress behind the curtains, until she was naked. Feeling her own smooth skin, her firm round breasts, she could think of nothing but the soft hairy chest of her Sam and his hardness against her small flat stomach each evening. The trauma of last night had changed Anna. Tonight Anna was going to love her Sam. It might be too late tomorrow.

Sam, who had been checking the lashings in the hold, replaced the covers and then had a wash. Not seeing anyone in the mess, he thought 'what am I waiting for' and parted the curtain over the side of the bed.

Astonished, he quickly closed the curtains, for Anna was standing in the small space by the sides of the bed, naked but for her engagement ring and the bandage on her arm. With only the glow of the night light, her soft golden skin and beautiful breasts he saw together for the first time. Sam believing what he saw was not surprised when Anna reached forward, placed her arms around his neck, at the same time pressing her breasts against his chest she kissed him passionately.

Sam attempted to remove his shorts, but Anna restrained him and commenced to do it for him. Anna wanted to give everything. Sam began gently caressing her breasts. She in a quiet controlled way had a strong desire to give herself to Sam tonight saying, "Will you join me in bed, I need to be loved tonight so much."

It was not easy, with a room full of people, but their need for the best of loving had overcome them and they were rapturously happy as they kissed, suckled, fondled and explored the mysteries of their naked bodies and made love.

In the morning, Cheng gently raised their curtains to see all was well, but like the babes in the wood, they were still fast asleep in each other's arms.

It was quite late in the morning when they eventually emerged from the poop, to stand shading their eyes in the bright sunshine. If another battle had taken place, they would never have heard it, they were too much in love.

Marcus, to protect the Petihoo, had suggested a change of name for the Petihoo as a form of cover after the fight with the raider.

Captain Chang shook his head and politely said, "Her spirit has guarded us in storm and tempest, we could not cast her back to the empty sea - from now on we will call her, 'Spirit of Petihoo'."

Marcus was happy with that and they embraced like true comrades.

The weather continued bright and breezy with the 'Spirit of Petihoo' cruising along like a happy spirit. The proposed new name seemed to have affected not only the junk, but everyone on board, for the sound of an Anglo-Chinese song that evening, must have frightened the fish for miles as they sang, toasted each other, with Mrs Chang's wine as they ate a festive supper.

The first thing that Marcus spotted as he came on watch at eight the following morning was a distant white spot dead astern coming up fast. Grabbing his binoculars, he breathed a sigh of relief as he recognised the sleek light grey hull of a destroyer cutting a clean bow wave at about twenty knots. Marcus was surprised when the Captain opened a locker and produced a battery Aldis lamp and pressed the trigger a couple of times, automatically thinking that Marcus would want to signal in morse, it being a warship.

His morse was not bad, but what do you say to a U.S. destroyer in a hurry. Thinking quickly he wrote out a suitable message that he thought might interest the destroyer's captain and ordered Wilson, who was on deck, to hoist the white ensign.

It would take but a few minutes for the destroyer to close on their position, so Marcus practised his morse on the trigger until the destroyer was in range of the lamp. To show he was no amateur although not a signalman, he flashed the destroyer up first with, "What ship - where bound." Much to his surprise the reply came back a little too prompt for Marcus. "U.S. destroyer 453 - bound Shanghai."

Quickly reading his scrap of paper to get the drill right, he flashed, "Have a message for U.S. Military Police. Major J. O'Brien, U.S. Army."

"Pass your message."

"Petihoo E.T.A Shanghai. Forty eight hours. L.I.T.A.M.A.N."

A final reply from U.S. 453 flashed, "Message received and understood - Will comply - Good sailing."

Increasing her speed the destroyer cruised ahead in a wake of foaming white. It was a fresh topic to talk about in the mess.

The sight of any warship is reassuring when they are on your side and just the mention of Shanghai brought it home how far and fast they had travelled in just over eight and a half days.

The Chinese always ready to gamble, began to bet with Mrs Chang as the bookie on the exact time they would tie alongside. The usual argument broke out about what the sailors meant by tied up alongside. Was it the first rope to touch the jetty or when they were all on. Would it be better at the first touch and the mate objected, he never bumped the old Petihoo alongside. Finally they agreed that the first heaving line to touch the jetty would be declared the winner.

That was not fair either, for the women would not stand a chance. Mrs Chang calling the girls together, they whispered amongst themselves then all began laughing. Mrs Chang had been at sea too long to fall for sailors' tricks. Prompted by Mrs Chang the girls raised the stakes to one hundred dollars. It wasn't a fortune but it was fun.

Enjoying a beautiful evening the girls each spent a while with the Captain sailing the ship and using the wheel. Cheng as usual had to have a little joke, as the Captain with his arm around her slim waist, said to her in answer to a question, "Do what you like."

Taking his cap and a horn he used to shout into, she called in a strong voice for a small women she shouted the order, "Down with the mainsail."

With a crash and a bump or two, the boom with the sail, hit the deck. Gathering the sail as it came down to stop it touching the water, all the crew in a mixture of Chinese and English gave the pretty Captain, a mock demonstration of a mutinous crew.

Feeling she had done enough damage for one day, Cheng gave the Captain his cap back which she had borrowed to play the part. In order to make amends for the work she had caused during her command, Cheng added her weight to the main halyards to re-hoist the mainsail.

As they were getting closer to Shanghai, the women decided to have a washday while the weather was sunny and warm. With the help of the crew as all the normal lines used in harbour for washing had been taken down. A new line was fitted from the shroud to the back to the poop to keep clear of the sails

Having washed their coolie clothing all the women, including Mrs Chang, changed into frocks which certainly pleased the crew. Mrs

Chang protested a little when Anna and Cheng suggested she, Mrs Chang, should put on a little make-up. With the girls help and a ribbon in her hair, Mrs Chang was a changed woman. Gone was the galley slave and instead a charming smiling woman, with a saucy Chinese wink.

It didn't take the sailors on board the three passing U.S. destroyers coming from Shanghai, to spot the underwear and ladies tit-bits hanging on the line, as they passed port side to port side to the Petihoo.

The women now standing on the poop, waving gaily to each ship as it passed, must have touched many a sailor's heart, for the girls they had left behind.

For all the problems that may lie ahead for Marcus and his crew, Captain and Mrs Chang were glad to be home for the sake of the children. With things as they are, Shanghai did not promise much of a future for them.

Living on a junk was great fun, but having seen a little of Hong Kong, it was now the time for them to think of the future. Their eldest son was now eleven, a difficult age for a child in Shanghai. Putting these thoughts to one side, Captain Chang prepared to alter course and enter the mouth of the Huangpu river where they had a permanent berth alongside.

Marcus had no idea how long he would be ashore settling his affairs, although he did promise that he would not be hanging around too long.

Captain Chang had his worries for although he had been paid for his cargo, he had to wait for it to be collected.

The Municipal officers were not renowned for their efficiency. Another worry, he wanted to get rid of his berth and buy another, away from where the Kia Kia had been berthed just ahead. If the Tong owned the boat, it followed that they also owned the jetty and controlled the rents. If there were any survivors from the boat they had left burning, he knew he had signed his own death warrant and possibly that of his beautiful family.

Before going alongside, they dropped the little dinghy with a member of the crew to land ashore and catch the heaving lines. These would be used to haul the heavier lines ashore and make fast to the bollards on the jetty. Mrs Chang of course was the sweepstake judge.

The run of the water down the river was not very fast and the rudder swung the Petihoo alongside her berth very easily. She was so close in fact that Anna abetted by Mrs Chang followed the position of the crewman ashore.

When the diesels gave a kick astern, helped by the run of the river, the Petihoo closed the jetty. With a piece of string on the end of a bamboo pole, Anna called the crewman ashore and reached out with her pole and handed the crew her piece of string. In no time the string was hauled in and the first hawse attached.

Cries of "Cheat" went up, but Mrs Chang wouldn't listen, and handed the money to Anna, thinking, "There you are dear, you'll need more than that when you get married."

On the jetty, standing quietly, were a small group of people, amongst whom were the Chang children, waving little flags of welcome, and racing up the gangboard as soon as it touched the jetty.

Leaving the mate to secure the Petihoo the Captain in his new cap and Captain's jacket, was mobbed by their overjoyed children to see them safely back. It was then Mrs Chang's turn, and picking up the smallest, she hugged them all in turn. The next on board was Joe, the Major, followed by Lita, who gave Marcus a passionate reception, hardly believing he had returned so soon. Captain Chang with a polite tap tap on the shoulder, also wanted to meet the pretty lady.

Joe always thoughtful brought along something to celebrate with when the families all gathered in the mess. Sergeant Borkowski and Benjamin soon arrived by jeep followed by Chung, Marcus's driver and the beloved ex-navy jeep. Chung the driver in Marcus's jeep had two passengers, Ma Pang and sister Lee. Mr Pang being detailed to look after the laundry.

The reception party was a big surprise to all the crew and it was all due to Borkowski who had deciphered the message from the Navy very quickly and acted on it straight away. Borkowski told them he would have brought Am Ling the cook, but Mrs Pang would never have travelled in the same jeep. She still thought Am Ling's evil spirit had something to do with Anna fleeing to Hong Kong.

Mrs Pang enjoying seeing Anna so soon was astonished how grown up her daughter had become. Worried about her husband, who was not a well man, she had to leave early. Lee, after much pleading to her Mother, was allowed to stay the night on board and sleep in one of the bunks.

Lee had grown up a lot since Anna had left, but seeing Anna she was soon her happy self after a small cup of Champagne.

Wilson was also staying on board for they had a lot to be grateful for to the Captain and his wife had made everything possible for Sam and himself. There were the children to welcome also with a pile of presents in the hold.

Marcus left in Joe's official car to stay with the Jung's at their restaurant.

The family party now began with Borkowski having a gamble playing with the children losing at dice and forgetting his drink. Sam, Wilson, Cheng, Anna, Lee, Benjamin, the Mate and crewman, were all present for supper whilst the children, all gathered on the Captain's bed, were busy undoing parcels of goodies with coloured wrapping paper everywhere. It was getting late but no one cared. They were home again.

Marcus did not mention diamonds to Joe or the others at Jung's restaurant, he merely mentioned that they had forgotten to clear the safe. Marcus had found Lita almost deliriously happy to have him back, for things had been horrific in his absence, with so called conscripts in uniform without officers walking into the restaurant on the pretext of looking for deserters or criminals.

It was them who were the criminals and fights with the police using firearms were quite common, when the civil authorities tried to keep law and order in this large metropolis.

Lita really thought that Marcus had come to take her away. Lita didn't seem to mind where, but she loved him and had despaired that she would never see Marcus again. In her own mind, she was prepared to return to Hong Kong with Marcus this time just to be by his side. Even Joe who for all his war-time experience, found the murders, riots and violence too much when your own loved ones are involved.

Una had already left and was home with the two boys in Seattle, and waited for Joe's tour of duty in China to come to an end.

Communism was as inevitable as the sunrise, although it might take a little longer.

Mr Jung could not bring himself to leave China forever. He was old and even Taiwan seemed to be on the other side of the world. Perhaps if Lita were to think more of herself, it may prompt them to follow their children before it was too late.

It is not surprising how quickly, everything seemed to revert to normal in the morning aboard the Petihoo.

Breakfast over, the children running around the junk, playing with their toys, with Sam and Anna waiting for Lee to say her goodbyes before Chung ran them all home by jeep to see Papa.

Chung who had slept with the crew last night, having joined the welcoming party and forgotten already it was no longer Marcus' jeep.

Captain Chang, dressed in uniform was anxious about his cargo. Wilson felt as a member of the crew he should go along with the Captain to the Custom Headquarters, taking Cheng with him to see if they could speed things up. It was a bit of a long shot, but a pretty face can make a difference, it was worth a try.

The 'Spirit of Petihoo' must have been with them, for Cheng wearing a classical Chinese frock, given to her by Yvonne, looked gorgeous. Sitting on benches in a grubby hall way in Customs Headquarters, Cheng became a little irritated by gawky officers looking and grinning as they passed. Seeing an important looking door with a sign saying, 'Chief Custom Officer' she tapped lightly on the door and walked in.

It was about ten minutes later that Wilson, worried about her, gently opened the door to peep in. Cheng sitting on the Chief's desk showing her beautiful legs was just finishing off some sad tale saying, "Daddy's been away so long, and you're such a comfort to me," allowing the Chief to fondle her thighs.

A little later, Cheng appeared at the doorway and waved the Captain to stand in the doorway. In his cap and coat he looked quite distinguished with his short grey beard and four rings of gold on each arm.

With a bow to the Captain and a smile to Cheng, the Chief of Customs quietly closed the door. Wilson, a bit perplexed looked at Cheng with a hurt expression, thinking she had sacrificed all. Cheng patting his cheek and waving a piece of paper under his nose, said cheerfully, "Don't worry, I did it for my sea-daddy."

Taking the Captain's arm, she left Wilson to follow.

Armed with the Custom clearance, the trio entered the Municipality Buildings, a sprawling mess of offices away from the Bund. The reception area was like a market, except it held cubby holed offices, with queues of people standing patiently to be attended to at a number of hatchways.

An undistinguished person in a drab uniform thought he was important until he saw the Captain standing apart dressed in his uniform with a humble foreigner cringing by his side.

He approached, but never reached the Captain, for Cheng like a good secretary, barred his way, at the same time asked Wilson to gabble anything in English but mention Hong Kong a lot.

Doing exactly what he was told, he held up his naval paybook as though is was a pass, returned it quickly to his inside pocket and recited a sailor's version of 'Shanghai Lil' with a lot of Hong Kong thrown in.

Automatically the doorman or porter or whatever he was, pointed to a door. Wilson said to himself, "I hope it is not a toilet" and following the pointed finger he headed for a distant door.

Once inside, Wilson followed by the Captain then Cheng, bowed and smiled with all the charm they had. The woman inside rose from her desk, and with a straight face, looked at the bar of chocolate Wilson had produced from his pocket and was now offering it to her.

It had been in the selection he had brought for the children in Hong Kong. It was a well known make and a great favourite with the Chinese in Hong Kong.

With a glance at Wilson's smiling face, she hesitated, opened a top drawer and then popped it in. Taking the Custom form from Wilson, she glanced at it, picked up the telephone and made two calls in rapid Chinese. Replacing the phone she then signed a copy of an authority to remove the cargo.

Handing the form to Wilson with a smile, he bowed slowly and in Chinese, with a strong English accent said, "Wo xiang Li Fa."

The lady looked at Cheng and then spoke rapidly in Chinese, the two women bowed and smiled, "I humbly beg you to forgive his mistake, he is learning to speak our language."

Taking the form, Wilson bowed as though she was most important.

Once they were outside, Captain Chang and Cheng were laughing at some huge joke which Wilson did not understand until Cheng said, "Why did you ask her for a haircut?"

Wilson smiled, "That was Sam, he told me to say that!"

Everyone seemed to be happy with the morning's work. Even Chung who hadn't a very interesting job just waiting, was grinning like a chinese cat. He too, had his bit of fun. He told the porter, "My Captain drives a battleship."

Having managed so well in the morning, Wilson told Chung to give the Captain and his family a tour of Shanghai, but avoiding the trouble spots.

They admired the large and crumbling buildings as they drove around the City. It was difficult to find Mrs Chang once they entered the Shopping area in the Nanjing Road. Although she lived here, this was a pleasure she had never enjoyed. A shopping centre and dollars in her purse. Her one desire had been a dressing gown, Mrs Chang bought two. One marked HIM and one marked HER, one with dragons, the other with water lilies..

When they reached Remin Park, the children never stopped running, for they had never seen such an open space to play before. There were small animals in cages, birds in aviaries, and flowers everywhere.

There were other parks too, but one was enough. Sitting in the jeep with the Captain in uniform gave them special pleasure. Many people bowed as they passed, and children waved. It was all great fun for the children.

That evening they dined with Wilson and Cheng as a family, while Anna and Sam were spending the evening with the Pang family.

The next day the cargo was removed without the crew doing anything much, apart from putting extra lashing on the two gangboards required by the coolies to unload the cargo.

Wilson and Sam were merely spectators as they watched the frail looking coolies lifting the heavy boxes with apparent ease. To protect their bodies they each allowed a piece of rag as a sweat rag. If Mrs Chang had been allowed, she would have provided tea or some refreshment, but a bucket of water with a tin mug attached was as much as the gang leader would allow,

Marcus, Wilson and Sam were all anxious to visit the workshop premises to see that it was still standing in one piece. Joe thought that unwise, knowing something about squatters. According to him they were nothing but gangs of villains, who infested the buildings they took over and one could just disappear once inside.

It was better to get a Chinese squatter and pay him to tell you who was in your own building. Any building like this left more than a week, would soon be occupied by these human rats. It took a whole night for the squatter to re-appear and report and even he had been beaten up.

It was occupied by three separate squats, two families and a gang. The gang collected the rent and forced other squatters to beg with tins they marked.

A slash across the face with a knife left a mark they could not hide when the callers arrived on their pitch to collect the cash. He the spy had been lucky. They just robbed him of the fee he had paid and allowed him to squat for one night.

Marcus looking at his bruised face felt a little guilty but the man had to eat and refunded the squatter and gave him a bonus. If you hired a Tong, there was only one price and that was the building became theirs.

There was one way of getting possession and Joe provided it. The Chief of Police who smoked 'Camel' cigarettes when he could get them. He was suspicious as soon as Joe offered him a 'Camel' cigarette.

"I've smoked the last lot you gave me, and they didn't last very long."

Joe then went into a rambling story about his friend Pierre who had left Shanghai in a hurry, who was a chain smoker like the Chief but he preferred his pipes.

He wasn't worried about the cigarettes in the safe, although he liked one occasionally. He was worried about his pipes, because a smoke is not the same when you have had your pipes for years.

Joe lying like a trooper said, "He told me I can have the cigarettes if I get his pipes."

The Chief said, "Don't worry about that, I'll go down and get them, just give me the keys."

Holding out his hand. Joe said, "I can't do that Chief," and then whispered in his ear.

The Chief of Police had a few little rackets, but despised the squalid work which he left to his juniors, particularly anything to do with sex. Looking at Joe with a straight face he said, "That is filth and disgusting, get them out before I inspect the safe."

The clearance of the squat began just before it began to get dark. A bus load of police armed with batons and iron tipped bamboo staves arrived and just charged straight into the building, shouting and hitting out at everyone they saw.

It became bedlam within a minute or two as they charged up the stairs to drive half naked bodies from the bedrooms. Those they couldn't move or deep into a drugged state were dragged and simply thrown down the stairs.

While this was going on, Joe and Marcus using Pierre's keys opened the steel doors to the inner lounge, told the policeman to stand outside on guard whilst they emptied the safe inside into one sack, and filled the safe with 'Camel' cigarettes from a box they had brought with them.

Joe then moved outside holding a couple of brown envelopes told the policeman to fetch the Chief. The Chief arrived, entered and cleared the contents of the safe with a sack provided and handed the sack to the policeman, with orders to guard the evidence with his life, until it was safely in the Chief's car.

The shouting and beating was still going on as Marcus and Joe drove away. Joe kept laughing to himself on the way to the boat and Marcus asked if he could share the joke, Joe replied, "The Chief hates dirty pornography, that is why I emptied the safe first - I told him the safe was full of nudes and naked photos of Yvonne, Pierre's wife, which he didn't want to fall into the wrong hands. I told him Pierre was French and funny that way."

To make the Chief's day more enjoyable still, as he sat at his desk puffing a cigarette with cupboard full of 'Camel' tucked away. The Chief had bagged two wanted murderers among the squatters raid and he might even get a medal, the lucky chap.

Following Pierre's instructions, Marcus showed the bag he had collected to Wilson who, after all was Pierre's representative.

Together they looked inside to inspect the contents.

Inside were numerous small chamois bags, all coded and brand new. Wilson selected one, gently pulled the knotted cord at the neck of the bag. Into his hand rolled a number of smaller bags each containing a quantity of sorted beautiful diamonds.

They looked in awe, at the fortune they were holding. Marcus thinking dolefully of his miserable service pay, said to Wilson with Lita in mind, "Do you think he would miss a little bag or two?"

Wilson made no comment at first, but still looking at the diamonds in his hand he said, "On behalf of the company, which I represent, I have the honour to present you with the Order of Petihoo," and tipped four diamonds into Marcus's hand.

Marcus holding more wealth in one hand than he had ever seen said sternly, "No, you can't do that!"

Wilson chuckled, saying, "You might have been able to say that last week Marcus, but I am a partner in the firm now with discretionary authority and am entitled to reward outstanding service to the company."

Looking at each other, Wilson was now the boss and he said hopefully to Marcus, "Why don't you marry Lita and we will treat it as an early wedding present - Don't forget the invitation!"

Marcus's eyebrows went up as he retorted, "What about yourself Wilson?"

Wilson glancing around, although they were alone in the wheelhouse said softly, "Do not tell anyone, only Pierre and I are suppose to be the only ones to know, but it's a partnership baby!"

They both nodded confidently and Marcus somewhat reluctantly pocketed the diamonds.

There were no tears or sadness at the restaurant that night, when Lita announced that she was returning to Hong Kong with Marcus when he sailed in the Petihoo.

It was only right that a mother and child should be with the husband. This was one out of the blue for Marcus but a natural outcome for two people like Marcus and Lita, so much in love with each other. It was not the break-up of the Jung family after all. With their eldest grandchildren already at school in Joe's home town, Seattle, a service base for the Major.

With Marcus's own family just across the San Juan Strait to British Columbia they were not all that far apart. It was but a short ferry to beautiful Vancouver where Marcus's Canadian father still lived. Mrs and Mrs Jung would travel with Joe when he returned to the States at the end of his tour of duty.

The excellent cuisine on which the restaurant had built its outstanding reputation, was impossible to maintain. The bothersome intrusions by hordes of flies from the smelling streets and drains, overcame the sweet smelling flowers in the surrounding gardens which had given them all so much pleasure under the watchful eye of Una and her friend the old gardener, was gone forever. Squatters had set camp and were too numerous to move.

That Petihoo was still a target for the Kia Kia Tong, did not deter Captain Chang in any way from sailing the China seas. Little did he know that his reputation had spread from Hong Kong to Shanghai and his junk was rumoured to be capable of sinking a warship. Marcus through his friend Sergeant Borkowski could have enough guns and ammunition to sink the Chinese navy. Marcus enjoyed sailing the Petihoo almost as much as Captain Chang.

He knew he could do something to increase her speed under sail, but did not want to offend a damned good shipmate.

It was a passing sea-going yacht, obviously damaged in the recent typhoon and on its way to the breakers that gave him the idea.

Taking the sampan, he and the Chinese mate found the breakers about a mile up river. With a lot of haggling between the Mate and the owner, Marcus and he came away with two aluminium booms, a Genoa, two foresails and a quantity of good quality running rigging and block suitable for sheets to attach to the booms.

Marcus was taking such an interest in the Petihoo, that the Captain and Marcus became like two contenders for the America with experimental sails being hoisted up and down on all masts as new halyards were fitted with one of the crew up the mast. Neat sheeved tackles for the sheets were fitted which improved the skill of those handling her. Safety lines for moving about the decks, gave special attention to the needs of the women and children.

Mrs Chang, apart from fresh vegetables, bread and things for the children was well stocked up from her shopping and the generous amounts of tinned food supplied by the base in Hong Kong.

Sleeping arrangements were still a little cramped, with Lita using the bridal bed with Marcus when he was not on watch.

The girls in the starboard bunks, with the children in the port bunks when not in mothers bed. Wilson and Sam used camp beds nearest to the girls side.

More often than not the children were found in the sail locker, in the stern building canvas tents like a camp, each to his own tent.

The day before sailing was rather quiet on board, with the Pang family having their last few hours with Anna and Sam, with a tearful sister Lee, comforted by the thought that she might be in Hong Kong herself for the wedding.

Am Ling for the first time invited to the Pang's home, wept.

Joe able to comfort Lita's mother with promise of photographs of Sam and Lita when they got married. With Sergeant Borkowski, Chung and Benjamin, Joe's Chinese drivers turned up with Anna's parents in one jeep and a happy smiling Am Ling and Lee in the other. Am Ling and Lee were now close friends and often got their heads together when lighting the copper.

Petihoo slipping the ropes, eased out of her berth without using the engines until they were well down stream. Heading out to sea they passed the fishing fleet at full speed to be past them by dawn hoping they had cleared Shanghai without notice of her departure.

Borkowski had brought enough toys to keep the children happy for a world cruise, whilst a new small boat that acted as a safe place for the children to play in the fresh air.

The hum of the diesels and bubble of the exhausts throbbing through the Petihoo, soon gave them plenty to see looking back on Shanghai, larger ships at sea and the moonlight and stars making it pleasant to be on deck. Lita was enthralled to see Marcus at the wheel in the morning after they had set the experimental rig to the sails.

There was little point in experimenting at night except for tuning in a radio that Marcus had been given by Joe. It had good batteries according to Joe and with a little sensitive tuning it could get most stations including some from America. It had to be put on a shelf with brackets to secure it because the children who had not played with one before, could not resist twiddling the knobs no matter how often they were told.

Captain Chang was joined on the bridge by Lita, Marcus, Sam, Wilson, Anna and Cheng, to watch Shanghai glowing in the distance, whilst around were ships like themselves bound for places far across the China seas.

There was a moon shining, encouraging lovers to cuddle, for the breeze was quite fresh, but not too warm. No one showed much inclination to go below, until a loud rattle on the roof of the galley below signalled that supper was ready. The mate, having already eaten, took over the watch so they could all eat together.

How Mrs Chang coped in that small galley, was a system based on neatness and fortitude for it was always hot and two portholes to get rid of leavings. The centre of the table was covered with a large fiddle, a device for holding all the food dishes still, but leaving enough room around the edge of the table for people to place their bowl and eat in comfort.

The only one who cheated and did not use chopsticks was Wilson. He had an excuse, for Chang's youngest daughter had developed a strong liking for him and on occasions like this, delighted on sitting on his knee and eating out of his bowl. Using a spoon, Wilson just about got a fair share of the food.

Everyone seemed to have a good night's sleep and at breakfast conversation became more general as duties had to be sorted out. With everyone in their coolie suits, headbands and scarfs, they couldn't really be taken for pirates, for they were all too clean.

It was important however, that they looked like junk dwellers. Even Captain Chang had discarded his uniform for a more disreputable appearance, whilst Marcus, Wilson and Sam, could have done justice as having been press ganged from some seedy dive in Shanghai.

Lita looking quite pretty even in a cut down camouflage shirt thought Marcus looked awful unshaven and with his brown hair blackened. She asked him, "Are you sure the Royal Navy is your chosen career, you look like the man who delivers the coal!"

Taking advantage of the remark, he seized a banana from the fruit bowl, for they were still seated at the table, he held it to her pretty throat, saying, "Kiss me Lotus flower and don't say no, I am a member of the dreaded Petihoo!"

His acting was corny, but he still got a kiss.

The Petihoo nice and steady with a good breeze, was ideal for Marcus and the Captain to try out their sail improvements.

The Captain from the bridge would order, "Change sails." With the crew and Marcus carrying out the change of sail as if they were competing in the America's Cup.

The Genoa, a larger curved sail did wonders twinned with the properly cut foresail on their present course and you could feel the extra surge, as Petihoo now straight, goose winged her way through the Pharmacy Straits.

Coaxing the extra bit of speed from Petihoo, resulted in Marcus becoming more musical as he began to sing sea shanties.

It was not long before the children picked up the opening line of, 'What shall we do with the drunken sailor' - 'Billy Boy' - 'Shenandoah'.

Then the girls joined in and it sounded as though the first bi-lingual choir to be heard on the China Sea had been born.

Captain Chang was heard singing to himself, when on his own watch. He had one line and that was, 'Where have you been all the day, Billy Boy', but he always stopped if he thought anyone was listening.

They were sailing closer to the centre of the Pharmacy Strait, with the wind veering a little to the West and the Genoa pulling and the speed and course steady. The sea itself was a little rougher with plenty of splash and thump as Petihoo breasted the waves with her rugged bow.

The shout, "Man Overboard" from Sam, struck a chill as he waved to the bridge before diving from the gunwale into the choppy sea.

Wilson went to join him, but Marcus said, "Hold it!" letting fly the main sheets, the Helmsman spun the wheel. The head of the mate, the Captain's cousin could be seen bobbing astern with Sam swimming strongly towards him.

The whine of diesels starting up and the shudder throughout the whole of the Petihoo as the screws began to churn at the water and stop the plunging junk. The flapping genoa was gathered in once free of the wind and swinging like a yacht round the mark, the Chinese helmsman straightened up and headed for the two swimmers now together in the choppy water.

Coming into the wind they approached the swimmers with Wilson already over the side with a life line to help in the tossing waters. Taking the mate from Sam they were hauled aboard together over the gunwale amidships. Sam needed a hand for although he had not been in the water long, he was quite exhausted. It was as well the accident had happened when it did in the Formosa Strait, for the wind began to back more westerly after the sails were set driving them on even faster.

These were dangerous waters and whilst the wind was favourable, it was as well to press on.

The Captain requested that before supper a candle to the 'Spirit of Petihoo' should be burnt briefly by all, to thank the 'Spirit of Petihoo' for handing back his mate.

The wine was passed that night and led by Sam and Wilson who were given an extra tot or two, the Petihoo Chinese chorus once again broke into song.

That was not the only noise that night as the wind increased a little and the pounding on the hull by the short, wind driven waves, defied all but the children to get a good night's sleep.

Cheng did not like the sleeping arrangements very much, for she found Wilson a tender and lingering lover. She had hoped there would be plenty of opportunity to encourage him to appreciate her obvious charm. Cheng half guessed that Yvonnes' pregnancy was no fluke, and the way Yvonne had looked at Wilson, throughout the previous trip, had tempted Cheng to tease Wilson by saying, "Hullo - Daddy!" but she never did.

Looking down on Wilson's sleeping form below her, she thought, "Wouldn't it be nice if I could get Anna, now sleeping in the bottom bunk, to change over. Wilson and I could make love for the rest of the trip."

Not being able to sleep, Cheng tried a few positions for sex within the confines of the bunk with Wilson, who was very well built.

There were many sleepy heads in the morning, although the sea had calmed down a little. The Petihoo with her extra sails was once again sailing on quite fast.

Cheng and Anna sitting at breakfast, both complained it had been a rough night, Cheng made the most of it, by saying, "I was sick twice last night, and found it terribly difficult to get out of the top bunk, to reach the toilet buckets, I really feel awful this morning. If I was tall like you, it would not be so bad!"

Anna, always thoughtful, suggested, "If you like, I will use the top bunk."

Cheng sounded grateful saying, "Anna I may get some sleep tonight, you are so sweet."

Cheng, having really had a bad night, stayed in her new bunk, resting.

Wilson noticed alright, for he often got a look at Cheng's gorgeous legs, whenever she climbed into the upper bunk, curtains, or no curtains. Cheng targeted Wilson for supper and sitting next to him, said softly, "I'm feeling much better now, the sea seems much calmer. Are we still racing along?"

Wilson tucking into supper, looked at her saying, "Cheng I am sorry, I didn't know you had been unwell, it was a bit blustery last night, but we have been sailing very fast, that's what all the bumping was about."

Cheng then mentioned Anna, "Anna knows I was not well, or rather, I was a bit scared last night, so we have changed bunks, she is taller than poor little me."

Wilson looked at her and wanted her as badly as she needed him, encouraging her he said, "Lucky little girl, you'll be sleeping next to me tonight."

Cheng looking in a way no man could mistake and feeling her breast, said softly, "You were so brave yesterday, I wanted to kiss you."

Wilson warming to her said, "That was nothing, Sam did all the swimming not me! He's the one to thank."

Cheng then said in a naughty tone, "But you're the one that nearly lost your pants, I saw your bottom as you were getting out!"

With a grin on his face, he said, "I'll see you later."

The wind changed in the afternoon and was now blowing from the North West. Captain Chang left the bridge and with Marcus, they decided to reset the sails.

Down came the Genoa and with a new large jib on one side and the mainsail on the other spread like wings, the Petihoo surged ahead with the stronger following breeze. The Captain commented, "I have never sailed her so fast since she was built, I think we could set a record if we tried."

Giving a token pull on the new sheets attached to the sail boom and testing the tension in the extra shrouds to the mast he said to Marcus, "All we have to do is steer her!"

A sighting by Marcus of a ship following from astern, was no more than the Captain had expected. It was probably known by every junk in the Huangpua that the Petihoo had slipped her berth quietly during the night and was heading South. Checking their position on the chart, the Captain left Marcus, who had the first watch, in charge. With a look at the billowing sails and a glance at the vessel astern, Marcus was confident that they were maintaining the lead by just using the sails alone.

The mess was a picture of dancing shadows in the glow of the dimmed night light.

Pushing aside the hanging net Cheng, in a brief slip, moved from the bunk two or three paces and showing a generous view of her shapely legs, tickled Wilson's nose with her toes. In the dimmed light beckoning him with her finger as she drifted back through the curtains.

Wilson who had been half expecting a call, slipping quietly through the curtains he joined her in the bunk. Cheng in a kneeling position at the bottom of the bunk took his right leg and placed it near to the ship's side.

Leaning forward until her warm nipples touched his chest she whispered, "Can I have a ride to Hong Kong!" as she eased herself gently forward.

With the gentle rolling motion of the Petihoo, they rose and fell to the rhythm of the sea. The spirit of Petihoo was with them.

Wilson was a little overcome when, after a vibrant session, Cheng whispered in his ear, something that brought their trip to Hong Kong to an abrupt end.

"Will you marry me if I am pregnant, we haven't used a French letter."

Wilson who had been having a wonderful time with this young beautiful girl, suddenly became panicky, as visions of Yvonne and his whole future with Pierre flashed through his mind. With a few sleepy platitudes, he eased his way out of the bunk, thinking to himself. "Now, what have I done?"

Wilson's troubles were not yet over. Sam who had been on watch as helmsman, with Marcus, had now been relieved by the Chinese crewman with the mate in charge of the middle watch until four a.m. It had been the practice of Sam when he came off watch to creep into Anna's bunk for a brief cuddle and kiss.

It was beautiful to hold each other if only for a while although Anna had forgotten to tell Sam that she had changed bunks with Cheng.

Marcus and Lita had gone to bed early and were asleep, by the time Sam got courting.

Sam and Wilson each wore a vest and shorts in bed and were similar in build in may ways.

It came as no surprise to Cheng, and thinking that Wilson had come back again, began to feel desire, but unlike Anna, she quickly removed Sam's pants and he in a state of disbelief, just laid back and enjoyed it.

Sam later in muffled whisper to his now sleeping partner said, "Anna, I love you" and dozed off.

Before he woke up to get his pants, a shouting voice called, "All hands on deck" and the banging of the plank followed by bonging of the gong from the kitchen, brought everybody out of bed at the same time.

Astonished cries from Anna were heard. "What are you two doing in bed together!"

Sam now dressed went to calm Anna, but she cried, "Don't touch me you filthy beast, to think I have kept myself for you."

Dressed, Anna made for the door.

Sam called desperately, "I thought I was in bed with you!"

Then they all ran out to answer the "All hands on deck" call.

It was the Captain, who coming down from the bridge informed them that there was more trouble astern. A vessel astern had overnight closed to within three to four miles by using her engines. It could be friendly but using your engines in that way at night was highly suspicious. It was not the first time Petihoo had been attacked, but they were now confident of protecting themselves.

Mrs Chang giving the girls a revolver each and a first aid bag, then sent Anna to the wheelhouse to act as interpreter for Marcus whilst Cheng with Mrs Chang armed prepared to repel any boarders.

The children stayed in bed, not interested in pulling up sails in the middle of the night.

CHAPTER 13

Preparing the guns, Wilson unpacked the mortar that Sergeant Borkowski had brought aboard. The projectiles seemed pretty big and Wilson had no idea of the range of the weapon. With the Captain's permission he rigged it up on the poop and fired one projectile over the starboard side. It travelled about eight hundred yards before exploding on touching the water.

"I'm going to enjoy this if anyone comes near us, they'll get more than they bargain for!"

All the guns were fired to test them. The after mizzen sail was taken down to clear the firing arcs and to avoid the swinging of the boom over the heads of the gunners. There was a great deal of tension building up in the Petihoo, which did not come from the fact that someone was following them.

Wilson was beginning to wish he had not slept with Cheng at all, after what she had said about marriage.

Anna had seen Sam with her own eyes in the bunk with Cheng who, having two lovers in one night, hoped it would all happen again. It was Lita with her worldly approach who soon put matters right when hearing of the change of bunks by the two girls. It was Yvonne who had sent Cheng to look after Wilson her lover.

Only Cheng knew that Sam had been seduced, for he had been rather innocent about sex, apart from his lesson from Cheng. His marriage would be all the better for that. Cheng advised by Lita to forget it ever happened between Sam and herself, for that was pure accident. Cheng did not want to ruin a perfect marriage.

Marcus was putting his heart and soul into sailing the Petihoo. With small adjustments and modifications to the sails and the rigging, he and the Captain coaxed the best from the Petihoo. Even if they were wrong and it was just another junk like themselves going about their lawful business, the thrill of competing, like the tea clippers of old was close to every sailor's heart.

Cheng, after last night and the call "All hands on deck" had retired to her bunk and had not joined the conversation at supper time.

Sam spoke with greater confidence. As far as he was concerned, he was tired when he came off watch, he went over to the lower bunk for what was a few moments with his fiance and fell asleep. That he had an erotic dream, was not a suitable topic for mixed company.

Anna herself was troubled, for having jumped to the conclusion that Sam would do such a thing. It was her fault for not telling Sam she had changed bunks.

Slowly the misunderstanding resolved itself and wanting to forget the matter, everyone was apologising to Cheng who was now seated for supper. Cheng didn't look unwell at all and smiled as though very pleased with herself.

Both Sam and Wilson were busy this evening checking the guns, making sure they were properly covered and the ammunition handy. Practising in the dark and rigging the mortar to fire astern was all good practice, but neither of them thought they had a chance in hell of ever hitting anything with it. Marcus thought otherwise.

It must have been a hangover from the war, but Marcus could not help scanning the horizon at night. He was alert and not likely to be caught napping and seemed to be keen for any action to begin. Suddenly, having decided the time was right, he pressed the starter button to run the engines. With the thrust of the propeller and the pull of the sails, Petihoo again began forging ahead into the dark night. He knew it was cheating if you were in a yacht race, but this game was something much more deadly.

Marcus never left the bridge that night, even when the Captain arrived at midnight to take over for the middle watch. Curling up on his bunk under the chart table, he managed a couple of uneasy hours dozing.

Marcus could only think, the Spirit of the Petihoo was working overtime tonight, for some unknown reason, he got up at roughly three twenty a.m. and picked up the binoculars. There astern, with a pluming bow wave, he could plainly see the low hull of a raider, no longer under sail, bearing down on them.

He touched the Captain, pointed, and opened the throttle of the diesels to full power. Mrs Chang immediately hit the gong. Within seconds, Wilson and Sam were on the poop, loaded and with guns already cocked, searching for the target. Marcus ordered them to hold fire until he had loaded the mortar.

The mortar sight was useless at night, but he estimated the range and elevation, removed the caps from three bombs and just let them go.

'Thump, Thump, Thump', Marcus heard them explode, but they could not be seen. Marcus adjusted the elevation to shorten the range and fired off three more bombs. Marcus saw the flash of one explosion, then another, each being short of the target. He now halved the range between the two last shots, and banged off half a dozen bombs. Marcus was sure, he had at least one or two hits.

With the engines now on full power the Petihoo was keeping her distance from the enemy. Wilson and Sam then began firing in short accurate bursts at a point above the pluming bow wave which could easily be seen.

There was the occasional whine of a bullet, but this gave Sam and Wilson a better target for the flashes made good aiming points.

Marcus, being a big gun enthusiast, began loading and firing continuously, fiddling with the ranging and bearing, with every few shots. The raider turned to disengage, but turning with her, Petihoo's Captain Chang showed better seamanship, knowing his own ship.

For the first time he interfered with Marcus's gunnery by screaming frantically like a Chinese war lord, "Fire, Fire, Fire," repeating it in Chinese as he took the helm himself, steering directly at the raider. Marcus continued to fire with everything. Sam now using one of the heavy machine guns but couldn't help thinking, "Oh God, the old man's lost his marbles!" as Captain Chang continued cursing.

The Petihoo looked enormous with her goose winged sails slopping and flapping like some giant bird of prey, as she bore down on the raider, driven by her powerful diesels.

The panic in the raider started long before Captain Chang slewed away, with all guns blazing. Getting well clear, the Captain did not waste time looking for survivors, he altered course, picked up the wind and sailed away.

It was not until they were well clear that Sam realized that Wilson had been shot and lost a lot of blood. Clearing the table used for navigation, they quickly stripped him and found the bloody track of a bullet down his back and through his buttocks. He also had a head wound. Lita, who had been a temporary nurse and Marcus between them dressed his wounds on the bridge. Wilson said he felt comfortable with the pillows from the bunk below. In the first aid bag (U.S. Army property) there were sleep inducing pills.

Tucked up for the night, laying on his stomach with a pretty nurse below in a bunk, it was as good as some hospitals.

Next morning he didn't get any sympathy from Sam or Marcus, who kept pulling his leg about getting shot in the backside.

Sam said, "Even if you tell your children you got the scar being chased by pirates, they would not tell their friends. Who wants a father who had been shot in the bum, they will think you were running away."

Maintaining a good rate of progress and still with a North West breeze, they were soon well away from the area where the attack took place.

Wilson had a steady stream of visitors, all willing to give him a towel bath.

The children were very serious about him being shot at first, but it didn't take long for them to get round to ask, "Where are the bullet holes?"

The children were very disappointed when Wilson turned back the blanket to show the bandaged bum. They couldn't see any bullet hole.

Candles were burnt to The Spirit of Petihoo and a special one from the children, to make Wilson's bum better.

Wilson's confinement to the wheelhouse gave him and Cheng a chance to talk things over for she admitted to wanting him badly and that she was a little jealous of Yvonne who seemed to get everything.

Wilson trying to think his way out of the possible trouble he was in, thought, "I wonder if Pierre would like another love child?" It would be a nice playmate for the other baby.

Wilson did not feel too bad about the bullet, it had the effect of keeping him from further trouble with the girls.

With less than seventy-two hours to go before they arrived in Hong Kong, everyone wanted to enjoy the experience of being a member of a deep sea crew of a fighting junk. The fresh air and physical work of tending the sails was now as much a pastime for the women as for the men. Today, for the fun of it, was women's day, with Mrs Chang and Lita taking charge and sailing the Petihoo with the girls repeating the order on deck, "sheet in" or "ease out" and generally controlling the shape and pulling power of all sails with a little extra pull now and then from the men. The children also joined in with much singing of, "What shall we do with the drunken sailor."

The Captain, who had been relegated to the galley, came up with his version of oriental fish kebabs with small, half-ripe tomatoes and onions with a pile of rice and vegetables. It must have taken all the afternoon to prepare the kebabs, the dishes were completely overflowing with food and woe betide anyone that stopped eating.

Leaving the memories of the Formosa Strait behind, they had now sailed far enough down the China coast to see the lights of Shant'ou to starboard, having left the light of Penghu now some distance astern to port.

With the wind still blowing steadily and without tacking, they altered course to starboard, making a dead reckoning bearing on the island of Hong Kong, although passing closer to the coast of China than at any time during the trip.

An air of excitement was already building up as the children saw distant lights and ships to starboard and made a game of running up and down the ladder to the Captain, asking, "Is that Hong Kong?"

It was much more interesting on the upper deck now, for although the fishing boats were out, the traffic seemed more varied with the sighting of a submarine flying a long paying off pennant to signal she was leaving the China station for good and returning to her home depot, HMS Dolphin at Gosport. There they would meet their wives and families still waiting for them to come home from the war.

At least Christmas 1946 was not too late for a little celebration.

Petihoo after a brilliant two days of sailing was now herself preparing to celebrate as the distinct shape of Hong Kong appeared in the distance. Every bit of bunting and flag of any description was tied to a halyard from the bow to the mainmast, now crowned with the White Ensign.

It might have been improper but nobody cared.

Freddie, the gunner at the naval base, was there to meet them at the small ship jetty as though they were a proper warship. It would be expecting too much to think there would be a bugler!

There were quite a number on the jetty to meet them, including a berthing party of sailors to take the berthing ropes.

Willy Willard, who had been sightseeing in the cathedral, had spotted Anna's and Sam's names on a notice displaying the banns of people to be married and couldn't wait to tell them the good news.

Marcus was the first one to a phone and rang Pierre to tell him that Petihoo had berthed with only one casualty. All was well, mission successful.

The fact that Wilson had received a bullet through the fleshy part of his bum sent Yvonne into a tizzy. Mr Quan was summoned immediately. Hardly giving Pierre time to dress, she bundled him into the car, saying, "Stop worrying about the diamonds, Teddie's got a bullet in his buttocks!"

Wiggy, Bungy, Black and Kemp were also there with a kiss from Cheng for each one of them. The same customs men who had cleared the Petihoo for custom duty on her last trip from Shanghai were again on duty.

With a wave from Captain Chang, to please themselves the Custom men made a cursory inspection of the junk not bothering to crawl into the hold where the children were playing cards on a table of sacks.

Each child had a handful of glass beads, with the youngest reaching into the neck of a sack to try and find more. Sam, a little hot under the collar, made them promise not to tell, whispering, "Anna, birthday," and hung a piece of loose string round his neck. They smiled and put their hands over their mouths knowing how to keep secrets.

Mummy had already told them that Sam would give Anna a baby soon.

With his head through the hatch where the covers had been, Sam was able to catch Marcus's eye. He called him over to look at the children gambling with the diamonds in the corner of the hold. Marcus wasted no time in grabbing a couple of pillow slips from the mess, passing them into the hold for Sam to cover the sack from which the children had winkled with their little fingers a small fortune.

Taking the sack from Sam as though it was an unexploded bomb, Marcus tightly wrapped the pillow cases around the sack and headed for the sick bay. After all, Wilson's boss owned them.

If they had all made an appointment to meet at Wilson's bedside, it could not have been timed better. Pierre and Yvonne had just arrived at the bedside, Yvonne snuggling up to the bandaged Wilson in his bed crooning, "Oh Teddy, to think you did all this just for me," and kissed him hungrily, adding, "It won't affect you, down there?" as she thought of the coming romps together on the new bed.

Pierre's thin drooping frame then stooped over the bed and planted a kiss suitable for a hero on Wilson's cheek, muttering in French something about a medal and pretending to pin a "Legion d'honeur" to his pyjamas.

Taking Wilson's hand from his wife's breast, Pierre shook it vigorously before replacing it, then enquired, "Are they safe?" meaning the diamonds.

Wilson was just about to say, "I don't know" when Marcus entered the room and dumped them on the bed. Looking at Marcus, Wilson leaned his elbow on the pillow, sat up with a jerk and said, "Is that them?"

Marcus nodded as Pierre, seizing the pillow case, felt inside, recovered the sack and was soon holding one of the small bags and diamonds in his hand. Pocketing it, he was about to pick up the sack and run, when Marcus reached out and placed a restraining hand on the sack, saying, "Don't be silly, Pierre, we have brought them all this way so let us get them through the gate first, there are Custom men at the gates and spot checks are made all day so let us do it my way!"

Wilson then asked for his crutches lying on the spare bed next to him. It was easy to remove the rubber feet and the tube inside was quite generous on each of the crutches. Refitting them he rang his bed bell and asked the sickberth attendant if he could have curtains around the bed for they wanted to discuss something rather private. Always willing to oblige, the screens were provided.

Being experts at handling precious stones, Pierre and Yvonne took no time at all to transfer the diamonds from the sack to the crutches. With an ample supply of large bandages and lint, the smaller gems, still in their chamois bags, were strapped to Wilson's waist.

With Yvonne's help he was quickly dressed in a naval singlet and tropical shorts and wearing an old hospital dressing gown, Yvonne asked the sickberth attendant if they could take Wilson for some fresh air. Who could refuse Yvonne anything... He even walked with Wilson, a little unsteady on his crutches, to the car and at the same time he informed the gate that it was in order for the patient to be taken for a bit of fresh air. With a friendly wave from the regulating Petty Officer, they passed through the gate.

With the diamonds now safely in the safe at home, Wilson, in the company of Pierre and Yvonne, was safely delivered back to the sick bay. He would be discharged within a day or two and they could then really celebrate with the wedding of Sam and Anna, his new business colleague.

Wilson had just got himself nicely back to bed when in walked Anna and Sam.

Anna kissed him full on the lips and he enjoyed that, whilst Sam, full of news, began with the story in the Hong Kong Times, giving a graphic account of the trip from Shanghai to rescue a beautiful young bride by the renowned Captain Chang with a splendid photograph of the Captain in uniform.

The follow up story of the bride when the wedding took place would be an exclusive feature of the young couple.

Padre Walters with his wife could see no objection to the Chang children being used as pages. Christ said, "Suffer little children to come unto me" and that was sufficient authority for them to be there.

There was also news that H.M.S. Battener was to arrive in Hong Kong tomorrow and will be flying the paying off pennant on her return to U.K. shortly.

The news of the return to Hong Kong by junk by the patrol pleased the Captain of H.M.S. Battener for he too wanted to get home and it saved him a trip to Shanghai.

The Captain of H.M.S. Battener was known as a bible puncher and held strict views about religion on board. A march to the cathedral would do the ship's company a lot of good, for everyone had been invited to the wedding including the officers.

Why not a wedding - According to the papers the young man is a peacetime hero by all accounts.

Sam said to Wilson, "What about the diamonds, are they safe and when do we get our money?"

Wilson, with the assurance of a rich man, said confidently, "Don't worry about peanuts, what do you want for a wedding present?"

The sun was shining and a gentle breeze blowing through the open doors gave a special welcome to the mixed congregation gathering for the wedding of Anna and Sam. Anna the bride was drawing more than the usual attention from the public, following fresh stories appearing in the press of heroine bride in daring escape from Shanghai.

They had hoped for a quiet wedding, but when you see sailors marching to the cathedral of St. John's it must be something special. Cameras clicked and the rather curious Chinese lined the streets to see what was going to happen.

The arrival of Pierre with Yvonne on his arm bowed with the dignity of De Gaulle as he braced his thin shoulders to enter the cathedral.

The girls, exotically dressed by Yvonne and wearing pretty pillbox hats looked like the glamorous attendants of a famous beautiful bride.

Sam and his best man, Wilson, were also immaculate in their new morning suits each with a definite Hong Kong cut and white carnations. They looked more like businessmen although there were lots of sailors there.

Welcomed by Wagner's Wedding March, Anna began her slow walk down the aisle on the arm of Marcus in naval uniform, sword and medals. Anna elegant and beautiful in an off the shoulder silk bodice dress with sequins and real pearls matched her pearl necklace, her first gift from Sam. She looked radiant as she smiled to the Rev. Walters when the ceremony began.

The service passed very smoothly, except for a minor incident as Anna and Sam left to sign the register.

The Chang children without the bride for a while were heard singing their own hymn in English

"What shall we do with the drunken sailor . . ."